THE

CRIMSON

QUERY

or

How the Squid Got Besuckered

THE
CRIMSON
QUERY

or

How the Squid Got Besuckered

Arlton Eadie

RAMBLE HOUSE

ISBN 13: 978-1-60543-521-3

ISBN 10: 1-60543-521-X

Cover Art: Gavin L. O'Keefe
Preparation: Fender Tucker

THE
CRIMSON
QUERY

or

How the Squid Got Besuckered

CHAPTER I

DETECTIVE-INSPECTOR LEE NORTON was in the act of fattening the straps of his travelling-trunk when there came a tap on the cabin door.

"A Marconigram, sir," announced the steward who answered.

"For me?" There was a note of surprise in Lee's voice. The liner had already passed through the Solent and was now steaming slowly up Southampton Water on her way to the docks which lay but a few miles ahead. "Rather late for a wireless, isn't it? In a few minutes the voyage will be over."

"I suppose whoever sent it didn't know we were so near berthing, sir," the man answered. "We're hours overdue on account of that fog we ran into last night, and for all the sender knew we might be still down-Channel. It was the last message that 'Sparks' got before he closed down. I knew it would be urgent, so brought it straight along."

"Thanks," said Lee, and slipped a coin into the man's expectant palm.

Left alone, Lee Norton opened the envelope. As he did so he noted, with that subconscious sense of perception which his profession had engendered in him, that the gum of the flap was still moist.

To the ordinary reader the message would have appeared like the alphabet in a state of anarchy and chaos:

SURFHHGZHVWGRZQLPPHGL
DWHOBLQVWUXFWLRGVORFD
OSROLFHVWDWLRQODPEHUW.

To one as familiar with the official code as Lee Norton, however, its meaning was plain enough. His features twisted into an expression of humorous resignation as he read it through.

"Ah, well, I suppose there is no rest for those who have the Eye-that-never-sleeps," he muttered with a laughing shrug. " 'Proceed Westdown immediately. Instructions local police-station. Lambert.' Well, the chief might have given me at least a pat on the back and a few days' leave after my having landed that shoal of

shoal of deep-sea confidence-sharks so neatly." Then his face
brightened. "But I suppose I ought to feel bucked. It must be a case
of some importance for the very unlamblike Lambert to summon
me from the vasty deep to undertake it. I wonder where Westdown
is, anyway? Must be somewhere near Southampton, or I shouldn't
have been ordered to proceed direct."

A perusal of the Railway Guide in the smoking-lounge brought
to light the pleasing fact that his destination was but a twenty-eight
minutes' journey from Southampton, and the depressing fact that
he would have a three-hour wait before he could get a connection.
By the time he had digested these pieces of information, the snort-
ing of the winches on deck told him that the boat was being
warped alongside the landing-stage. So, consoling himself with the
reflection that there was no need to hurry ashore, he lit his pipe and
stepped out on deck.

"And why so sad and thoughtful, Mr. Norton?" said a laughing
voice behind him. "Did your wireless message tell you that all the
poor crooks, whom you delight so much in hunting, have gone on
holiday, or that a close season has come into force?"

Lee turned, and his grey eyes lit up as they encountered the
mischievous blue ones of the girl who had addressed the bantering
inquiry.

"No, Miss Chalmers," he answered, and there was a rather grim
note underlying his jesting tone. "Contrary to the general idea,
crooks are most hard-working people. Their only holidays are the
ones they take at the Government's expense and their only close
season is when they're in close confinement."

"Really?" Beryl Chalmers was the kind of girl who looks most
bewitching when she laughs, and now she seemed positively bub-
bling with merriment. "I suppose you keep each other busy—a
kind of mutual give-and-take arrangement."

The smile which twitched the corners of his mouth was one of
pity rather than of self-satisfaction as he made answer:

"Yes, poor devils! They give themselves away and we take
them in charge. The average crook is a most unimaginative and
incompetent person."

"I'm sorry to hear that you've been disappointed with them up
to now," she returned lightly; "but I suppose it would not be proper
for me, as a law-abiding citizeness, to wish you better luck in future. But, seriously, I hope you have not received bad news."

"But I have—the worst possible." His twinkling eyes belied his
tragic tone. "I've just been ordered to a place called—let me

see . . ." He made a dramatic pause while he searched for the Marconigram and consulted it. "It's a place so unspeakable that it's literally unpronounceable, and I shall have to spell it. It's called Z-H-V-W-G-R-Z-Q!"

She gave an exaggerated shudder.

"How frightful! A place with a name like that must be too bad even to talk about! Where is it—Russia?"

"It certainly has a Moscovitish sound," he answered with a smile.

"I'm sorry that you have to leave England again so soon, Mr. Norton."

On the face of it, it was an ordinary enough remark; but something in her voice as she said the words caused Lee to glance sharply up with a sudden catch of his breath. Was it only his conceited fancy, or was there really a note of lingering regret in her tone? They had met five days since, as fellow members of the inevitable "entertainment committee" which seems to spring into being on even the briefest sea-voyage, and till now their conversation had been limited to the usual commonplaces of shipboard life: the weather, the ship's daily run, and so on. But Lee had felt himself irresistibly drawn towards this light-hearted, butterfly-like creature who had chanced to flutter across his path. But his longings had not materialized into the vaguest of hopes. It did not need a detective's acumen to tell him that Beryl Chalmers belonged to an entirely different world from his own. True, there had been a time when they might have met on a more equal footing; for he had been an Oxford undergraduate with an allowance which far exceeded his present salary when the crash came which changed his father's valuable Russian oil-shares into so much waste paper; but Lee Norton was not one to let past might-have-beens influence his present conduct. But now—if she cared ever such a little . . .

He turned towards her again and felt his heart thumping curiously as he noted her flushed face and the eyes which seemed dim with wistful regret.

"It's good of you to say you are sorry, Miss Chalmers," he began, "but I am really not deserving of your sympathy on that point. You see . . ."

"Any more for the shore?" bawled a voice from the gangway. "Hurry along, please, or the boat-train'll be gone before you've passed the Customs."

Looking up, Lee saw that, save for the impatient quartermaster, the deck was deserted.

"Are you going to London?" he asked; but she shook her head.

"My car is waiting," she returned. "Poor Captain St. Quentin will think I am never coming."

She turned and passed quickly down the gangway. Lee, snatching up his bag, hastily followed.

"Anything to declare, sir?" asked the Customs officer as he passed through the shed on the dockside.

The excited young man had a whole lot to declare—but not to him.

"Yes—no—that is, of course not," he answered absently as, his eyes and thoughts still on the girl ahead, he made to pass through the barrier. To the lynx-eyed official, however, his agitation seemed the very embodiment of conscious guilt.

"I should like to have a look inside that bag, sir, if I—you don't mind," he said politely but firmly. "Kindly step this way."

Under other circumstances Lee's professional admiration might have been excited at the thoroughness of the search to which his belongings were subjected, but now every second of delay was torture. It seemed ages to him before the man handed him back his bag with the intimation that he was free to go. Dashing out of the shed, he saw that his worst fears were realized. The only sign of Beryl Chalmers was the tail-end of her car disappearing in the direction of the dock gates.

"And that's that!" he said with a wry smile. "And I didn't even see the number of the car. What rotten luck to welcome me back to the Old Country!"

He started to follow, only to be arrested by the sound of his own name being shouted behind him. Turning, he saw the Customs officer running towards him with an envelope in his hand.

"Is your name Lee Norton?" the man asked.

"That's me," said Lee, his surprise for the moment getting the better of his grammar.

"Then this letter must have fallen out of your bag. I found it on the floor near the barrier."

With a word of thanks, Lee took the envelope and broke the seal. Inside was a sheet of paper bearing a few roughly printed words:

Why go to Westdown and lose your life—why not sham ill and quit while you are safe?

Underneath, by way of signature, or to give emphasis to the grim warning, a large note of interrogation had been drawn in red ink.

Lee frowned thoughtfully as he folded the paper and placed it carefully in his pocket-book.

"It seems as if there were people on board that ship who know a good deal more than is good for them—or me!" he muttered grimly.

CHAPTER II

BY THE TIME that Lee Norton had registered his bag through to his destination and emerged from the Dock Station, the rays of the sinking sun were striking across the broad estuary, cutting a path of virgin gold across its waters and lighting up the high medieval walls which still rear their sturdy, though obsolete, ramparts at the waterside. The tall arc-lamps were beginning to burst into sizzling brilliance as Lee, turning his back on the docks, skirted the walls and, passing beneath the ancient Water Gate, made his way rapidly through the narrow streets which lay beyond.

The young detective was a great believer in the power of brisk physical exercise to induce a corresponding mental activity, and just then he felt the acute need of doing some hard thinking.

What was the meaning of the message that had been slipped into his bag? Was it the warning of a friend or the threat of an enemy? How had the unknown sender become aware of his intention of visiting Westdown—a fact which he had not known himself until shortly before the ship reached the docks? Had the wireless message been intercepted, or the operator bribed to reveal it? Granted that it had been written in code, but no code is proof against a patient decipherer, for the mere recurrence of the cypher which represented the letter E would supply its key. Again, who on board was likely to know?

He started suddenly as memory supplied the answer to the half-formed question. Had he not jestingly told Beryl Chalmers that he had been ordered to the place with the unpronounceable name, and read to her the ciphers which stood for Westdown in the code? What if she were the unknown author of the message?

"If so, then I'll stake my life that it was meant for a friendly warning," he said half aloud. "But the whole idea is impossible—absurd!"

He was angry with himself for his foolish indiscretion in naming the code-word of his destination, but still angrier at the thought that would persist in thrusting itself into his mind. Let it not be imagined that he was a blind believer in the idea that the human countenance is an infallible index of its owner's mind. Stern experience had long since exploded that picturesque fallacy. He had helped to obtain a well-merited life-sentence for a woman whose face might have served as a model for a martyred saint, and had seen the most repulsive-looking man he had ever met sacrifice his life in an attempt to bring in a wounded comrade. Yet, in spite of this, the mere thought of Beryl Chalmers as an associate of crooks seemed like sacrilege.

Busy with his thoughts and speculations, Lee had walked almost at random through the gas-lit streets. He had crossed the two main thoroughfares of the town and, after making a wide circle, had returned to the neighbourhood of the docks. The air of the street through which he was passing had a distinctly nautical flavour; such of the houses as did not offer to provide "Good Beds for Seamen" were devoted to the sale of the wherewithal to quench their thirsts. It was while passing a particularly disreputable-looking specimen of these latter that Lee caught sight of a face which sent his thoughts abruptly into another channel.

It was one of Norton's boasts that he seldom forgot a man who had once passed through his hands. Momentary though the glimpse was, as the light of the half-opened door fell upon the man's face, it was enough for the detective to have recognized and placed him before he had taken two strides. But "Swab" Simson was now dressed far differently to what he had been when he had stepped from the dock of the Central Criminal Court to undergo his sentence for dope-running. Then he had been attired in the grease-stained dungarees of a tramp steamer's donkey-man; now he was arrayed in a style which seemed to indicate that he toiled not, neither did he spin. And Lee knew his job well enough to realize that sign of affluence in a man of "Swab's" antecedents was a highly suspicious thing. His lips pursed into a silent whistle of admiration as he contemplated the back view of the loud check suit.

" 'Swab' is evidently in funds just at present," he thought. "Has he taken up bookmaking, or is he up to some game which calls for a little looking into? My old friend must have altered considerably if he came by that rig-out by the sweat of his manly brow!"

But, in spite of his suspicions, it was more for the sake of the distraction which the chase would give him that Lee quietly dropped behind and began to shadow the unconscious ex-convict. If "Swab" had forsaken his illicit dealings, Lee would have been one of the first to rejoice at the fact; but if the contrary was the case, then his hours of waiting would not be wasted.

Meanwhile, Simson had proceeded on his way in blissful ignorance of the interest which his movements had for the man who,
had he chanced to look round, would have seemed to be strolling
in the same direction on the other side of the road. But the suspicion that he was being followed did not seem to enter his mind.
With never a backward glance, he hurried on with the air of one
who has some definite object in view, and his destination seemed
to lie in the lowest quarter of the town.

Gradually the mean streets through which they were passing
grew meaner still; the houses more squalid; the passers-by more
furtive and suspicious-looking. When he at last turned into a maze
of narrow and ill-lighted alleys near the waterside, Lee mentally
congratulated himself on the impulse which had induced him to
take up the chase. It was a quarter given over to the less desirable
foreign element of the great sea-port; the place where the China-
men and Lascars off the ships were accustomed to spend their
spare time and cash in diversions dear to the Oriental heart. If
"Swab" still had dealings in the dope line, here was the very place
to get him with the goods.

So absorbed had he become in the chase, that it was only the
sound of a distant clock striking the hour that recalled the fact that
he had other work on hand. His train was due to leave in twenty
minutes' time, and the direction in which his quarry was heading
led in the opposite direction to the station. The keen desire to see
the outcome of his present adventure fought against the instinctive
respect for the orders of his superiors which was a legacy of Lee's
military service during the late war. He resolved on a compromise
between the two desires.

"I'll trail him for another five minutes," he decided, "then I'll
nip back to the main street and chance getting a taxi—"

His thoughts were interrupted by the sounds of a scuffle coming
from the dark alley into which "Swab" had plunged a moment before. Puzzled at this new and unexpected development, Lee instinctively slackened his pace. A hoarse cry for help urged him
forward at a run. Rounding the corner, he saw his quarry struggling
in the grasp of three men.

In spite of the odds against him, the little crook was putting up a
plucky and by no means unskilful fight. His fist crashed home
most scientifically on the chin of one of his attackers, sending the
fellow to the ground, but in doing so "Swab" left his back exposed
to the others. Before Lee could reach him, or even shout a warning,
a heavy "cosh" rose and fell on his unprotected head. As he sagged

limply sideways under the savage blow, his other assailant lunged forward, and now there was a glint of steel in his upraised hand. At the sight, the detective's automatic came into his hand as though by instinct, and two ear-splitting reports echoed down the narrow passage.

Lee purposely aimed wide, for he dared not risk a running shot into the knot of struggling men. But the mere sound of the weapon served its purpose. With one scared look at the approaching detective all three turned and ran for their lives, scattering and diving into the maze of waterside alleys where pursuit would be hopeless. Lee pocketed his weapon and bent over the prostrate victim.

"A close call that, eh, 'Swab'?" he said genially.

The man stared up at the face of his rescuer with a look of ludicrous amazement.

"Why, if it ain't Mr. Norton!" he gasped. "Who'd ha' thought to meet you in a place like this!"

"Lucky for you that I was handy to meet!" was the other's grim retort. "Your friends seemed mightily desirous of making you the subject of a sensational inquest."

"Swab" spat disgustedly on the ground as he tenderly felt the back of his head.

"Don't you abuse the sacred name o' friendship, Mr. Norton," he said in a tone of severe reproof. "They were just dock-rats who downed me for what they could pinch. I tell you I never set eyes on 'em in my life," he added, in a voice of unnecessary loudness.

Lee smiled to himself as he remembered the old French proverb, but he did not pursue the subject. "Are you hurt much?" he asked instead.

"Just a bit dizzy-like from that cosh on the 'ead." "Swab" straightened himself up as he spoke, only to stagger and seek the wall again.

"Here, lean on my shoulder," said Lee, placing himself beside him. "I'm thinking a dash of brandy wouldn't do you any harm, my man."

"There's a pub just round the corner to the left, sir," said "Swab" with sudden animation. "I think I might manage to get that far."

"Come on, then."

With an inward chuckle at the new role which fate had thrust upon him, Lee drew the arm of the ex-convict over his shoulder and, half leading, half carrying him, steered his tottering footsteps in the direction indicated.

The "Eight Bells" was a modest establishment whose chief trade was done in the early morning and dinner-hour, its patrons consisting mainly of dock-labourers and stevedores. When Lee shepherded his charge into what purported to be the saloon bar he found, to his satisfaction, that they had the place to themselves. Lowering "Swab" on to the cushioned settee that ran along one side of the room, Lee rapped on the counter and called for a double brandy.

"My friend has met with a little accident," he explained as he noted the suspicious glance which the red-cheeked barmaid shot at his companion's limp attitude.

"Ain't had too much already, has he?" she asked doubtfully.

"You can take my word for it. He's a life-long abstainer," said Lee unblushingly.

Under the reviving influence of the raw spirit, "Swab" soon began to take an intelligent interest in his position. The dazed look gradually faded from his eyes and in its place there came a gleam of furtive cunning. The immediate danger past, several disturbing factors in the situation began to intrude themselves on his mind. Lee's most opportune appearance had surely been something more than a mere coincidence. It was clear that the detective must have been shadowing him. But how long had he been on his trail, and how much did he know? Obviously it was a situation which, though not without its humour, needed careful handling.

"I must say that I'm surprised at you tailing me, Mr. Norton," he began by declaring with an air of injured innocence. "I've quitted that 'sniff-stuff' lay long ago. I'm going the straight and narrer path, I am now. You ain't got nothing on me 'cause there ain't nothing you can get."

"I'm very pleased to hear it," said Lee, but without enthusiasm. "If at any time I can assist you in keeping to the straight and narrow path you just mentioned, I shall be only too happy to do so. No, I haven't got anything against you, 'Swab', and I hope I never shall. But I had a few hours to spare and thought I would employ them in doing a guardian-angel stunt."

"It's a mercy for me that you did, sir," the other declared as he drained his glass with evident relish. Then he leant confidently towards the detective. "You always were a genn'eman, Mr. Norton. You've just done me a good turn and I'll do you one in return. I'll give you a bit o' advice."

Lee Norton looked at the man curiously. It was fairly plain that his excess of gratitude was not wholly unconnected with the mellowing influence of the generous dose of spirit which he had consumed. Lee shook his head.

"I think I can worry along without any advice from you, 'Swab'," he said shortly.

The other wagged his head slowly as he regarded him with a knowing leer.

"So you may think, but that's just where you make your bloomin' little error," he declared gravely. "Anyway, here's my advice, and you can take it or leave it, but it's the straight tip, and no mistake." He paused for a moment, then added in a lower tone: *"Don't go to Westdown!"*

Lee sat suddenly upright, his eyes snapping with surprise. So here was another who knew about his new mission. But how had he come by his information? But he did not fall into the mistake of asking a direct question. Instead, he gave a smile and shook his head.

"But, my dear man, I have not the slightest intention of going there." He merely made the assertion in the hope that its denial might lead "Swab" to betray the source of his information.

"Oh yes, you are, Mr. Norton." The little crook laughed in the manner of one who is sure of himself. "You're going straight to Westdown on a special mission. Well, all I can say is—don't go there! Or, if you must, don't be out on the moor at night."

"Moor? What moor?" demanded Lee quickly. "It seems that you know more about the place than I do myself."

"Swab" sank his voice to the merest whisper.

"I mean Abbotsmoor, the gawd-forsaken stretch of waste land that lies between Westdown and the aerodrome on one side and Abbot's Towers on the other. Don't you try and cross there alone at night, for if yer do—"

There came a dull, muffled explosion and "Swab" slipped sideways on the settee with a spreading patch of crimson on his check waistcoat. Lee started up in amazement, scarcely able to credit what had happened; for, except for themselves, the little room was empty. But even as his feet touched the floor, a spurt of flame licked from the wooden panelling against which his back had been resting a second ago, and a bullet shivered a mirror on the opposite wall.

In an instant Lee Norton understood. Somebody had overheard their conversation from the adjoining bar, and had fired through the wooden partition in the hope of silencing them both.

Pistol in hand, Lee dashed into the street. There was no need for him to look into the compartment whence the shot had come—the speeding figure, twenty yards down the street, told its own tale. Instantly Lee gave chase. But the fugitive had come well equipped for his getaway. His light running-shoes enabled him to draw rapidly ahead, and when the detective reached the end of the street he was nowhere to be seen.

Although the street had been deserted a few moments since, there was a little crowd jostling around the door of the "Eight Bells" when Lee returned. Forcing his way through without ceremony, he pushed open the swing-door and stepped inside. A policeman who was bending over the body looked round as he entered.

"That's 'im!" cried the girl behind the bar, her voice shrill with excitement as she pointed at Lee. "That's the bloke what was with the one that was shot!"

The constable straightened up and came forward, feeling in his tail-pocket as he approached Lee.

"There's no need to bring out the 'snaps,' Constable," said the detective, pulling out his official card. "He was shot from the next bar, and I narrowly missed getting a bullet myself."

He raised his hand to indicate the second bullet-bole in the wood, then suddenly paused as his eyes fell upon the murdered man.

"Did you search him?" he demanded sharply, turning to the policeman.

The man shook his head. "Didn't have time, sir. Why?"

"Then who unbuttoned his waistcoat?" Lee asked with a puzzled frown.

"It must have been that gentleman in the light overcoat," said the barmaid suddenly.

Lee swung round and faced her. "What gentleman?" he asked sharply. "Where did he come from—and go to?"

"Why, he was in here when I ran in after hearing the shot," answered the girl. "He said he was a doctor. He just looked at the poor feller for a moment or two—examining him, I thought. Then he said as how he was badly hurt and that he must get help. Then he hoofed it into the street."

Lee Norton stooped over the huddled body and turned back the edge of the open vest, and as he did so an exclamation broke from him.

Outlined in blood on the front of the dead man's shirt was a large crimson query.

CHAPTER III

A FEW MINUTES after the fatal shot had been fired, a tall man was making his way through the dingy streets which lay between the "Eight Bells" and the waterside. He was smartly dressed in a blue double-breasted suit and carried on his arm a light fawn raincoat. His features were clean-shaven, but a close observer—had there been one, and sufficient light by which to make his observations—might have noticed that his chin and upper lip bore traces of spirit-gum where a false beard had been hastily removed.

He walked quickly and with an apparent intimate knowledge of the district; for, though he carefully avoided the well-lighted main thoroughfares, he soon arrived on the broad open space which abuts on the town quay.

Leisurely strolling across to the stone steps which lead down to the water's edge beside the Royal Pier, he took out a cigarette-case, selected a cigarette with care, and produced a patent lighter. Had anyone chanced to have been interested in his actions they might have set him down as a very inexperienced smoker; for, in spite of the fact that there was scarcely a breath of wind, he found it necessary to flash his lighter three times before the cigarette was drawing to his satisfaction.

Scarcely had he exhaled the first puff of smoke, however, before a small motor-dinghy put off from a steam-yacht moored on the farther side of the fairway, heading straight as an arrow for the landing-steps. Swinging round a few yards off, the man in charge backed neatly alongside, and the stranger stepped aboard.

"Cast off," he ordered curtly.

The man hesitated.

"How about 'Swab'?" he asked.

"I guess he's not coming this trip," said the other. "Get her going."

The coming of the tall man must have been awaited, for the yacht had been made ready for sea, with navigation lights burning, accommodation ladder stowed, and anchor hove short for hoisting. No sooner had the dinghy made fast alongside than there came the rattle of a winch forrard, followed by a jangle of bells in her engine-room, and to the tune of her slowly beating propeller the *Lapwing* begun to slip down the dark reaches of Southampton Water.

On gaining the deck the new-comer immediately descended the companion and tapped on the door of the state-room in a peculiar manner.

"Enter!"

It was a curious voice that called out the invitation. Either its owner must have suffered from an impediment in his speech or was deliberately disguising its natural tones.

It was a small cabin, luxuriously and tastefully fitted, yet it did not differ from the accommodation usually to be found in pleasure-craft of that class and tonnage, save in one important respect. Its walls and ceiling showed no signs of port-holes or skylights, the ventilation being supplied by concealed fans, on the same principle as the forced draught of a ship's stokehold.

"Well?"

The solitary occupant did not attempt to rise from the table as he jerked out the word of inquiry in his shrill, artificial voice. Apparently he was a man of middle age, with a broad, impassive face, the lower part of which was concealed by a full grey beard. His hair, which was also thick and grey, was worn rather longer than is customary in this country, and this probably accounted for the fact that, although his voice betrayed no trace of foreign accent, a stranger, upon being asked to guess his nationality, would have answered unhesitatingly, "Russian." And in his guess he might just as likely have been right as wrong—at least there would be none to deny its correctness. For the birth and antecedents of the person who styled himself "Count Ravangar" were mysteries known to himself alone.

"I came aboard to report—" began the tall man.

"But you came alone, is it not so, my good Rawlins?" interrupted the man who called himself Count Ravangar, in a tone which made his words seem more like a confident assertion of a fact than a question. "Ah, I see that you are wondering how, sitting in this windowless cabin, I know that you were by yourself when you came aboard. It puzzles you, does it not? But you will find, as we get better acquainted, that there will be many things about me that will puzzle you even more. And if you are wise, my good Rawlins, you will be content to remain puzzled. Those who seek to know too much about me have a way of taking their knowledge to a realm where it will not profit them." He paused for a moment to allow that suavely veiled threat to sink home in the mind of his hearer, then: "And where is my esteemed 'Swab' Simson?"

"I left him in the 'Eight Bells'—dead," answered Rawlins sullenly.

Not the faintest flicker of a muscle broke the uncanny immobility of the Count's face.

"So . . . it was . . . necessary?" he asked softly.

"You bet it was—why, the swine was going to let out a squeal that would have been heard from here to Scotland Yard!"

"But—in a public-house . . ." The Count spoke in the tone of a connoisseur whose artistic susceptibilities had been hurt. "Surely a man of your experience could have hit on a plan less crude—and risky?"

Rawlins shook his head.

"I only just got him in time," he growled. "Another second and he'd have blown the whole plan."

"To whom, pray?"

"Lee Norton."

The sudden start which the Count gave was the first sign of emotion that he had exhibited. But his face remained as impassive as ever as he started to his feet and took a few turns up and down the little cabin.

"So Lee Norton is here, is he? The man for whom was intended the wireless message to the *Oramic* which we intercepted. But how came he to have an assignation with 'Swab'? He had only just arrived from America."

"If you ask me, Count, I should say that their meeting was just an accident. In accordance with your instructions, I shadowed Lee Norton from the moment he left the dock gates. First of all he crossed to the station and checked his baggage, but I couldn't get near enough to hear where to. Then he came out into the town and seemed to walk about just at random. It seemed to me as if he was just killing time until his train left, for he seemed to be simply fooling round the side-streets until, passing a little drive in the lower part of the town, he saw 'Swab' Simson."

"As I said—a pre-arranged meeting," said the other, nodding his head.

"If it was, then Lee ought to be a movie-star instead of a 'busy'!" declared Rawlins. "Anyway, the whole thing must have been cleverly timed if it was a put-up job. I'm not exactly a simp where such things are concerned, and to my mind it seemed as if

Lee recognized 'Swab' and started off to trail him. After a bit, the
"busy" glanced at his watch as though undecided whether to give
up; then there came a shout from round the corner. 'Swab' had
been set on by three of the 'cosh-boys' who hang round the docks
on the look-out for anyone worth downing. Of course, I couldn't
show myself until they moved on again, and then I saw that 'Swab'
had evidently got a swipe on the head which had knocked him half
silly. Lee took him into the saloon bar of the 'Eight Bells' and I
nipped into the public bar to see if I could hear what they were
talking about. There was only one other man in the bar, and anyone
with half an eye could see that he had 'cheap crook' written all
over him. As soon as I'd heard enough to know that 'Swab' was
going to squeak, I called for another drink, and in paying for it I
was careful to see that the crook in my compartment had a good
look at the wad of notes that I lugged out of my pocket, and when I
made to put it back in my pocket I purposely let it fall on the floor
and turned my back.

"Well, you can guess what happened. The fellow snatched up
the money and was out of the door like a flash. That was what I'd
been waiting for. I pulled out my automatic and fired two shots
through the partition against which 'Swab' and Lee Norton were
leaning. I missed the 'busy,' for he sprang to his feet at the first
shot, but I got the other all right."

Although there was not the slightest change of expression on
Ravangar's features, it was apparent, by the way in which he
rubbed his gloved hands together, that he was not unappreciative
of the finesse which his henchman had displayed.

"Very ingenious indeed, my good Rawlins. Norton, of course,
seeing the running crook who had stolen your money, at once assumed that he was the gunman, while you made off in the opposite
direction?"

"But not without first making sure that 'Swab' could tell no
tales," said the other grimly. "But he had passed out all right. So I
just put the sign on his chest to give Norton a hint what he was up
against, and came off to the yacht."

"You did wisely by not attempting to reach our headquarters by
road," Ravangar said thoughtfully. "Probably all outgoing cars
would be stopped and searched. Yes, you did quite right."

"I shall need another 'gat', though, Count," said Rawlins.

Ravangar looked up sharply. "You left your pistol on the scene
of the murder?" he asked slowly.

Rawlins gave a derisive laugh.

"Think I'm an amateur? No, I dropped it overboard as soon as I reached this yacht. The Yard has got hold of a new stunt of tracing guns by means of the rifling-marks on the bullets that have been fired from them. You can provide me with another 'gat'—"

"But not with another neck, eh?" The sound of a dry chuckle came from beneath the heavy beard, but no sign of mirth appeared on the Count's set features.

At this unexpected hint of geniality from his chief, an ingratiating grin spread over Rawlins' coarse features

"Not a bad bit of work, that of mine, Count?" he said with a self-satisfied air. "You ought to be very satisfied—"

Count Ravangar raised his head and looked fixedly at the man. Such was the expression in those coldly gleaming eyes that the boastful words faltered on the other's lips.

"The moment I cease to be satisfied with you, my good Rawlins," he said very softly, "that same moment you will cease to be a man. You may go to your quarters.'

And the man, whose hand had not faltered when he had sent his fellow to his doom, now slunk from the room without a backward glance.

During the whole of this interview not a single flicker of feeling or emotion had disturbed the marble-like repose of the Count's features. But this was not due to his self-control, iron-willed though that was. In point of fact the face that Ravangar showed to the world was but a cunningly modelled mask, with hair and beard equally—false. If anyone had ever known the real identity and lineaments of the man who called himself Count Ravangar he had assuredly not lived long enough afterwards to pass on his information.

CHAPTER IV

mEANWHILE, THE *LAPWING* was slowly slipping down the narrow arm of the sea which lies between Southampton and the Isle of Wight. With every light shrouded, except the necessary mast-head white and the red and green on either side of her bridge, she glided like a dim white-sheeted ghost between the twin lightships which mark the shoals off Calshot and, leaving the quick-flashing white light of the Nab on her port quarter, rounded the cliff-girt shoulder of the Wight until the beam of the lighthouse on St. Catherine's Point was winking steadily away to starboard.

But the cruise was destined to be a short one. Scarcely had the yacht quitted the shelter of the island and began to dip and curtsy to the rollers of the Channel, than Count Ravangar rose abruptly from his chair.

"Yes, I think it had better be tonight," he muttered softly to himself. "It is very evident that this Lee Norton is too smart to allow an opportunity to slip past—and I must be the same."

He closed the book that he had been consulting—a book, by the way, whose closely written pages would have afforded much food for thought to the officials of the C.I.D had they chanced to have caught sight of them—and locked the precious volume in a safe beneath the desk. Crossing to the aft bulkhead, he pressed a certain portion of the carved frieze, and instantly three of the rosewood panels swung outwards, revealing a telephone instrument and a small switchboard by means of which the unseen manipulator could either give orders to any part of the ship or overhear what was being said there.

Pressing down one of the numbered levers, he rang through to the wireless operating-room.

"Connect me up with the instrument," he ordered. "I wish to send out a message."

"Very good, sir," was the answer, and a second later there sounded the unmistakable click which told him that the connection had been made.

It certainly seemed a strange manner of message which the Count prepared to send. Instead of speaking into the mouthpiece, he carefully selected a record from the cupboard beneath the large cabinet gramophone standing near, placed it in position, and set the machine in motion. Instantly the opening bars of Schumann's *Symphony in B Flat Major* were being broadcast on a wavelength which he had no right whatever to use. For ten seconds the music continued; then through the earpiece which he held to his ear there sounded three high-pitched howls in quick succession, as though some amateur on shore was badly oscillating. It was the signal that his message had been heard and understood; so, disconnecting the gramophone, he switched on to the navigation bridge and gave a sharp order.

The helm was immediately put over, and the *Lapwing,* again veering to starboard, pointed her gracefully curved bows towards the Needles Light and, making a wide half-circle round that red-and-white beacon, entered the Solent Channel. Half an hour later, having almost completely circumnavigated the island, she dropped anchor im Lymington Roads.

But that sleepy little port was not Count Ravangar's objective. Scarcely had the yacht lost way than the motor-dinghy was lowered, and the Count, accompanied only by Rawlins and one member of the crew, embarked for a cruise in shallower waters than the *Lapwing* could navigate.

The tide was now in the last quarter of its flood, enabling them to hug the shore closely as their little craft drove eastwards with the current, rounding the long spit of sand off Needs Oar Point and entering the mouth of the Beaulieu River. It seemed as though the man at the tiller was well acquainted with the devious channel of the little stream. Turning sharply N.W. as he came opposite the Coastguard Station on the right-hand bank, they traversed three-quarters of a mile of comparatively straight river, only to turn northwards again and head straight for what looked like dark woods barring all further progress. Just when it seemed as if the next few yards must inevitably see them fast aground, there came a glint of silver to the left—the moonlight reflected on a further reach of the river. Emerging from the shadows of the tall pines, they slipped silently past a tiny cluster of red-roofed houses which seemed to be standing guard over a tumbledown little quay.

Three miles above this, the bright headlights of a car came into sight on the road which here follows the right-hand bank. Immediately the dinghy was headed for the shore, and Ravangar and his companion sprang out and entered the car. No words were spoken, nor were any needed. The loitering car immediately picked up speed, heading up the hill which leads to Abbotsmoor; while the boat, swinging neatly round, disappeared in the direction of the sea.

It was not until the car had nearly reached its destination that Count Ravangar broke the silence.

"By the way, my dear Rawlins, you did not tell me how you managed to convey my warning to Lee Norton as he came ashore from the *Oramic.*"

A slow smile appeared on the lips of the other man.

"It was the girl who did it," he answered. "She gave the letter to one of the Customs men on the dock-side and asked him to say that it had fallen from Norton's luggage. She gave him to understand it was a tender missive of love which she was far too bashful to deliver herself, and he believed every word of the tale she pitched. When that girl really spreads herself, she can make a man take her word against that of an angel from heaven. I suppose it's her eyes that does the trick."

Ravangar stroked his beard thoughtfully.

"H'm, she's very clever—very clever indeed," he mused aloud. "Probably she will be very useful to me . . . later on."

CHAPTER V

"A ND NOW, SERGEANT, I should be glad to have some particulars of the case," said Lee Norton, glancing across the breakfast-table at the tall, military-looking man seated opposite.

It was the morning after the murder of "Swab" Simson. The formalities and inquiries which had followed that crime had detained Lee in Southampton until it was too late to reach Weston that night; but in spite of his efforts and those of the local police nothing further had come to light, and there had been no other course open to him but to proceed to his destination by the first train that morning, leaving the case in the hands of the local superintendent. Upon calling at the little police-station at Westdown he had been referred to Detective-Sergeant Hattersley of the C.I.D., who was already on the spot in connection with the case on which Lee had been detailed.

"This is a watching job," he explained. "We've got to keep a certain Captain St. Quentin under observation."

Lee paused in the act of raising his coffee-cup to his lips. The name sounded vaguely familiar to him. When and where had he heard it mentioned lately? Then suddenly came the memory of Beryl Chalmers' parting words as she had hurried down the gangway of the *Oramic*: "Poor Captain St. Quentin will think I am never coming," she had laughingly declared, and the tone which she had used left little doubt in Lee's mind that she was referring to someone whom she knew well. It was an unusual name. What if he had been ordered to keep observation on one of her closest friends? Lee pushed aside his untasted breakfast and bent forward eagerly.

"Quentin?" he repeated. "What has he been up to that the Yard wants him watched?"

Sergeant Hattersley laughed. He was a huge, broadshouldered man, with hair already turning grey at the sides, and a short, close-clipped moustache. Lee knew him to be an officer of proved courage and resource, but this was the first occasion on which they had acted on a case together.

"It seems that you've got things a bit wrong," said the sergeant. "Captain St. Quentin isn't a crook—he's the inventor of a new aeroplane in which the Government is unofficially interested. I say 'unofficially' because the new 'plane has not been purchased by them as yet; but they are only waiting until the trials are completed before taking it over. It being a secret invention, I naturally do not know in what respect it differs from the usual run of such things. But I do happen to know that it marks a great advance over all existing types of machines, and it doesn't need much brains to realize that there is more than one foreign Power who would be glad of a little inside information about her design. And that is just what you and I are here to prevent them getting."

"I understand," murmured Lee Norton. Somehow or other he did not feel that glow of satisfaction which he should have felt when he heard that the captain-friend of Beryl Chalmers was not a prospective quarry.

"I have here a large-scale Ordnance Survey map of the district," Sergeant Hattersley went on, "and I can put you wise in a few minutes to facts which have taken me over a week to ferret out. The village public-houses are fairly well patronized hereabouts, and I've been haunting them for the past week, standing treat and listening to the local gossip. and I've learnt quite a lot about the people living round about."

He cleared a space on the table and spread out the map before his colleague. Glancing at it, Lee saw that it represented the whole of Abbotsmoor, with a part of the New Forest to the north and the Beaulieu River lying like a short, twisted snake in the right-hand corner. It was an excellent map, for it showed every building, however small, and even the numerous prehistoric tumuli, or burial-mounds, with which the moor was dotted. Almost in the centre of the map a rough circle had been drawn in red ink, and to this the sergeant first pointed.

"These are Captain St. Quentin's hangars and workshops. They're not marked on the plan because they were only built at the beginning of the present year. The buildings are surrounded by a high wooden fence topped with barbed wire. When the 'plane is brought out for an experimental flight—which is always at night, by the way—a section of this fence is removed, and is replaced as soon as the machine returns. A company of picked men of the Hampshire Light Infantry are permanently situated within the enclosure, and these provide the sentries which patrol the fence night and day. Captain St. Quentin has his own quarters in a hut adjoining the hangar where his 'plane is housed."

"The place seems to be guarded rather better than most convict prisons," Lee remarked, looking up. "It looks as if my job is going to be a sinecure."

Hattersley gave a smile in response, but it was a somewhat grim one.

"Don't make any mistake, Mr. Norton—the Yard didn't send us here for a change of air! It's not so much the new 'plane that we're here to guard, as Captain St. Quentin himself. The people at the War Office have got the idea that he may be kidnapped—or killed."

"I should have thought that a more likely event would be an attempt to steal the plans of the new machine."

Hattersley shook his head.

"There are no plans in existence. Captain St. Quentin has resolutely refused to commit his new gadgets to paper, and such rough notes as he has made for his own guidance are purposely in such a form as to be unintelligible to the cleverest mechanical engineer. His own brain is the only safe he uses, and, indeed, it would be hard to find a better one."

"That's so," agreed Lee. "There's many an old lag contemplating four stone walls at this present moment and regretting that he did not do the same thing. My own experience is that a secret is only half a secret when it's put into black and white."

"Still, the plan has its disadvantages in a case like this," continued the sergeant. "Should the captain chance to be killed—accidentally or otherwise—then the secret will be lost to the British Government. Or should he be abducted by the agents of some foreign Power, there is a chance of the new 'plane being used against us."

"Provided that Captain St. Quentin can be induced to reveal it," interposed Lee.

Sergeant Hattersley gave him a queer look.

"If the captain should chance to mysteriously disappear, I should not like to gamble on that not happening," he said slowly. "An ordinary European spy would go to some pretty long lengths to extract a secret worth millions, but I suppose he would not resort to torture to gain his end. But if St. Quentin were to fall into the hands of a gang of Orientals—for the East is quite as alive to the value of air supremacy as the West—then I think that the chance of the secret not being extracted would be a poor one."

"You mean that the process would not be one of 'painless extraction', I presume?" Lee observed.

"I mean that he would be tortured until he talked!" said the other bluntly. "And that's why we've got to guard the gallant captain like the apple of our eyes, and the job is not going to be child's play, either! The captain is a young gentleman who has a great idea of his own ability of looking after himself. He refuses to have an escort to accompany him wherever he goes, and that will mean that we'll have to hang about and shadow him secretly. That would be difficult enough in an ordinary case in open country like this, but when I tell you that our charge is courting a girl hereabouts, you will begin to realize that you're not on such a feather-bed job as you thought you were!"

A vague premonition began to form in Lee's mind as his subordinate made the explanation. There was a pause, during which Lee slowly charged his pipe and lit it. Truth to tell, he almost feared to ask the question which was hammering at his brain. Not until his pipe was drawing freely did he turn to Hattersley.

"May I ask the name of the young lady who is the object of the captain's attentions?"

"Certainly," was the ready answer. "She's the daughter of Sir Raymond Chalmers, who lives at Abbot's Towers, the big stone house on the further side of the moor. See—here it is—" and he indicated a spot on the plan with his forefinger.

But Lee Norton scarcely glanced at the place indicated.

"But her name, man—her name!" he cried, throwing all pretence of indifference to the winds. "What is her name?"

Hattersley looked his surprise.

"What's the excitement?" he said. "The old man is a widower, and he's only got one daughter. Her name is Miss Beryl Chalmers, and she and St. Quentin are engaged to be married. Ah, I can see you're rather surprised at the news. It rather complicates matters, doesn't it?"

"It does," agreed Lee in so quiet a voice that the sergeant never suspected the raging turmoil of the young detective's heart.

Captain St. Quentin was engaged to the girl whom Lee would have given his life to possess, and he himself had been deputed to shadow his every movement and to be the guardian of his rival's life.

"Ah, well, it's a small world and a funny one, after all," said Lee with a little twisted smile on his clean-shaven lips.

His colleague looked up, puzzled.

"I don't see your point," he said.

"Of course you don't, Sergeant," was Lee's cryptic reply. "And . . . I hope you never will."

CHAPTER VI

T HE MAJORITY OF THE HOUSES in Westdown are gathered in two long straggling rows on either side of the highway which forms its main street. They are mostly single-storeyed cottages, and present the greatest diversity both of alignment and architecture. Some have their doorsteps on the main street, while some coyly peer forth behind gardens gay and fragrant with summer flowers and climbing-roses; some are of time-mellowed red brick, others of black-and-white half-timbering; a few of the older ones have the mouse-grey chalk walls, the making of which is now to be numbered among Hampshire's lost arts.

Lee Norton's occupation of crook-catching had not deadened his soul to its perception of the picturesque, and it seemed to him as though he had never beheld a more quaintly pretty view than that which met his eyes as he stepped out of the door of the ivy-covered cottage where he and Sergeant Hattersley had taken lodgings. The only note which jarred upon its old-world charm was the very up-to-date automobile which stood outside the little shop, which, judging by the miscellaneous array of goods visible through its small-paned Georgian windows, seemed to be a combined general stores and post-office. As they were passing this emporium Lee got the second surprise of that morning.

"Why, it's Mr. Norton!"

Turning at the sound of the voice, he saw, framed in the low-pitched door-way, the figure of the very girl whom they had been talking about a few minutes before.

For a moment Beryl Chalmers stood there, the bright morning sunshine glinting on the masses of hair which escaped from beneath her small felt hat, the lines of her slender, tweed-clad figure outlined against the shadows within. Then, slipping the letters which she held in her hand into the red-painted box, she came eagerly forward.

"Well, this *is* a surprise! Fancy meeting you here of all places!—why, I thought you would be well on your way to that place with the unpronounceable name by now. But I hope you are not visiting us in your professional capacity—we should never be able to hold up our heads again if we thought that we had merited the attentions of the crack detective of Scotland Yard!"

As she ran on in her bantering, light-hearted voice, Lee felt his face growing red. For what had, a moment before, seemed an almost deserted, sleepy village street, now seemed much too crowded for his liking. The chauffeur at the wheel of the car had cocked a listening ear in his direction; a butcher's boy had paused in the act of mounting his bicycle and was staring at him open-mouthed; the two old cronies outside the post-office had ceased their gossip and were eagerly attentive.

Lee was in a quandary. As a man, his heart was dancing at the sight of Beryl Chalmers, but as a police officer he felt like cursing the fate which had thrown them face to face at that particular moment. To have acknowledged his identity at that moment would be fatal to the task on which he was engaged.

"I—er—that is, I—" he began, and, catching her eye, he twisted his features into what he hoped would be interpreted as a warning expression.

Her eyes opened a trifle wider as she noted his contorted face.

"Are you feeling ill, Mr. Norton?" she asked anxiously.

He shook his head slightly as he repeated his performance. But the result was only a grimace which seemed to the girl to indicate sudden and intense agony. The look of concern deepened in her eyes. She came a step nearer.

"There is a doctor near—" There was no hint of laughter in her voice now, but a tremor which made Lee despise himself for being the cause of it. "Get into my car—"

With an effort that he hoped would not be apparent, Lee drew himself up and composed his features in a frigid stare.

"I fear you have made a mistake, miss," he said, allowing his words to fall with icy precision. "I have not had the pleasure of meeting you before. You are evidently confusing me with somebody else. My name happens to be Coleby."

In his confusion he had adopted the first name that had come to his mind. It was only when Sergeant Hattersley exploded into a violent fit of coughing that he realized that he had taken one of the aliases of a well-known counterfeiter who was at present undergoing a well-merited stretch at Dartmoor.

For a moment the girl remained staring fixedly at him. Then a wave of scarlet rushed into her cheeks as she dropped her extended hand to her side and drew back, an expression in her clear blue eyes which made the young detective feel like a particularly debased species of worm.

"I'm sorry," she said slowly. "It was a foolish mistake for me to make." Turning abruptly, she entered the waiting car and drove off without a backward glance.

Lee groaned as he watched it disappear in the distance.

"Friend of yours?" asked Hattersley dryly.

"She *was,*" replied Lee, with a rueful emphasis on the past tense. "What rotten luck to meet her in the street like that! Do you think she believed me when I denied being myself?"

The sergeant stroked his moustache dubiously.

"Couldn't say, sir," he answered, with the caution for which his profession was noted. "I rather fancy that she was a little bit annoyed and disappointed. But of course you couldn't do anything else with all those people looking on. I hope her recognition of you isn't going to complicate matters," he added thoughtfully.

Lee shook his head a little sadly.

"No fear of that, Sergeant. The next time we meet she will most probably look straight through me as if I didn't exist!"

If Sergeant Hattersley's own opinion agreed with his superior's he did not give any indication of the fact as he turned and fell into step with him as they traversed the village street and entered on the rolling moors beyond.

The day was perfect; the hot sunshine which fell from the sky of unflecked blue was tempered by the brisk south wind, which stirred the pink and white blossoms of the brambles, bringing a tang of the sea which lay but a few miles away, where, of a blue so ethereal as to scarcely be distinguished from that of the sky, the headlands of the Wight hung in the shimmering haze.

For a long time the two men walked in silence; then the sergeant startled his companion with a curious question:

"Do you understand anything about fishing, Mr. Norton?"

Lee looked at him searchingly for a moment, suspecting some obscure reference to his late encounter lay in the remark. Apparently satisfied that Hattersley was in earnest, Lee shook his head.

"Not very much. Why?"

"I had an idea of posing as an amateur angler in order to have an excuse for hanging about the moor," answered the sergeant. "There's a small stream running within sight of the aerodrome, and fishing's about the only sport at which a man can moon about for hours doing nothing. The trouble is that I don't know enough about it to keep up the character—folk are so apt to gather round and ask fool questions. I bought a book on the subject, but it didn't seem to help me much."

"What was the name of the book?"

The seeker after piscatorial knowledge gave a snort of disgust.

"I might have known that the book was no good—why, the blighter who wrote it didn't even know how to spell! It was *The Complete Angler,* by Izaak Walton. Only he spelt it c-o-m-p-l-e-a-t."

"You were disappointed, eh?" smiled Lee.

"Sheer waste of money," declared the other moodily. "The goop who wrote it seemed to think more about buttercups, and ale, and flirting with milkmaids than he did about catching fish!"

"You were certainly unfortunate in your choice of an up-to-date text-book," laughed Lee. "But I'll soon initiate you into the mysteries of casting the dry-fly."

They had quitted the high-road and were following a faintly marked footpath which struck obliquely across the moor. Presently Hattersley pointed to a large red-gabled house which stood by itself by the side of another road to their left.

"There's a queer old card living in that house over there," he informed Lee. "You're sure to meet him grubbing about among the prehistoric mounds on the moor. His name is Gideon Wilfer, and he's the President of the local Archaeological Society, and no end of a big bug at the British Museum. He's got a permit to excavate the tumuli, which are to be found in dozens hereabouts, and spends most of his time digging up the bones and measuring the skulls. Queer kind of a hobby, isn't it? But, then, he seems a queer kind of a man. I came across him a couple of days ago, and he kept me there for hours jawing about burnt and unburnt interments, long-headed and round-headed skulls—he called 'em names about a yard long, Greek, I suppose; but he was good enough to translate into English for my benefit. They tell me that he's got enough old bones in one of the rooms at Moor Lodge to stock a village churchyard. Well, well, I suppose there's no accounting for taste."

As they progressed, the rough moorland began to give place to smoother country, with stretches of level turf gradually merging into a flat grassy plain. Set almost in the centre was a range of low wooden buildings, approached by a narrow bridge spanning the stream, which at this point made a broad hairpin loop, forming a natural moat round three-quarters of the structure.

"Those are Captain St. Quentin's hangars and work shops," said Hattersley. "The landing-ground is on the farther side—"

"Well, that's very curious," said Lee suddenly.

Glancing at his companion, the sergeant saw that he was looking at something in the opposite direction to the buildings which he was in the act of describing.

"What is curious?" he demanded.

Lee did not appear to hear the question as he stood staring at a small clump of bushes about a hundred yards to their right. The young detective was a keen observer of trifles which the average man might have passed by unheeded, and something in the behaviour of the flock of crows which fluttered above the bushes was vaguely reminiscent of something which he had seen on the shell-pitted fields of France and Flanders.

"There's something lying dead under those bushes," he declared presently.

"A rabbit, maybe—" began Hattersley, but Lee was already walking rapidly towards the spot.

With something like a contemptuous smile on his lips, he watched the receding figure. But his expression changed when he observed Lee break into a run, and quickly stoop over something which lay on the ground. Then he in his turn began to run, and in a few minutes had reached the scene of the tragedy.

For a tragedy it undoubtedly was. The man who lay face downwards among the bracken had evidently been felled by a savage blow on the head, and it did not need a second glance at the terrible gaping wound to realize that he must have been killed immediately.

It was equally apparent that his death was the result of foul play. Not only was the wound in such a position as to rule out the possibility of it being self-inflicted, but the body had been stripped of its outer garments, even to the hat and boots.

Careful notes were made of the exact position of the body, and the ground in the vicinity vainly searched for footprints or other indications which might give a hint as to the identity of the murderer. Then Lee knelt by the side of the still form and gently turned it over on its back.

Sergeant Hattersley gave an exclamation as he pointed downwards.

"This man is a soldier—there's his regimental number!" He indicated several figures stamped in black ink on the man's clothing. "463694—he is probably one of the Hampshires who guard the aerodrome. If so, it will be easy to identify him—Why, what's the matter?"

For Lee Norton was staring at a narrow curved bloodstain on the front of the man's grey shirt.

"What's that?" the sergeant went on. "Has he been stabbed as well?"

Lee shook his head as he rose to his feet. His lips were set in a straight line and there was a hard glitter in his eyes.

" 'Swab' Simson spoke the truth after all," he muttered, half aloud.

Hattersley grasped his arm.

"You mean that you know who is responsible for this?" he gasped.

"I know that it is the work of the gang who murdered 'Swab' to prevent him giving information—the gang who ask their questions in the blood of their victims. And this is their sign. . . ."

And Lee Norton pointed to the large crimson query on the breast of the dead man.

CHAPTER VII

HALT! WHO ARE YOU?"
The brisk challenge, emphasized by the point of a bayoneted rifle held at the "ready", brought Lee Norton to an abrupt standstill as, having left Hattersley to guard the body on the moor, he approached the main-guard of the aerodrome.

"I wish to speak to your company commander at once," he answered.

"Guard . . . turn out!"

Lee nodded approvingly as he noted that the sentry did not relax his vigilant attitude as he called out the order. Evidently the men had received orders to take no chances with unknown visitors. He repeated his request to the sergeant of the guard who appeared in response, and, after stating his business and showing his card, was conducted by a lance-corporal to the officers' quarters.

"Captain Mansel will be off parade in a few minutes, sir," said the man, raising his hand to his sloped rifle in salute.

Lee nodded his approval once more as he saw the man, instead of leaving him, smartly "order arms" and stand at ease, keeping a watchful eye on him the while. It was clear that the discipline of that picked detail was such as to satisfy the most exacting of sergeant-majors.

Captain Mansel made his appearance soon afterwards. He was a capable and energetic officer, who was not in the habit of wasting words. He listened in silence to what the detective had to say, then gave his orders with promptitude and decision. A stretcher-party was dispatched to bring in the body, and the records in the orderly-room searched to discover the name of No. 463694. In a few minutes the company clerk entered with the desired information. The man who bore that number was Private John O'Connor of B Company.

"Was he reported absent from camp last night?" asked Lee.

Captain Mansel turned to the regimental sergeant-major.

"Parade the sergeant of his hut and the men who sleep there," he ordered.

An examination of these men elicited the amazing fact that O'Connor had entered his hut a few minutes before "Lights out", and had immediately put down his bed-boards and gone to sleep. Lee Norton's brows drew down into a puzzled frown as he listened to their evidence. He had already noticed that, whereas a slight rain had fallen late the previous night, the ground beneath the body was quite dry. It was clear, therefore, that the man must have been lying in the same position for at least ten hours. He turned to the men again.

"Did any of you men actually speak to O'Connor?" he asked.

There was no answer, and the suspicion which had been slowly forming in the detective's mind became a certainty. There could be but one explanation—the murderer had dressed himself in his victim's uniform, had entered, the aerodrome and answered O'Connor's name when the roll had been called. It would have been a simple matter for him to have quitted the hut later without raising suspicion. . . . Lee felt his heart turning to ice as he realized the full meaning of the plot. He could scarcely summon up courage to ask his next question.

"Can I have a word with Captain St. Quentin?"

Captain Mansel shook his head. "That's impossible. He went on leave last night—"

"Thank God for that!" cried Lee fervently. "Oh, I beg your pardon—of course you do not understand. If you will lead the way to Captain St. Quentin's quarters, I may be able to explain."

The airman-inventor occupied a small hut adjoining the hangar and workshops. In a few seconds the little party came to a halt before the door, and the sergeant-major made as though to lead the way inside.

Lee laid a detaining hand on his arm.

"Not on your life, Major," he said. "And you can take it from me that my warning is not a mere figure of speech."

Motioning the others to remain where they stood, he threw open the door; then, passing round to the side and rear, he threw open every window that he could reach.

Captain Mansel regarded his proceedings with raised brows.

"Gas?" he queried laconically.

"It is something even more deadly than that," was the reply. "Did you notice the faint smell of almonds as I opened the door? But you shall see its effects for yourself. I think it's safe to enter now, especially with this wind blowing."

The first room they entered was the captain's office. Everything seemed in perfect order; it was not until they opened the door of the room where he had been accustomed to sleep that they noticed anything unusual. There, beside the plain camp-bed, a few fragments of curved glass lay upon the floor. At first glance that was all. But the little fox-terrier that lay curled up on the hearthrug did not raise its head at their approach, and the only tenant of the gilt bird-cage hanging in the window was a little heap of ruffled yellow plumage lying motionless at the bottom of the cage.

Lee Norton pointed to each in turn.

"If Captain St. Quentin had been sleeping here last night he would be as lifeless as his pets are," he said to his astonished hearers. "The man who had killed Private O'Connor earlier in the evening crept later to this bedroom window, pushed it up a few inches, threw in a glass ball filled with a concentrated solution of cyanide of potassium, then closed the window and made his escape, probably waiting till daylight before passing the main-guard. And now I should be obliged if you will allow me to use your 'phone for a few minutes."

Lee rang up the local headquarters and apprised them of the tragedy, requesting them to forward the news on to the Yard. As he was preparing to leave the aerodrome, Captain Mansel drew him aside.

"I noticed a peculiar mark on poor O'Connor's chest," he said. "It seemed to me like the mark that one sees at the end of a question."

Lee nodded.

"You're quite right, sir; it *is* a question. But, please God"—he spoke in a quiet, passionless voice, but his eyes had hardened into two points of gleaming steel—"it is a question to which I intend to find an answer!"

CHAPTER VIII

THERE CAME A DISCREET KNOCK on the door of Sir Raymond Chalmers' study at Abbot's Towers, and the butler entered, a sheaf of newspapers and letters in his hand.

"The mail and newspapers, Sir Raymond."

Having made this rather unnecessary announcement, Riggs laid the articles on the desk and waited for the remark about the weather with which his master invariably prefaced any orders that he might wish carried out. This particular morning, however, Sir Raymond's thoughts seemed to be centred on a more important topic. He was searching among the papers which were strewn about his desk, and at the sound of Riggs' voice looked up, his bushy grey brows drawn down in an irritated frown.

"I wish, Riggs, that you would instruct the maids to carry out their cleaning duties in such a manner as to leave my private papers undisturbed. I am most particular in the way I arrange them, and now they're all mixed up."

James Riggs' features took on an expression of the deepest concern. He was an old servant who regarded the smooth and orderly running of the establishment over which he had charge as one of the immutable laws of Nature. To him the slightest hitch or friction seemed to hint at anarchy and revolution, and was as wormwood and gall to his order-loving soul. The tone in which he answered might have been that of a bank manager who had been suddenly informed that the contents of the strong-room had been abstracted.

"Indeed, Sir Raymond, you surprise me," he said, nervously washing his hands with invisible soapsuds. "I was particularly careful to instruct the new parlour-maid to refrain from touching them. I trust there is nothing missing, sir?"

Sir Raymond shook his head.

"Nothing of any value, Riggs, and certainly nothing that would be of interest to the new parlour-maid, whoever she may be. The letter I cannot find is one from Captain St. Quentin, giving the address at which he is staying in London. I was looking it up in order to write to him."

Riggs rubbed his close-shaven chin.

"Maybe Miss Beryl would know his address, sir," he suggested.

Sir Raymond shrugged irritably as he threw the papers back on the table.

"Maybe, maybe. But, still, it's very annoying to find one's papers have been disturbed. I suppose that new maid is quite trustworthy, eh?"

"I think so, sir," the butler answered readily. "She seems a most diligent and respectable person. She was engaged through a most reputable agency and bore excellent references, showing that she had been in the service of a certain Count Ravangar for quite a number of years. Would you like to question her, sir?"

"Oh no, no. The affair is of really no importance, but you must impress upon her the fact that my correspondence is not to be touched." He seated himself at his desk and began to open his mail. Whilst in the act of slitting open the first envelope he suddenly looked up. "By the way, what is this new maid's name?"

Riggs put his forefinger to his forehead for a moment, then shook his head.

"I really do not remember, sir. You see, the first parlour-maid is always called 'Susan', just as the first footman is always called 'John'. It saves confusion should the servants be changed, and those names are much more suitable for their station of life than some of the newfangled ones which parents give their children nowadays. Only the other day I engaged a lad to clean boots and do odd jobs, who rejoiced in the appellations of Claude Gustave. Now," he added grimly, "he is just plain 'Joe', the same as the last one."

Left alone, Sir Raymond rapidly ran through the dozen or so letters. It was his custom personally to examine his correspondence, making pencilled notes on the margins of such letters as could be attended to by his private secretary and setting aside those of a more intimate and confidential nature to be answered later.

Half an hour later he pressed the bell-push at the side of his desk and his private secretary appeared.

"Please attend to these, Miss Maune," he said. "I have already noted an outline of the form in which I want them answered. There is one, however,"—he selected a large foolscap sheet from the pile and held it up—"which you might answer more fully. It is from a gentleman—a total stranger to me, by the way—who signs himself Amos Aintree. He states that he is engaged in writing a history of the ancient religious houses of England, and asks me if I can supply him with information regarding the old Abbey of St. Nicholas, whose ruins stand in my grounds. I believe I am right in saying that you take an interest in these—er—somewhat ancient and musty details of the past?"

A slight wave of colour, which might have been a flush of gratification, appeared on Hilda Maune's usually pale cheeks. She appeared to be a young girl of about twenty-five; her dark, pale-olive complexion, and the unfamiliar style in which her raven hair was drawn back from the broad, intellectual forehead, all tended to give her a slightly foreign appearance. She was dressed in a plain grey frock that was almost Quakerish in its severe simplicity.

"Yes, Sir Raymond," she answered, after an almost imperceptible hesitation. "It is true that I have taken some interest in the old records relating to the Abbey. You will remember that you gave me permission to look through those old deeds and parchments in the ancient muniment-chest which I unearthed in the old-store-room above the library."

"Yes, yes, I remember." He raised his eyes and looked into her face with a smile. "Good lord! Fancy you wasting your spare time poring over mouldy manuscripts, and straining your eyes trying to read that crabbed, black-letter Latin! But there—I suppose you're interested in these things?"

"I find the subject very interesting, Sir Raymond."

"Indeed? Then you and this Mr. What's-his-name?—Amos Aintree—will be two kindred souls. By the way," he asked, with a note of deeper interest, "I suppose you did not happen to discover anything startling in that old chest, did you? Nothing relating to the hiding-place of the treasure?"

"Treasure?" Her finely pencilled brows rose the slightest fraction as she repeated the word. "No, I fear I cannot claim to have unearthed anything so romantic. Is there really a treasure hidden hereabouts?"

"Oh, I suppose it's merely a legend," he answered carelessly. "There's been a sort of tradition handed down through our family ever since the first Sir Randolf Chalmers came into possession of the estate at the dissolution of the monasteries in the reign of Henry the Eighth. In those days the Abbey of St. Nicholas was reputed to be the richest of the Cistercian Order, with jewelled tabernacles, golden pyxes and chalices, and, in particular, one immense diamond which had been brought home by one of the Crusaders. According to the tradition, it was as large as a hen's egg—though you may take that piece of information with a pinch of salt!—and it had once adorned the turban of Saladin himself—which may perhaps require another grain of the same condiment! However that may be, the whole point of the story is that when the King's Commissioners came to take over the Abbey and its contents, they found the place as bare as a barrack-room. The jewelled vestments, golden plate, richly woven embroideries, the 'Child of Light'—which was the pet name of Saladin's diamond—all had disappeared."

Hilda Maune tapped her white teeth thoughtfully with the end of her pencil.

"I wonder where?" she said softly.

Sir Raymond gave a short laugh.

"You may have your choice of about half a dozen theories, all equally probable—or improbable. The Abbot may have hidden the treasure to prevent it falling into sacrilegious hands. Or the Commissioners may have quietly appropriated it without the formality of noting the fact. Or one of the merry freebooters who levied 'travellers' toll' on the moor may have looted it before they came. Or—it may never have existed at all! But one thing is certain—from that time each successive head of the House of Chalmers has had a spell of grubbing about the ruins of the old Abbey—one of them razed three-parts of the place to the ground and built the present 'Abbot's Towers' with the material—but, for all the treasure they found, they might have spared themselves their trouble."

"And did you have a search made, Sir Raymond?" asked the girl.

It was no business of hers, and it was an impertinence to ask, as she knew. But Sir Raymond merely laughed as he nodded his head rather dolefully.

"Oh yes, Miss Maune, I had my share in the family foolishness. I came into the title while I was still at Oxford, so I invited a party of my fellow-students down for the treasure-hunt and we had the time of our lives. I do not think there was a panel that they did not tap, or a cellar that they did not explore—or a rabbit that they did not unearth in the grounds! And that, I may say, is all they *did* unearth. After that, I allowed the tale of the treasure to sink into the oblivion of the other fairy-tales of my youth. But all the same—" He gave the girl a steady look as he went on in a more serious tone: "If you *should* discover anything in those old records—anything tangible, that is—I should like to hear of it at once. It would be very handy to have a nice hen's-egg diamond just now."

There was a very thoughtful look in Hilda Maune's eyes as she quitted the room a few seconds later. There had been a wistful eagerness in the old man's voice as he had uttered his last remark that had set her thinking. It was the first hint she had received that he was in need of ready money.

She made her way to the room in which she worked and, taking the cover from her typewriter, sat down, and for the next two hours busied herself in typing the replies to the letters which she had received. It says much for her strength of mind that, although she was burning with impatience to know the nature of the information that the unknown Amos Aintree was so anxious to obtain, it was not until her other work was completed, and she was able to give her undivided attention to it, that she took up the blue-grey foolscap sheet and slowly read it through.

Coming to the end, she read it through again, and then a third time. And at each successive reading the look of speculative interest deepened in her eyes. Finally she opened a drawer at her side and took out a small memorandum-book and laid it on the table. For an hour she read through the closely written lines, occasionally referring to the foolscap, as if comparing parallel passages. Then she folded the letter, placed it in the note-book, and locked it away in her desk.

Lighting a cigarette, she sat back in her chair and slowly and thoughtfully smoked it through.

"Now, I wonder who this Mr. Amos Aintree is—and how much he knows?" she murmured to herself.

Coming to a sudden decision, she placed a sheet of plain paper in the machine and with deft fingers tapped out the date. Then she paused. Typewriters, unless they be brand-new, are apt to be more easily identified than handwriting. She withdrew the paper and tore it into pieces. Then she selected another sheet, slowly printed a few words in a disguised hand, addressed the envelope, and placed it among the others to be posted.

The next morning Amos Aintree, opening his mail in his bedroom at the quiet Bloomsbury hotel where he was staying, found a missive which gave him considerable food for thought. It was in printed characters, and ran:

You may learn all you wish to know by reading the epitaph on Chaucer's monument in the Poet's Corner of Westminster Abbey as the clock is striking three on Thursday next, at the same time holding a guide-book in your hand—upside-down.

Most people, on receiving such a message, might have set it down as emanating from the brain of a madman. But not so Amos Aintree. Something like satisfaction spread over his hawk-like features as he read it through.

"Well, that's certainly a new one on me in the way of assignations," he thought. "But I'll be there all right. It looks as though there's somebody else been reading up ancient history besides myself."

CHAPTER IX

T HE INQUEST ON THE BODY of the unfortunate Private O'Connor was held in due course, only to be adjourned after formal evidence of identification had been given. During the days which followed, Lee Norton devoted his energies in an endeavour to trace the movements of the victim on the night in question. His inquiries brought to light the fact that O'Connor had been seen by one of his comrades shortly after dusk, in the vicinity of Abbot's Towers.

"You are certain that you are not mistaken?" Lee asked the man.

Private Howard, an intelligent-looking man of about thirty, shook his head decisively.

"It was O'Connor all right," he told the detective. "I had gone for a longish tramp across the moor after tea, and was returning along the high-road which leads past the ruins of the old Abbey. There's a gap in the fence there, where some of the palings have been torn down, and when I came opposite this I saw a chap in uniform standing there as though he was waiting for somebody. I recognized him at once as a man in my platoon named O'Connor— the man who was found murdered the next morning.

" 'Cheerio, Con!' I shouts across to him. 'Coming back to billets?'

" 'Not yet,' he called back, 'I've got to see a certain party first.'

"Well, of course, in those circumstances I knew that my company would be *de trop,* as the saying is. So I went straight on along the road, as I'd been warned for guard the following day and I wanted to clean up for inspection. But I hadn't gone above twelve paces before I heard him speak to somebody, and, looking back, I saw him talking to a girl who'd just come through the opening in the fence."

"How do you know that?" asked Lee. "Did you see her come through?"

"No, sir, I didn't actually see her, but she could have come no other way. The road is straight just there, with the open moor on one side and a high fence on the other, and she had not been in sight a moment before I heard him speak."

"Do you think you could give a description of her?"

The man looked doubtful.

"Well, it was dusk, as I have said, and I only had the merest glimpse, so to speak, as I didn't want to stand staring at a fellow when he's talking to his girl—as I supposed he was. She was dressed in a long dark coat, with one of those small felt hats like the girls wear now, which hide their hair. She was about middle height, rather slender, and young—"

"Then you saw her face?" the other interrupted eagerly.

Private Howard laughed.

"No, but he'd hardly be waiting there for an old woman, would he? But since you have mentioned it, as far as I actually saw, she might have been any age."

Lee Norton closed his note-book with a disappointed snap.

"Do you think you would recognize her if you saw her again?" He asked the question as a forlorn hope, and was scarcely surprised when Howard shook his head.

"Not unless she was dressed in the same clothes and standing in the same half-light. Then I might. But I wouldn't like to take my oath on it one way or the other."

"Did her manner—her general appearance—the way she walked and behaved—did it strike you as being that of a servant?"

"Well, sir, that's a hard question to answer—nowadays." The soldier rubbed his chin reminiscently. "I remember meeting a young lady once—we were quartered in Portsmouth at the time—I could have sworn that she was—"

But Lee had no desire to listen to a disquisition on the deportment of the young lady of Portsmouth. With a few words of thanks to Howard for his information he quitted the hut in which the interview had taken place and, passing the main-guard of the aerodrome, set his face towards the village of Westdown.

His return found Sergeant Hattersley in close consultation with a man whom Lee recognized as one of the detectives attached to the Southampton police.

"They've found the missing uniform!" cried the sergeant, pointing to a bundle of clothing which lay upon the table.

Lee's eyes glistened. Here, at last, was something tangible.

"Where was it found—on the moor?" he asked.

"No, sir. A man tried to sell it to a second-hand clothing dealer in Southampton. But the shopkeeper was rather smart. He'd read about the murder in the papers, and happened to remember the regimental number of the dead man. He looked inside the tunic and saw that the number stamped there tallied. He kept the man in conversation while his assistant rang up the station, and we sent a couple of plain-clothes men round and pulled him in."

"Is the prisoner a local man?"

"Well, he is—in a way," answered the police officer. "He's a gipsy fellow who travels the country selling brooms and such-like. He's been through our hands once or twice for poaching game on Sir Raymond Chalmers' preserves, but he doesn't seem to be a very desperate character, by all accounts. He said that be found the uniform under a bush (together with the boots, which he was wearing when arrested) as he passed across the moor on his way to Southampton, He described the place, and I'm now on my way to check up his statement. I looked in to ask if you'd care to come along with me?"

"Nothing would please me better," returned Lee Norton, "especially as I have a little journey to make across the moor. I saw your car at the door as I came in. If you will be good enough to wait a few minutes while I make a little purchase at the village general shop, I'll be glad of the lift."

In a few moments Lee had transacted his business and had returned with a small brown-paper parcel under his arm, and the car set off. The drive was a short one. Halting at the first large clump of trees on their left, the local man alighted and began to walk slowly to and fro, his eyes intently searching the ground for some expected sign. Presently he halted and beckoned to Lee and Sergeant Hattersley.

"It looks as though Nat Marks was speaking the truth. He said that he camped just here, and there's the ashes of his fire still there. It was under this holly-bush that he says he found the uniform. Let's see if that part of his story is true too."

Lee Norton raised his eyebrows slightly, but it was Hattersley who spoke.

"Have you been laying out your spare cash in detective thrillers, Sergeant?" he inquired sardonically. "It's something new to me to hear of a bundle of clothes leaving indications of where it was found."

The younger man seemed to resent his tone.

"Well, one's never too old to learn," he returned with a grin. "If you had waited until I'd finished my explanation you would have seen my point. Naturally, the first thing that Nat Marks did was to go through the pockets of the clothes. According to his own account, he found a packet of cigarettes—which he smoked; a sixpence and two pennies—which he spent; and a white card, which he threw away—and, by all that's wonderful, there it lies!"

The man was in the act of darting forward towards the square of white pasteboard which lay among the grass, when a hand fastened on his shoulder with a grip of iron. Turning, he saw Lee Norton regarding him with grim amusement.

"Go careful, my lad," warned Lee. "When you've been on this case a little longer you'll realize that every card you see with a red query drawn on it needs very watchful handling."

The local officer looked his surprise.

"A red query—?" he began.

"Didn't you notice it? Come with me, but don't attempt to go near it, as you value your life."

The card lay in a little path which ran between two clumps of bushes. Keeping carefully clear of this track, Lee pushed aside the branches of the prickly holly and drew his companion nearer to the grim symbol.

"The most natural manner in which anyone would approach that card would be along that path," he said, "in precisely the same manner as you were about to. Now watch, and see what would have happened if I had not stopped you in time."

He stooped and picked up a large stone which lay dear by, and, aiming it carefully, dropped it on a small grassy hummock which rose in the middle of the path, distantly there was a flash from the bushes on one side, Followed by a loud report and the sound of a bullet ironing harmlessly away in the distance.

The young policeman turned to Lee a face which had suddenly gone white.

"A spring-gun!" he gasped.

Lee Norton's lips were no longer smiling.

"A booby-trap would be a better description," he said grimly. "I rather fancy it was set for me . . . and I am not flattered!"

"Well, let's have a look at the contrivance, anyway," said Hattersley, coming towards the bushes which concealed the gun, only to pause at a sudden exclamation from Lee.

"No, don't disturb it," said the latter. "I have an idea. You, Sergeant Hattersley, will remain here to see that nobody interferes with that secret gun. Our young friend here will motor back to Southampton as fast as the legal limit allows—faster if he likes— and tell Nat Marks that he is unable to find the spot he means. Possibly Marks will offer to show him where it is; if not, then the suggestion must be made to him. Anyway, you will bring him here and ask him to show you the card he found. If he goes straight to the card without hesitation, you will know that he knows nothing of the hidden gun. If, on the other hand, he shows fear, you will know that he is one of the gang I'm looking for. Have you got that? Good! Now hustle."

Lee waited until the throbbing of the car had died away; then he took up the paper parcel which he had brought from Westdown and prepared to go.

"What, aren't you going to stay to see the way in which Marks behaves?" cried Hattersley.

Lee shook his head.

"You can carry on from now with regard to him," he said. "If he picks up the card, I will take the responsibility of your turning him loose after giving him a little sermon with the text 'Findings are *not* keepings'. If he funks it, you can put him back and see if he can be made to talk pretty."

Hattersley nodded; then he looked at his companion queerly.

"And you . . .?"

Lee smiled.

"I'm about to try my hand at a few casts—but of a different kind from those which used to delight the heart of your friend Izaak Walton."

And, leaving Sergeant Hattersley to ruminate in solitude over his cryptic remark, Lee Norton emerged from the bushes and set off along the road which led to Abbot's Towers.

CHAPTER X

IT WAS AN HOUR LATER when Lee Norton crossed the narrow strip of sward which lay between the high-road and the tall, close fence of the Abbey grounds, and, after a preliminary glance through the gap where two of the palings were missing, slipped cautiously inside.

He quickly realized that this most convenient method of entry and egress to the domain of Sir Raymond Chalmers was not due to accident. The spot had evidently been carefully chosen. The belt of brushwood which screened it from view from the windows of the house was, while dense enough for that purpose, yet not so tangled as to prevent the easy progress of anyone who wished to pass unobserved from the rear of the house to the gap. And the trodden state of the long grass seemed to indicate that somebody was in the habit of passing that way frequently.

His eyes constantly searching the ground, Lee began to follow the faint trail, mentally noting the significant fact that, turn and twist as it might, it invariably led in such a direction that whoever used it would be screened from observation. But his hopes of gaining any information of its mysterious frequenter seemed small, for the nature of the ground was not favourable to the retention of footprints. He had traversed fifty yards before his drooping hopes suddenly soared aloft. He had caught sight of the thing he had been hoping for—a patch of damp ground intersecting the trail he was following. But still no footprints met his eager eyes; and the reason was not far to seek. A series of rough stepping-stones had been placed at intervals across the muddy patch. Lee examined them carefully and came to the conclusion that they had been brought to that spot from some little distance, for many of them were squared masonry, and one still bore traces of carved foliage which showed it had originally formed the capital of a Gothic pillar.

"It seems that O'Connor's unknown lady-love had a great disinclination of getting her shoes soiled!" he muttered to himself. "She has evidently been utilizing the loose stones from the Abbey ruins for the purpose. This means that she must have carried an electric torch if she came this way by night—unless she was in the habit of coming here so frequently that—Hullo, what's this?"

He had been carefully stepping from stone to stone; now he paused abruptly at the sight of a single footprint deeply indented on the soft soil. Apparently the unknown girl had missed her footing on one of the stones, and had come down with all her weight on the mud beside it. The impression was perfect. There was the dainty, pointed sole, the high, fashionable heel—even some sort of a maker's embossed trade-mark could be discerned stamped on the instep. Lee's face lit up as he noted the clue which seemed to have been literally dropped at his very feet. It was such a stroke of luck that he had not dared to hope for in his most sanguine dreams.

But the discovery did not find Lee Norton unprepared. Quickly retracing his steps to firmer ground, he drew from his pocket a small tin which, from the label still adhering to it, had originally contained golden syrup of a well-known brand. Placing this upon the ground, he undid the parcel which he had bought at the village stores and poured some of the plaster of Paris into it, adding water from his pocket-flask until it was of the consistency of thick cream. Again making his way to the footprint, he leant over and poured the mixture into the depression. Then he concealed the empty tin and the unused portion of the plaster under a neighbouring bush, lit a cigarette, and sat down to wait until the cast had hardened sufficiently to enable it to be safely removed from its muddy matrix.

Under ordinary circumstances this would have taken about ten minutes, but he was too much alive to the importance of his find to risk its destruction by undue baste. It was twenty minutes later by his wrist-watch before he rose and drew from the ground the dainty white cast which was an exact replica of the shoe which had made the impression.

As he held it up and noted its perfect outline, Lee mentally blessed the memory of the reformed coiner who, in a garret in the slums of Deptford, had initiated him into the possibilities of plaster of Paris as a casting-agent.

"We progress, my dear Lee Norton!" he murmured to himself with a chuckle. "Here's the first real clue since I came on the case."

Carefully placing the fragile object in his pocket, he leant over, obliterated the footprint, and raised his bead—to meet the eyes of a huge Alsatian dog which had silently approached from the direction of the house.

For a moment man and hound stared at each other without sound or movement. Then Lee, still keeping his gaze on the beast, slowly drew himself erect. Under normal conditions, Lee was very fond of dogs, especially the larger kinds; but just at that moment he found it in his heart to curse the individual who first took it into his head to import that particular breed. For there were a watchful menace in the brute's glowering eyes and a tenseness of its splendid muscles that warned him of impending trouble.

"Hullo, boy!" he called out, with a confidence which he was far from feeling. "Good dog . . . good dog!"

But the "good dog" was proof against such blandishments. He greeted the tentative advances with a low, ominous growl, and, baring two rows of gleaming fangs in a manner which left no doubt whatever as to his intentions, began slowly to advance.

Lee was armed, but he was loth to slay a creature who, after all, was but carrying out his canine notions of what was fit and proper. He looked round for a weapon less deadly than the Browning he carried at his hip, but there was none in reach. But above his head the branch of an old elm jutted across the path. If he could reach that . . .

Both man and dog sprang at the same instant; the one forward, the other upward, and the man won by a short margin which was represented by the five square inches of trouser-leg which he left in the jaws of his "runner-up". A moment later, before the dog could repeat his leap, he had drawn himself up and was sitting astride the branch well out of reach, while the infuriated dog was raising canine Cain at the foot of the tree.

"Treed—by the faithful friend of man!" was Lee's disgusted comment as he watched the antics which the dog was performing in his efforts to make his closer acquaintance. "I wonder what's going to happen next?"

He had not long to wait before being enlightened on that point.

"Brutus! Brutus!" cried a voice which almost caused him to tumble from his perch in surprise. "To heel, sir!"

The bushes parted and Beryl Chalmers stepped into view.

A momentary look of alarm showed on her face as she looked from Brutus to the figure of the man in the tree; then a fleeting smile twitched the corners of her lips.

"Why, it's Mr.—Let me see, what did you say your name was? Oh, I remember—Mr. Coleby." She glanced calmly up at the fuming and discomfited detective, the light of mischief shining in her eyes. "How do you do, Mr. Coleby? I perceive you have experienced a rise in the world since I last had the pleasure of meeting you." Then her feelings quite overcame her gravity, and she buried her face in her handkerchief and burst into peal after peal of laughter.

For a while Lee viewed her most unbecoming levity in silence, his face assuming an expression which was intended to convey dignified reproof. But he found it very difficult to be dignified whilst sitting straddle-legged on the branch of a tree, with a yelping dog making delighted leaps at his ankles.

"I am pleased to see that my unfortunate predicament affords you food for laughter," he said, regarding her sorrowfully and endeavouring to conceal the rent in his trousers and at the same time retain his balance on his leafy perch. "It would be more seemly, however, if you were to temper your mirth with at least some slight feeling of gratitude to me for risking my life at the hands—or rather the teeth—of your dear Brutus whilst prosecuting investigations which may result in the apprehension of a gang of miscreants who might have done you serious bodily harm."

Her blue eyes opened wide as she listened.

"Gracious!" she cried in well-simulated admiration. "You must have been perched up there for hours and hours to have thought of all those long words! To hear you talk one would think you were a detective—like my friend Mr. Lee Norton," she added slyly. "Maybe you have heard of him? Most of the criminal classes know him well."

"Oh, I guess I know him right enough—and so do you, Miss Chalmers. It distressed me more than you know to have to cut you dead in the village the other morning, but, really, I had no other choice. If it had got to be known that we were keeping Captain St. Quentin under observation, our efforts would have been greatly hampered, and perhaps—"

"You are watching Stephen?" Her surprise was genuine enough now; her eyes filled with an expression that looked like fear as they looked up at him. "So that is the reason for your presence here—to spy upon him!"

"But only for his own safety, Miss Chalmers," Lee said eagerly, for the tone of cold contempt in her voice had stung him like a whip-lash. "There's a gang out to prevent his new aeroplane becoming an accomplished fact. But for the merest accident that Captain St. Quentin happened to go on leave just when he did, he would be dead by now."

It was clear that his news had come as a sudden shock to her. Hastily slipping a leash on the dog's collar, she motioned the detective to descend and faced him squarely.

"It seems as if I have been acting like a foolish child," she said. "Please tell me everything."

Lee Norton quickly gave her the outline of the facts, beginning with the mysterious warning that had been discovered in the Customs shed and ending with their adventure with the hidden spring-gun on the moor that afternoon. But some instinct seemed to warn him not to tell of the footprint he had found a few minutes since. Her beautiful forehead was creased in a puzzled frown when he came to the incident of the girl who had met O'Connor at the gap in the fence.

"That's strange," she said. "Daddy was complaining only the other day that his private papers had been tampered with. One of them was missing—yes, I remember now—it was a latter from Stephen—Captain St. Quentin, that is—giving the address at which he was staying in Town. I wonder if there is any connection between the two incidents?"

"It's certainly worth looking into." Lee's statement was rendered more emphatic by the memory of the footprint-cast which reposed in his pocket. "Would it be possible for me to have a look at the ladies of your household—unofficially, of course? You might ask me over to tea, for instance, say tomorrow."

She thought for a moment; then shook her head.

"Tomorrow is Thursday, and I remember that Daddy said that Miss Maune, his private secretary, had asked for that day off, to do some shopping in London. We'd better decide on the day after."

"Friday will suit me admirably, Miss Chalmers. And I wish to thank you, first for saving me from the attentions of the too zealous Brutus, and, secondly, for helping me with the case."

She smiled up at him rather wistfully.

"Pray do not thank me, Mr. Norton. It is the duty of every law-abiding person to assist the police, is it not? And I suppose in this case, seeing that I am engaged to be married to the man whose life is threatened, I should be doubly anxious to help."

Lee looked at her keenly. There was a note of lingering pathos in her voice that set his heart leaping wildly. Was it possible, after all, that she did not love this airman-inventor to whom she was engaged? Perhaps she read the thoughts reflected in his face, for she started suddenly and bent over the tiny watch on her wrist.

"I must be getting back to the house," she said quickly. "They will be thinking that I am hatching conspiracies if I stay away much longer! Good-bye, Mr. Norton."

Lee grasped the slender hand which she held extended and held it for an instant.

"Good-bye—till Friday!" he smiled.

For a long time after her dainty figure had disappeared among the bushes Lee stood in deep thought. At last, with a sigh, he turned to retrace his steps. As he did so, his eyes fell on the patch of ground at his feet. There, on the spot where Beryl Chalmers had been standing a moment or two before, were several well-defined footprints on the soft ground. For a full minute he remained staring at them like a man in a dream; then, moved by a sudden, unaccountable impulse, he took the cast from his pocket and laid it in one of them.

A slight vibrating tremor ran over Lee's stalwart form.

"Impossible!" he cried aloud. "It's unthinkable!—absurd!"

Yet before his eyes was evidence silent but irrefutable. Line for line, curve for curve, the imprint of Beryl Chalmers' foot tallied with that of the unknown girl who had been speaking to the soldier a few minutes before he had been done to death.

CHAPTER XI

THE HANDS OF BIG BEN were approaching the right-angle which indicates three o'clock when a thin-faced, under-sized man emerged from Westminster Station and, dodging the traffic of the intervening streets in a nervous manner suggestive of one unfamiliar with London, made his way towards the north entrance of Westminster Abbey and, pausing only to purchase a paper-covered brochure which described the glories of the ancient fane, stepped within.

Most people would have immediately set him down as a sightseer from the other side of the Atlantic, inasmuch as he wore the horn-rimmed glasses and low-crowned felt hat which a certain famous film comedian has impressed upon the minds of the British public as constituting the outward and visible signs of the American city-dweller. The removal of the latter head-gear, which was of a peculiar shade of mauve in keeping with the tweed lounge suit, revealed the fact that its wearer's head was nearly bald. Such hair as still remained was light and fluffy in texture, and of the intermediate shade of flaxen turning to grey; the eyes which blinked short-sightedly behind the huge glasses were of a pale, watery blue.

The stranger evinced none of that insatiable curiosity which usually marks the American tourist "doing London". He hurried up the lofty aisle with scarcely a glance at the monuments of the illustrious dead with which it was lined, and not until he had reached the south transept known as the "Poet's Corner" did he take the slightest interest in his surroundings.

"Say, can you direct me to the grave of Geoffrey Chaucer?" he inquired of one of the black-robed vergers who were passing.

"Certainly, sir," answered the man. "You are standing by it now."

"Right here, eh? Thank you."

For a few minutes the stranger stood motionless, as though paying silent homage to the dust of the "Father of English Poetry", and as he stood, the deep-throated bell of the neighbouring clock began to chime the hour.

Very deliberately, Amos Aintree turned his guidebook upside down and a gleam of suppressed anticipation came into his watery eyes.

A low, clear voice sounded at his elbow:

"As you were saying, Poppa, there is no doubt that Chaucer was the first poet who wrote in what is now the English language," it said, apparently continuing a conversation. "But I think I've seen enough of the Abbey. Let's go."

Turning, Amos Aintree saw that the remarks had been addressed to him by a young dark-haired girl who stood at his side. Was she his unknown correspondent?

"Yes, it is very interesting, as you say," he returned deliberately, "but not so interesting as the muniment-chest at Abbot's Towers."

A flash of understanding lit up her dark eyes.

"I guess you've said it, Poppa," she said, with a quick smile. "Let's come somewhere where we can talk."

He fell into step beside her, and together they passed out into the brilliant autumn sunshine which flooded the streets.

"Shall I call a taxi?" asked Aintree, as they passed across Victoria Street, but she shook her head.

"We can talk quite well in the park," she returned.

A shade of disappointment crossed his sallow face.

"I was going to suggest a cup of tea—in a private room. . . ."

"Nice girls do not take cups of tea in private rooms with perfect strangers," she answered gravely. "And I happen to be one of the nice girls."

"You're sure that!" he exclaimed, with an admiring glance at her profile as she walked beside him. "I'll tell the world—"

"The less you tell the world, and the more you tell *me,* the better I shall like you, Mr. Aintree," she countered promptly. "But here we are."

Save for a nursemaid or two and a few somnolent figures lying on the grass, that portion of St. James's Park was deserted. The girl led the way to a couple of green seats a little apart from the rest and looked at Aintree long and critically.

"Now, Mr. Aintree," she went on in her quiet, self-possessed voice, "as an opening to our conversation, we'll have what they call in your country a 'whole-piece showdown'. We'll put all our cards on the table, beginning with you, and if you've got any aces that don't belong to the pack, you'd better keep them up your sleeve. Is my meaning quite clear, Mr. Aintree?"

The American nodded slowly and a bland smile spread over his hatchet features.

"I get your meaning all right, miss, but I don't think that you've got mine. Your manner seems to suggest that you regard me as some kind of crook or other who's out to sell you a gold brick when you're not looking. I'm sure that my intentions and aims will bear the strictest investigations."

Hilda Maune did not seem to be much impressed.

"Let's have them," she said.

"In the first place, I had better introduce myself more fully. My name you already know, but it will probably be news to you that I am the originator, controller, and also the director of The Two Hemispheres Film Corporation of Chicago. May I ask, Miss—er—"

"Smith," she answered promptly.

"A thoroughly British and non-committal name," he commented dryly, with a little bow. "Well, may I inquire, Miss Smith, if you have ever witnessed a performance of one of our productions?"

"I cannot say that I remember doing so."

"H'm, I guess that's a pity." He gave a depressed shake of his head as though deploring that she had missed one of the chief joys of life. "But if you had done so, Miss Smith, you would have realized that our productions are marked by a refined, a scholastic—I might almost say an archaeological atmosphere that is lacking in all other films. We—or perhaps I should say I—for the controlling interest in the company is in my own hands, and I dictate its policy—I aim at providing film dramas which, though they hold a vital and human interest, are at the same time of a highly aesthetic and educational standard. I am at present engaged in writing, or adapting, a scenario which will accurately reproduce one of the ancient 'moralities' or 'mystery-plays' that were acted in England from the eleventh century down to the time when the regular theatres of Shakespeare's day superseded them."

"A very laudable ambition, Mr. Aintree. Well?"

"I naturally looked round for a manuscript of one of these old plays to use as a basis for my film. Of course, I did not wish to use any well-known play, such as *Everyman,* or *The Castle of Perseverance,* or *The Shepherd's Play.* No, my aim was to unearth an old play which, though unknown to the world at large, still contained matter which might be utilized in a film. During my researches, in your British Museum and elsewhere, I found several references to a miracle-play called *St. Nicholas and the Three Poor*

Maidens, which in pre-Reformation times was performed annually on the feast of that saint at the Abbey of St. Nicholas in Hampshire. I could, however, find no copy of this old play, and I naturally thought that it, like so many others, was entirely lost. One day, however, while looking through the State papers in your Record Office, I chanced to glance through a copy of the report made by the Commissioners of Henry the Eighth when they took over the Abbey at the dissolution of the monasteries. There, among the list of missals and illumininated manuscripts, I found that a copy of the old play, inscribed on vellum and illustrated with pictures of the characters in the play, was mentioned as being handed over to the first Sir Randolph Chalmers when he took over the Abbey and lands. This, you will understand, was the very thing I had been looking for. I lost no time in writing to the present holder of the title, Sir Raymond, requesting that I might be allowed to make a copy of the old manuscript. But, greatly to my surprise and mystification, the only answer I received was an assignation in Westminster Abbey."

The girl gave a short, silvery laugh.

"You must have been surprised," she said carelessly.

"You're right, miss, I was."

"And mystified, I think you said?"

"Right again."

"Yet not sufficiently so that you wrote to Sir Raymond for an explanation?" He was silent, and the girl went on: "I think that why you failed to do so was because you had a shrewd suspicion that there was somebody who knew almost as much as you about that very curious old play?"

Amos Aintree shot a keen glance at the face of his companion, then dropped his eyes and sat silently and thoughtfully chewing the butt of his cigar.

"I think there are a few more cards to be placed on the table, Mr. Aintree," Hilda Maune continued, after a long pause. "You might, for instance, tell me of what other facts of ancient history your researches brought to light."

He leant towards her and laid an eager hand on her arm.

"See here, miss, I want to propose a business deal with you. I don't know who you are, and I don't care. But let me have the original manuscript—the original, mind you—in my hands for half an hour, and there's a thousand pounds—pounds, not dollars!—waiting for you the moment I've finished with it."

Hilda Maune looked thoughtfully at the birds wheeling above the distant tree-tops.

"A thousand pounds is a lot of money," she said softly.

"It's sure a tidy pile—and easily earned if you do what I ask. A smart young girl like you could do a lot with a thousand, eh?"

"I could do a lot more with a quarter of a million," she said, without the least change of tone.

Amos Aintree jumped as though he had been stung.

"A quarter of a million! My sakes, you're crazy, girl!"

"It might be worth it—to you," she said, eyeing him steadily.

He flung the butt of his cigar from him with a fierce gesture.

"The sum you ask is absurd!" he cried. "Besides, what right have you to dictate terms? I have but to go to Sir Raymond and tell him all I know—"

"And *I* have but to go to him and tell him all *I* know—and then it would be good-bye to your chances of ever handling that manuscript. And now I think I'd better leave you to think the matter over." She rose to her feet and buttoned up her gloves. "I must be going, as I have some purchases to make before the shops close."

He rose in his turn.

"But where shall I find you if—"

"If you decide to accept my offer? An advertisement in the Agony Column of the *Morning Wire,* addressed to Miss Smith, will be seen by me. And now . . . good afternoon."

There was a thoughtful frown on his face as he watched her figure disappear. Then he selected a cigar from his case, lit it, and drew from his note-book a piece of paper and slowly read the words written on it. Coming to the end, he carefully replaced it and for a while sat staring thoughtfully at the spot where Hilda Maune had disappeared.

"The pretty little shark wants a quarter of a million, does she?" he murmured. "I thought to play her for a sucker, but it seems she's just as cute as I am. A quarter of a million's sure some money, but"—he rose to his feet and started to walk towards the park gates—"it might be worth it, after all. I'll ask the Count. . . ."

CHAPTER XII

I T IS A MAXIM of the professional crook not to tempt Providence by breaking the law when he has money in hand, and although "Dippy" Nolan professed a supreme contempt for all maxims, good or bad, in the ordering of his shiftless and lawless existence, the one which said "Steal not—unless you are stony-broke" was one that he faithfully obeyed. It was not until he had changed the last note of the roll which he had snatched from the floor of the "Eight Bells", that he ended the prolonged and glorious carouse which his sudden accession of funds had enabled him to indulge in, and sallied forth, blear-eyed and shaky, to replenish his depleted exchequer.

Dippy Nolan had neither the brains nor the courage to shine as a super-crook. His activities—as indicated by the familiar prefix to his name—were confined to picking pockets. It was with mingled feelings of anger, fear, and outraged innocence that he gathered from the newspaper reports that he—a harmless, unaspiring "dip"—was generally credited with having fired the shot, through the partition, which had killed "Swab" Simson.

The fact that he was not mentioned by name gave him but small consolation. He was familiar enough with police procedure to know that his arrest on suspicion would be immediately followed by his identification by the girl behind the bar, with probably fatal results to himself. More than once during the days which followed the crime he had been tempted to seek an interview with the officers who had the case in hand, openly confess to the theft of the notes, and trust that the description of the real murderer, which he would be able to supply, would not only atone for his crime, but would be deemed worthy, in addition, of the usual monetary consideration which he knew by experience to be the reward for such "information received".

A dozen or more times he had bent his steps in the direction of the police-station, but always his resolution had given way at the critical moment. That instinctive distrust which is ingrained in the mind of every crook would bid him halt before taking the plunge. What if his story were not believed? What if he should find himself in the dock charged with the capital crime? He realized, by the adroit manner in which he had been made the cat's-paw, that the real murderer was a clever fellow who might be quite capable of turning the tables against a witness with such a record of convictions as Dippy had against him. On the other hand, he would be compelled to give up his ill-gotten money in order to prove the truth of his story, and Dippy, though he had probably never heard of *Æsop,* was quite alive to the risk of relinquishing the substance for the shadow. So it happened that, while every detective in the division had been hunting for the murderer, the one man who could have put them on the track was carefully concealing his knowledge.

But even now, although three weeks had passed since the crime, an impulse urged the pickpocket to tell what he knew. He was turning the matter over in his mind as he passed along the busy High Street of Southampton, gazing aimlessly in the shop windows and threading his way along the crowded pavement. He had almost come to a decision to reveal all he knew; had actually turned in the direction of the station to carry out his good resolution, when Fate, in the shape of a bulky purse lying exposed in a woman's shopping-basket, decreed otherwise.

Almost instinctively, Dippy sidled alongside. A minute later the purse was in his own pocket, and the elated Dippy turned to go.

"Good morning, Dippy," said a voice that he knew only too well.

The crook turned and stared coldly at the keen-faced young man who had addressed him.

"I think you're making a mistake, sir," he said politely. "I don't think I know you."

The plain-clothes detective grinned.

"Oh yes, you do, Dippy—and I know you!" He laid his hand affectionately on Dippy's arm and propelled him gently but irresistibly in the direction of the woman with the basket. "Have you lost anything, madam?" he asked.

The woman glanced into her basket and gasped.

"My purse—it's gone!"

"If you'll kindly follow me to the station you'll probably have it restored to you," answered the detective. "Quick march, Dippy, and don't fall into the error of trying to drop anything as we go along."

Arrived at the station, the sergeant in the charge-room greeted the prisoner with a look of pained surprise.

"What, you here again, Dippy? I hadn't seen you for such a long time that I thought you'd reformed, or emigrated, or been run over. What's the charge—theft from the person, as usual?"

The prisoner drew himself up.

"You may not believe me, Sergeant—" he began impressively.

"You're a good guesser, Dippy," interrupted that officer, with a grin.

"But I was on my way here when that 'busy' took me," continued the crook impressively. "I wanted to tell you—"

"Tell it to the magistrate in the morning. Give him a rub down, Taylor."

Dippy was "rubbed down" accordingly, and the deft fingers of the gaoler brought to light the purse which had just been stolen, a copy of a racing-paper, a packet of cheap cigarettes, and lastly a brown leather wallet.

"Who does this belong to, Dippy?" asked the detective, holding it up.

The prisoner's shifty eyes narrowed in thought. If he was going to make capital out of his misfortune, now was the time to act. His cringing mien grew of a sudden arrogant.

"Never you mind whose it is, my man," he answered loftily. "I want to see the superintendent."

"You'll see him soon enough," was the grim answer.

"I tell you I've got some important information that I want to tell him privately."

"You'll see him in good time, depend on that. What I'm asking you now is where you got this wallet?"

"Never you mind," was Dippy's answer, accompanied by a sulky shake of his head. "I knows what I knows, and what I knows ain't for the likes o' you to be told."

The sergeant shrugged his broad shoulders and, opening the wallet, shook it face downwards on the desk before him.

"There ain't nothing in it, Sergeant, because I—Blimy! What's that?"

Dippy's face had suddenly gone white as he stared at the object which had fluttered to the desk. It was a small square of white pasteboard and on it was a large crimson note of interrogation.

There was a dead silence as the sergeant bent over and scrutinized it closely. When he raised his eyes, Dippy read the unspoken accusation in them, and a hoarse cry of terror broke from his lips.

"Strewth! If it ain't the same mark as what was on the corpse of 'Swab' Simson!" he cried. "But it ain't nothink to do with me. I thought the wallet was empty, but that there card must ha' been sticking in one of the corners. I didn't know it was there—I swear I didn't!"

"I can well believe that!" said the police officer grimly.

Dippy wilted under the suspicious gaze of the three men who confronted him.

"For God's sake, don't look at me like that!" he wailed. "I didn't do 'Swab' in, and I never set eyes on that card afore this very minute. I pinched that wallet in the 'Eight Bells' a few seconds before the shot was fired, and—"

The sergeant held up his hand suddenly.

"It's my duty to warn you that you're now charged with complicity in the wilful murder of the man commonly known as 'Swab' Simson, and that anything you may say is liable to be used in evidence against you. If you did really steal that wallet, and are able to give a description of the man—"

He broke off in surprise as he saw that the prisoner had slipped to the ground.

"Has he fainted?" he asked quickly.

The plain-clothes man was bending over the limp body. There was a queer expression in his eyes as he straightened up and looked round.

"Where's the woman who preferred the charge?" he rapped out. "She should have followed me to the station. Did any of you see her?"

The others shook their heads.

"Why?" they demanded in one voice.

"Because I noticed that one of his fingers started bleeding as soon as he picked that purse out of her basket," was the excited answer. "I thought he staggered a bit as we came along, but I put it down to the drink; but now—"

"Well, what now?" the sergeant exclaimed impatiently, as the other paused and again bent over the prostrate form of the prisoner. "Here, carry him into the cells while I ring up the divisional surgeon. I want to get his statement as soon as I can."

The detective loosed the prisoner's hand and it fell to the floor with a thud.

"I'm afraid the statement will have to wait, Sergeant," he said slowly. "There isn't any more information coming from Dippy, either now or ever. The man is dead—murdered by the gang whose sign is the Crimson Query!"

CHAPTER XIII

WHEN INSPECTOR NORTON AND SERGEANT HATTERSLEY arrived at Southampton in response to an urgent summons from Headquarters, they found no less a person than Sir John Lambert, the Chief Commissioner of Scotland Yard, in conference with the local chief of police. Sir John lost no time in plunging into the business which had caused his hurried journey from London.

"There is every indication, gentleman, that a new and very sinister force has of late come into being in this country—a combination of clever and relentless criminals who feel so sure of their immunity from detection and arrest that, far from seeking to disguise the authorship of their crimes, they openly proclaim them to the world by means of a recognized symbol. I refer, of course, to that fantastic and seemingly theatrical sign which is beginning to be known to the public at large as 'The Crimson Query'. It is difficult to understand their motive for thus proclaiming their guilt. The first and most vital consideration of the ordinary criminal is to conceal the fact of his complicity in his crime; but these men, on the contrary, seem to glory in their deeds. There can be, to my mind, but one explanation of this apparently senseless 'trademarking'—if I may be permitted to use the term—of their victims. The leader of this formidable league is desirous of creating a similar reign of terror over the inhabitants of these islands as the dreaded Camorra once did over the Italian populace. I do not think it is necessary for me to add that he will not succeed!

"But still, that does not lessen the immediate danger. Let us review the series of murders and attempted murders which have taken place in the short space of three weeks. First, we have the man known as 'Swab' Simson shot dead in the 'Eight Bells' at the same time as Inspector Norton here narrowly escaped the same fate. Secondly, there was Private O'Connor battered to death on Abbots-moor, and the life of Captain St. Quentin attempted the same night. Next comes the attempt on Inspector Norton by means of the hidden spring-gun. The third victim was the pickpocket, Dippy Nolan, who met his death through snatching a purse which

had been fitted with a series of hollow needles, so arranged that
upon being grasped they would inject a concentrated solution of
Aconitum Napellus, or some closely allied alkaloid, beneath the
skin. Finally we come to the dastardly attempt on the life of Captain St. Quentin last night."

The Chief Commissioner paused as a simultaneous gasp of surprise arose from his hearers.

"Last night, sir?" It was Lee Norton who spoke, and his set features alone showed how deeply the news had affected him. "Was it
here—on the moor. . .?"

Sir John Lambert shook his head.

"No, no, you were not to blame, Norton. It happened in London.
Shortly after the lunch-hour yesterday afternoon Captain St. Quentin left his friend's house in Portman Square with the intention of
visiting his club in Pall Mall. He had just reached the corner, when
a large grey touring-car emerged from a side-street and made directly towards the spot where he was standing. Fortunately a passer-by had time to shout a warning, otherwise the captain would
have been crushed against the railings and instantly killed. As it
was, he jumped, and escaped with a broken arm. In the confusion
the driver of the car jumped out and got clear away. There cannot
be the slightest doubt that it was a deliberate attempt at murder. It
is clear that the gang are out to get him, and get him they will—
unless we get them first. So I have thought out a plan whereby
their eagerness may be made the means of their own undoing. I
want a man of the same height and build as Captain St. Quentin to
impersonate him in order to draw them off his trail. The question
of disguise will be simplified by reason of the fact that yesterday's
'accident' will give an excuse for the man who takes his place to
have his face partly concealed by bandages or surgical plaster. The
captain's height is five feet ten, and to indicate his build I have
brought one of his old tunics down with me."

As Sir John paused, every eye was turned towards the stalwart
figure of Lee Norton. It did not need a second glance to see that he
alone of those present would be able to assume the role. Yet for a
brief instant he felt himself hesitating. It was not the prospect of
danger that held him back; rather was it some vague premonition
of the complications and misunderstandings which his masquerade
might engender. He turned to the Commissioner with a question.

"Will Miss Chalmers, the captain's fiancée, be told of our plan,
Sir John?"

A decisive shake of the head prefaced the reply.

"No—absolutely no! In a case like this the fewer who are aware of our intentions the better. The only person outside the service who will be aware of the substitution will be Captain St. Quentin himself. He is to leave tomorrow night for a nursing-home in the South of France, and by the time he has recovered from his injuries I trust all danger to him will be past."

Outwardly unmoved, Lee Norton took off his coat and donned the blue-grey tunic belonging to the airman. It fitted him like the proverbial glove.

"Capital! Capital!" cried the delighted Commissioner. "Not a wrinkle to be seen! If you can but assume his identity as neatly as you do his clothes we'll fool these scoundrels yet! You will report at 15A Portman Square at ten o'clock tomorrow morning. That will give you time to settle up your business here. Tell your friends that you have been ordered on a mission abroad, and do not let a living soul—not even your nearest and dearest friend—suspect the real reason for your disappearance."

Lee Norton had much to occupy his thoughts as he accompanied Sergeant Hattersley back to Westdown. The situation was already complicated enough, in all conscience, yet here was another factor which bade fair to render it, as far as he was concerned, chaotic. He did not seek to conceal from himself the fact that his feelings towards Beryl Chalmers were far deeper than those of a mere chance acquaintance. Yet this would not have troubled him much had not something in the girl's manner conveyed to him, in the unspoken yet unmistakable manner in which such things are conveyed, that he was not indifferent to her. Yet he was about to assume the identity of the man to whom she was engaged to be married. In his character of Captain St. Quentin he would be bound to meet her again and again. Would she recognize him? Would her subtle woman's instinct reveal him for the fraud he was, and kill whatever feeling she might have had for him? Would he be expected to play the lover in his new character? Would she . . .?

"I wish to heaven that our esteemed Commissioner had been run over himself before he came down here with his fool stunts!" he exclaimed loudly and irritably.

Sergeant Hattersley looked across from the other side of the railway carriage with a grin.

"What's up now, Lee? Getting the wind up already?"

"Yes," returned Lee.

For a moment the sergeant looked at him in open and undisguised disbelief. Then he laughed.

"Oh, I see what you mean? You're thinking that you'll be expected to take the 'plane up for a flight?"

Lee Norton shook his head.

"You're a bad guesser, Sergeant. When I spoke I was alluding to something much more dangerous than flying."

"Oh, and what's that?" asked the interested sergeant.

"Flirting!" said Lee curtly.

Sergeant Hattersley, who was a married man, leaned across and slapped the other encouragingly on the shoulder.

"Cheer up," he said heartily. "Why meet trouble half-way? After all, you've only got to go and get killed in place of Captain St. Quentin—you haven't got to marry his girl!"

By the time Lee had finished his lunch and had packed his bag it was high time for him to set out for Abbot's Towers to keep his appointment with Beryl Chalmers.

After an hour's sharp walking along the high-road, he began to realize that he had cut things rather too fine. It was past four o'clock, and he was less than half-way to the Towers. The road, as he knew, made a wide sweep before it reached the old house. Why not take a short cut across the moor, guiding his steps by the grey turrets which showed above the trees, seemingly not more than two miles off in a direct line?

No sooner did the idea occur to him than he stepped off the road and struck across the open ground, only to be arrested by an urgent shout behind him.

"Hoi! Hoi, maister! Hoi! Coom back—coom back, maister!"

Turning, Lee saw an ancient, white-bearded countryman standing up in a cart and gesticulating wildly in his direction.

"Why, I'm not trespassing, am I?" Lee called back. "I was just about to take a short cut—"

A strange wheezing sound came from between the old man's lips, and after a moment Lee realized that he was laughing.

"He, he, he!" crooned the ancient. "Taking short cut for Kingdom Come you weer, maister, for sure! It's only folk as be tired o' life as takes short cuts to Abbot's Towers!"

"What do you mean?" Lee demanded irritably.

The old man peered at him with his dim eyes.

"Never heerd o' Abbot's Mire, maister?" he asked. "There be ne'er a living thing as gets out o' the Mire when once it be trapped. Ponies, cattle, deer—ay, and men!—lie yonder, sucked down and choked by the soft black mud. And 'ee weer making straight fer it, 'ee weer. Lucky as I be heer to stop 'ee."

Lee Norton examined the stretch of moorland with a new and closer interest. Yes, now that he knew what to look for, he could see that the grass took on a fresher and more luxuriant green in the hollows between the scattered mounds. If all the stories that he had heard about the treacherous swamp were true, he had had a fortunate escape.

"Thanks for your warning," he said gratefully.

"And thank 'ee, too, zur," answered the man as he transferred to his pocket the silver coin which Lee had just pressed into his horny palm. "If so be it ye're in a hurry to get to the Towers, just 'ee jump in and I'll give 'ee a lift theer."

When the old horse between the shafts had been urged into a lumbering trot, Lee turned to the old man.

"Is there no path at all across there?" he asked with a jerk of his head towards the swamp.

"Ay, theer be a way, so folks do say," he answered deliberately. "But there's few that know the path, and they as does 'ud have to have certain death behind 'em afore they'd cross it after a day or two o' rain. I mind the time when little Jenny Murray wandered on theer, picking flowers and such-like, an' her only a child of eight year old and knowing no better. Right in the middle o' the mire she weer, zur, afore summun come flying back to Westdown with the news. And then we all goes up and stands by the road—her mother among us, nearly distracted, poor soul, expecting every minute to see her Jenny sink down, yet dus'sent call to her in case she should run to her and be swallowed up. For more'n an hour we watched the child wandering to and fro, and then she came out with not so much as a splash o' mud on her little shoes. Some said as how the angels must ha' been guiding her innocent footsteps that day, zur."

"Maybe," said Lee soberly.

"But theer weer others as weren't so lucky," the ancient went on. "Theer weer a horse as took fright and dashed off the road afore his rider could turn 'un . . ."

The old man rambled on, one grisly legend following the other, until by the time they came to the lodge gates of Abbot's Towers it was a source of wonder to Lee that there were any inhabitants at all left in the village of Westdown.

"Ah, zur, do'ee keep away from Abbot's Mire, 'specially arter rain," was the parting piece of advice as the old man drove off. "I was borned and breeded in these yere parts and I knows!"

Lee was soon to find that taking tea at Abbot's Towers was both an impressive and depressing function. The first Sir Randolph had built with an eye to security rather than comfort. Although it was still broad daylight, deep gloomy shadows hung about the oak-panelled walls of the Great Hall, lighted by a sudden gleam here and there as the light of the rose-coloured table-lamps was reflected from some mailed effigy or trophy of ancient arms.

Lee, in apologizing for being late, mentioned the fact of his narrow escape from attempting to cross the swamp.

"It's indeed fortunate that there was somebody there to warn you," said Sir Raymond. "The place is a veritable death-trap. There has been talk of having it railed off, but nothing has been done by the local authorities. I, at least, have done my share, for there is a high fence all along that part of my grounds which abut on the Mire. You see, Mr. Norton, that part of the moor is very seldom visited, as it leads to nowhere. It has existed from very ancient times—in fact," a smile flitted over his face as he added, "it is so venerable that it had a traditional spectre all to itself!"

Hilda Maune, who was seated directly opposite Sir Raymond, looked up quickly.

"Do you know whose ghost it is that is supposed to haunt the Mire?" she asked.

The old baronet turned to Lee with a smile.

"Miss Maune, my secretary, is quite an enthusiastic collector of old legends connected with the Towers; sometimes I cannot help thinking she has some ulterior object in view, and that I shall wake up one morning and find that she has published a book on the subject—"

"All complete with photographs of the ghost!" interrupted Beryl laughingly.

"After all, it's only natural that an old place like this should have its ghost," said Lee. "Indeed, I should be rather disappointed to find that it had not one—especially as it has a ruined abbey in its back garden, as you may say."

"Have you seen the ruins, Mr. Norton?" asked Beryl.

Lee shook his head.

"My time has been too fully occupied to indulge in the pleasure of sight-seeing. But as this is my last night in this part of the country, I should like to have a look at them before I go."

He had been watching Beryl's face as he made the announcement, and he could have sworn that a shadow passed across it.

"So you are leaving us?" It was Sir Raymond who put the inquiry. "Does that mean that the mystery of that young soldier's death has been cleared up?"

"Unfortunately, it does not, Sir Raymond. The mystery remains as deep as ever, but I, personally, will have no interest in it after tonight. I have been ordered abroad."

Sir Raymond pushed back his chair.

"In that case you might wish to have a look over the ruins before it gets too dark?"

"I should be delighted."

"There's a glorious sunset!" Beryl cried with a light laugh, as she glanced at the ruddy glow on the windows. "The old place will look quite romantic! Come along, Mr. Norton, and we'll have time to get our sight-seeing over before the ghost begins to walk!"

"Who is he—or is it a she?" asked Lee as they quitted the Great Hall and made their way on to the long terrace which was one of the glories of the old mansion. But Beryl shook a laughing head.

"Oh, you must ask Hilda that question," she declared. "She is the antiquarian of this household."

Lee glanced inquiringly at the dark-haired girl, half expecting to see a smile on her face. To his surprise, however, she answered in quite a serious tone.

"Legends, because of the mere fact that they *are* but legends, are apt to be vague and contradictory," she said gravely. "Some say that the white-cowled figure which flits about the roofless chapel, or traverses the treacherous swamp, was a certain Brother Nigel who was expelled from the Cistercian Order for some grave breach of their rules, and was condemned to pass the remainder of his days in a cave on one of the knolls of firm ground in the depths of the swamp. Others say that it is the wraith of the Abbot Falayse, during whose term of office the Abbey was seized by Henry the Eighth. Rather than allow the treasures of the Order to fall into the King's rapacious hands, he gathered them together and bore them to a piece of firm ground in the centre of the Mire and there buried them. Others, again, say that both treasure and prelate were swallowed up by the swamp. These are the current legends; you may take your choice of the most probable. But one thing is certain—at times a white-robed figure is to be seen crossing the ground where no mortal man could tread without being engulfed."

He stared at her in silence for an instant. Her dark eyes were shining strangely in the crimson rays of the setting sun; there was a rapt, almost reverent expression on her pale face.

"And do you honestly believe that, Miss Maune?" he asked.

She threw up her head with a challenging gesture.

"I myself have seen it," she said quietly.

"Seen it?" Startled, he jerked out the question urgently. "Where?—when?"

"Crossing Abbot's Mire—on the night that O'Connor was killed!"

Then, before he could ask the torrent of questions that surged to his lips, Hilda Maune had turned and re-entered the house.

CHAPTER XIV

THE RUINS OF THE ABBEY OF ST. NICHOLAS lay about a quarter of a mile distant from the Towers. Lee, who had expected to see a few crumbling pillars and, maybe, a tottering fragment of wall, was amazed at the sight which greeted him as he emerged from the belt of trees and saw the venerable pile standing in solitary grandeur on the slight eminence above the winding river. Originally the Abbey must have been of enormous extent, for, in spite of the fact that it had been freely used as a quarry to supply the materials for the building of the Towers, enough had escaped the hand of the spoiler to tell, silently but eloquently, of its departed glories. Of the domestic buildings of the monastery little but the foundations remained; but the cloisters and the great chapel, save that their roofs were open to the sky and their walls overgrown with ivy, were as perfect as they were when the white-habited friars trod their worn flagstones or chanted their midnight orisons beneath the lofty Gothic arches.

"This was a famous place in its day, Mr. Norton," said Sir Raymond, who had followed Lee and Beryl out into the grounds. "It was generally credited with being the largest and the richest Cistercian monastery in this country. St. Nicholas, as you probably know, was looked upon as the patron saint of sailors, and seldom a ship put out on a long voyage but what the master, and maybe his crew as well, made a pilgrimage here to pray for fair winds and profitable cargoes, and I suppose they did not forget to suitably record their gratitude on their safe return. Tradition has it that many a rich jewel and piece of massive plate found their way into the Abbey's coffers after a sharp sea skirmish in the Narrow Seas."

Lee Norton looked at the speaker with sudden interest. The note of eagerness in his voice as he had described the rich offerings had not escaped the detective's quick ear.

"Indeed, Sir Raymond? And what became of all this wealth?" he asked.

The old man shook his head testily.

"Ah, I'd be a very happy man if I were able to answer that question, sir. But, wherever the treasure went to, it certainly did not go into the pockets of my ancestors, for every one of them has had his turn at trying to find it." He stood looking moodily at the ruins before him, then looked towards his companion with a sudden smile. "Now there's a chance for you, sir. You detectives are generally credited with being able to see a bit farther through a brick wall than most people—why not have a shot at solving the mystery of the Abbot's treasure! I'll pay you any fee in reason if you're successful."

"But I was always under the impression that such 'treasure trove' would be claimed by the State?" said Lee.

Sir Raymond shook his head.

"That only applies to the discovery of money or valuables that have no owner. My case is very different. You must understand that the Abbey of St. Nicholas was given to the first Sir Randolph Chalmers by Henry the Eighth, together with its contents, and each head of the house has specifically mentioned the lost treasure in his will. Oh no, sir, I have not the slightest doubt that I would be able to make good my claim if the treasure should be unearthed. Why not have a shot at solving the mystery?"

Lee laughed at the suggestion, but there was a thoughtful expression on his face.

"I'm afraid that I have enough mysteries already on my hands to keep me occupied for some time to come, Sir Raymond. Perhaps later on I may possibly . . ." His voice died away with the sentence unfinished, and he remained staring intently at the shadows behind the pillars of the roofless nave. When he spoke again it was to ask a question. "Are the public admitted to view these ruins?"

"No—they are my private property," answered the old baronet. "Why do you ask?"

"Because I caught sight of a face peering between those pillars over there." Lee pointed as he spoke. "Yes—there it is again. It seems as though somebody else is desirous of seeing the old Abbey at sunset."

"Then he is trespassing!" Sir Raymond returned angrily. "I should like to have a nearer look at this enthusiast who visits my property at sundown. You go round that way, and I'll go this, so that he can't escape."

With a slight shrug, Lee nodded and commenced to make his way across the short stretch of grass and through the arched doorway which led to the interior of the chapel. A deep, almost uncanny silence hung over the great structure. The rays of the westering sun, striking through the lofty windows, painted bars of ruddy gold across the worn flags with which the nave was paved, leaving the remainder in an obscurity which seemed even deeper by contrast.

Entering the aisle, Lee advanced and cautiously peered round one of the Gothic pillars which had formerly supported the roof. For a moment his eyes, dazzled by the sudden change from the glare of sunlight to semi-darkness, could distinguish nothing. Then he was aware of a figure descending the flight of broad shallow steps from the sanctuary. Carefully keeping in the shadows which lay between the squares of sunshine streaming through the side windows, Lee advanced, and at the same moment Sir Raymond came forward from the opposite side of the chapel.

"Good evening," said the baronet blandly. "May I inquire the reason for your presence here?"

The stranger swung round sharply at the sound of his voice, and for an instant seemed to hesitate as though contemplating flight. The frown of annoyance which passed across his sallow features as he saw his escape was cut off by Lee changed instantly to a smile.

"Sir Raymond Chalmers, I guess?" he said in a voice which left no doubt as to his nationality.

"You have the advantage of me in knowing my name," said the baronet stiffly.

"Maybe my own name is not quite unknown to you, Sir Raymond. Do you remember receiving a letter from a Mr. Amos Aintree a few days ago?"

"Aintree? Oh yes, to be sure I did. You asked about some old mystery-play or other, if I recollect rightly. Is your present visit in connection with that?"

The American paused before replying, his pale eyes blinking thoughtfully behind his horn-rimmed spectacles. Then he shook his head.

"Not exactly. I am the chief director of 'The Two Hemispheres Film Corporation', and I am at present searching for a suitable location for some of the scenes in my forthcoming production. One of those scenes is an old ruined abbey, and—subject, of course, to your approval—I guess I've found it right here." Amos Aintree glanced round at the ancient walls with an approving smile. "Yes, sir, I reckon this is a genuine old sure-enough hoary ruin, and it'll suit me down to the ground."

Sir Raymond Chalmers made an ironical inclination of his head.

"It is very gratifying to me to know that my property meets with your approval," he said quietly. "I think, however, it would have shown better taste on your part to have called on me and asked my permission before trespassing on my private grounds."

The film producer gave an apologetic smile.

"I'm sure sorry if you're riled any, Sir Raymond, and I hope you'll accept my word that I intended no harm to your old ruin. But what was the use of troubling you needlessly? We happened to be passing, and saw that there was a gap in your fence, so the Senorita suggested that we should just slip quietly through and have a look at the place without troubling you. For all we knew, it might not have been at all suitable; but as it is, well, it's the real goods. The Señorita is fair crazy over it."

Sir Raymond looked puzzled.

"The Señorita?" he repeated, with raised brows.

"My leading lady, the rising star who's going to cause a universal eclipse among the other orbs in the film firmament. She's around here somewhere, exploring the ins-and-outs of the old place, as happy as a child with a new toy." He raised his voice and called: "Señorita! . . . Señorita!"

A light footfall sounded on the sanctuary steps as a vague white figure appeared.

Aintree stepped forward with the air of a showman.

"Gentlemen, allow me to present to you Señorita Clotilde La Zorita."

There was a moment's pause, and then into the golden radiance of the dying sun there stepped a figure that made the two men catch their breath in admiration. Each had his own preconceived notion of what a film star looked like in the flesh, but the young girl who appeared before them caused these notions to be hurriedly revised.

She was clad from head to feet in spotless white. The slender grace of her girlish figure was accentuated by the soft folds of the cloak which fell from her shoulders to the ground, almost nun-like in its severe simplicity. Her corn-gold hair, parted in the centre, fell in two thick plaits over her shoulders almost to her waist, framing a face Madonna-like in its serene purity and repose. Eyes of deepest violet, half veiled by their golden lashes; a mouth shaped like a tiny scarlet heart; a throat whose satiny whiteness vied the single strand of pearls by which it was encircled—she seemed, as she stood there, so still and aloof, like a stained-glass picture of some medieval saint suddenly and miraculously endowed with life. When she spoke, her voice was like a silver vesper bell.

"I am pleased to make your acquaintance, sirs." She spoke
without the slightest trace of foreign accent, but the care with
which she chose her words only seemed to add to their innocent
and child-like charm. "I was so overcome with the charm of this
beautiful place of devotion that I quite forgot that we were trans-
gressing in entering it. I beg you will forgive me, Sir Raymond?"
And she raised her eyes for the first time and fixed them on those
of the baronet.

"Forgive you? Of course—of course—delighted to be of service
to you, miss—er—that is, Señorita." The old man was stammering
like a bashful schoolboy. "I'm sure I shall feel highly honoured if
you will use the old place to—er—take your photographs in—that
is if you think it good enough."

She shook her head sadly as she clasped her hands on her
breast.

"Good *enough!*" she cried. "Nay, it is too good! It seems almost
like sacrilege to use these ancient walls, hallowed by the prayers of
the monks of old, for a mere background for a film drama. What
would those holy monks of old say were they to know that their
loved Abbey was so profaned? Would they not rise from their
graves and drive me from the sacred ground?"

The old baronet laid a reassuring hand upon her slim shoulder.

"I shouldn't let that worry you, Señorita," he said with a smile.
"I don't suppose it'll trouble them. They've been a longish time
dead, you know."

"Dead?" She repeated the word with a rapt light shining in her
eyes. "What is the significance of mere earthly time to those who
have passed across? Who shall say that the shades of the friars do
not visit their earthly home, to tread the cloisters they loved—to
watch over the treasures they gathered?"

"Eh, what's that?" An eager look had mounted to Sir Raymond's face as he jerked out the question. "What do you know
about treasures?"

For a moment she stood silent, her face upturned, her eyes
closed, her hands folded across her breast. Then she began to speak
in a low, rapid voice:

"I see much gold and many jewels lying in a great stone coffer.
Great goblets set with many jewels—a cross of emeralds—a mitre
sewn with pearls—a chalice of hammered silver, black with age—
a golden tabernacle containing a relic of the Abbey's patron saint.
And among them, wrapped in many folds of fine linen, is a great
diamond—the 'Child of Light'—"

"The 'Child of Light'? Heavens above!—" It was Sir Raymond who spoke, his voice but little louder than an awed whisper. Then he came forward and caught her by the hand. "Who are you, child? And how came you to know of the things of which you speak?"

It was almost as though she had not heard. Motionless, as in a trance, she stood, her lips moving slightly.

"But they are not for mortal hands to touch," she went on. "Above that secret hoard there hovers the shade of a mitred abbot. It is the spirit of the Abbot Falayse, guarding for all time the treasure that he hid."

The baronet was trembling with excitement.

"Where?" he cried. "Hid where?"

She turned slowly, her hands outstretched like one who walks in sleep. "It is near here—I know it—I feel it! Near . . . near . . ."

"Where? Show me the place—point it out!" Chalmers begged eagerly.

As she stepped forward as though to obey the frenzied appeal, her foot caught in a crevice of the broken floor. With a low cry, she staggered and seemed about to fall. But in an instant Aintree had caught her in his arms. She lay there for an instant; then her eyes opened and she looked dazedly round.

"Where am I? What has happened?" she murmured faintly.

Aintree smiled reassuringly.

"It's all right, Señorita; I guess you've been overtaxing your strength some." He turned to the two men with a warning look. "She's psychic, you know," he whispered, "and highly strung. It would be rather interesting to have a séance another time, eh? But, there, I guess you'll just think she's been talking nonsense."

"Far from it, my dear sir," Sir Raymond hastened to assure him. "Her description of the lost treasure tallies word for word with the old Abbey records. I should feel honoured if the Señorita will make my house her headquarters while the film is in the making."

"That's real kind of you, Sir Raymond," returned the American, with real feeling. "On her behalf I thank you."

And taking the girl's arm he led her towards the house.

Unknown to the others, there had been a fourth spectator of the strange scene. Beryl Chalmers had been watching through a lancet window of a small gallery which overlooked the body of the chapel. No sooner had Señorita Clotilde and the two men quitted the building, than Beryl ran quickly down the narrow winding staircase and touched Lee Norton on the arm.

He turned with a smile.

"I've been trying to get a word with you ever since I arrived," he said. "I want to know if you had ever previously passed by the spot where your dog had me treed."

She considered for a moment; then shook her head.

"Never," she answered firmly. "I should not have taken that path then had I not been attracted by the dog's barking. Why do you ask?"

He looked her full in the face.

"Because I found a footprint there which tallied in every respect to the shoes that you were wearing."

"I?" She drew back as she gasped out the word; then she burst into a laugh. "In that case I can provide you with a clue. On the same morning as the murder on the moor occurred, the new boot-boy mixed up all the shoes. I remember that we had to have a general sort-out the following day."

A great load seemed to be lifted from Lee's heart as she made the explanation.

"Can you tell me who wore yours on that night, Miss Chalmers?"

She looked at him curiously.

"Why are you so anxious to know that?"

"Whoever wore them had an appointment with the victim a few minutes before he was killed, and I should like to know her movements on the night in question."

"I'm afraid," said Beryl after a moment's hesitation, "you will have to question the girl herself."

Lee looked up quickly. "And she is—?"

"My father's private secretary—Hilda Maune."

CHAPTER XV

I T WAS A VERY DEJECTED LEE NORTON who made his way towards the Towers through the gathering dusk. The moment that Beryl Chalmers had revealed the name of the girl who had worn her shoes on the fatal night, he had realized that he had, as far as the footprint clue was concerned, come to a blank wall. The details of the case were still fresh enough in his memory for him to know that Hilda Maune had a complete and unassailable alibi during the hours when the crime must have been committed; every inmate of the Towers would be prepared to swear that she did not leave the house after nightfall. Yet, seeing that she had met the victim a few hours before his death—was, in fact, the last person to speak to him—it was strange that she had not come forward voluntarily to make a statement to the police. True, the interview at dusk at the gap in the fence might have been nothing more than a clandestine lovers' meeting; but, on the other hand, if she had loved the young soldier, why had she not tried her best to assist the police in bringing his murderer to justice?

He fully realized that there was something un-English in the series of crimson queries which had been marked upon the victims of the wave of crime that had swept over that part of the country. Sir John Lambert, the Chief Commissioner, had compared it to the Italian Camorra—and Hilda Maune's pale-olive complexion and raven hair seemed to hint that in her veins there coursed some of the hot, passionate blood of the South. Obviously, he concluded, she was a young lady whose past history and future movements might well repay a little investigation.

He had been so absorbed in his own reflections that he had almost forgotten the presence of the girl who walked by his side. It was not until they had reached the steps of the stone terrace that Beryl recalled his wandering thoughts with a laughing remark:

"I will not insult Scotland Yard by offering the ridiculous sum of a penny for the thoughts of one of its chief ornaments, but I would willingly know the reason of the most portentous frown which you have worn for the last ten minutes."

The frown changed into a smile at her words.

"I think you hit upon just the right expression when you called me an ornament, Miss Chalmers," he said; "for up to now it strikes me that my presence here has been more ornamental than useful to the interests of law and order. In other words, I am as far off a solution of the series of crimes as ever."

"Is that the reason why you are being taken off the case?"

He started at the tender sympathy which had sprung into her voice. Of course, she would look upon the story of sudden recall, which he had told to facilitate his coming impersonation of Captain St. Quentin, as indicating that he was in disgrace at Headquarters. He hated to gain her sympathy by deceiving her, but the circumstances in which he was placed rendered it impossible to tell her the truth.

"Well, Miss Chalmers, the powers that reside on the Thames Embankment do not exactly shower bouquets on unsuccessful detectives," he temporized; "but I'm not likely to loose my professional reputation just yet. I have not given up the mystery as hopeless; and, although you will not see me around here for the next few weeks, I will still be hovering about."

"In spirit?" she asked jestingly.

He did not smile as his eyes sought hers.

"Exactly—in spirit, Miss Chalmers."

For a few moments there was silence. Then Beryl Chalmers broke into a contemptuous laugh.

"It seems as if our beautiful Spanish clairvoyant has quite thrown her spell over you—Why, we shall all be seeing visions soon!"

"I wish to goodness that she could see a vision of the man who committed those murders," Lee muttered grimly.

She turned to him, her eyebrows raised.

"Surely you do not take that nonsense seriously," she cried with, it seemed to him, as much annoyance as derision in her voice. "A man of your experience must have seen that she was only trying to create a sensation. If her press agent knows his business, we shall have notices in all the morning papers giving a perfectly thrilling account of the wonderful psychic gifts of the incomparable Señorita Clotilde la Zorita. Quite a romantic name, by the way, isn't it?"

Lee Norton nodded his head slowly.

" '*La zorita*' means 'the dove' in Spanish," he informed her casually.

"The dove!" she repeated, her eyes turning towards the lighted windows of the Great Hall before which they were standing. "Let us hope that she does not belie her name!"

Turning abruptly on her heel, she passed beneath the low arch of the ancient door-way and entered the Great Hall; and Lee, after a moment's hesitation, followed.

"What a beautiful old house this is of yours, Sir Raymond!" There was no mistaking the tones of the silvery voice which fell upon his ears as he entered the Hall. "How I love its peaceful charm—its old-world restfulness! It reminds me of the old convent of Santa Leocadia at Toledo, where I was educated by the good nuns. Ah, those were happy, happy days that I spent there, before I came out into this great world, with its empty pomp and worthless riches. When my work here is finished, oh, how gladly will I retire again to those secluded cloisters, to find the real happiness that this world cannot give!"

Señorita Clotilde had removed the long cloak and was now attired in a long white dress whose simple lines showed to perfection the outline of her slender form. As she sat in the great, throne-like oaken chair, one elbow resting on its carved arm, her chin supported by her palm as she gazed pensively into the smouldering logs in the wide fire-place, she looked like one of those beautiful but unfortunate figures that have flitted across the stage of History: those victims of the axe or guillotine whose matchless beauty has but rendered their tragic fate the sadder.

Amos Aintree looked across at her rather anxiously.

"I hope you won't think of giving up your profession for a good many years yet, Señorita," he said. "I hate to mention business to anyone with an artistic temperament such as yours, but there's a little matter of a three-year contract to be worked through before there's any chance of your quitting the business."

"I know, I know." She gave a deep sigh as she spoke. "One should always do one's best to carry out one's obligations, no matter how irksome they be. Were I an ordinary actress, I should not dare to face the ordeal of the years of make-believe before me. It is only the assistance and support that I receive from those who have passed over that enable me to keep on."

Sir Raymond, who had been hanging on her words as though enraptured, now bent forward in his chair.

"Am I really to understand that you claim to receive the help of—er—disembodied spirits when you act?"

Her violet eyes grew wider as she turned them on the speaker.

"But, Sir Rayomnd, I do not act."

"But the parts you play—"

She slowly shook her head.

"It is not I who play those parts," she replied seriously. "You must understand that the only parts I undertake are those of actual historical characters—Marie Antoinette, Lady Jane Grey, Joan of Arc, and other less famous, but none the less real, persons. And it is they themselves who play their own parts before the camera—I am but the medium whose earthly body is controlled by their spirits."

"It's very obliging of them to return to the earth just at the right times for the pictures to be taken!" observed Hilda Maune dryly. "Pray, what would happen if the studio were waiting for a close-up, of, say, Queen Elizabeth, and the ghost refused to walk?"

"That is a contingency which has not happened so far," interposed Aintree hastily.

"And it never will so long as we enact the plays on the actual spots where the real persons lived and moved during their lives on the earth," said Clotilde, rising to her feet. "But I trust you will excuse me, ladies and gentlemen; I have had a rather fatiguing day and I should be glad to rest."

Sir Raymond bounded eagerly to his feet.

"Certainly, certainly, my dear Señorita. I have already ordered your room to be prepared."

He pressed the bell and a maid appeared.

"Susan, show Señorita Clotilde la Zorita to her room."

The maid shot a quick, searching look into the face of the Spanish girl, then, with a murmured, "Be pleased to follow me, madam," led the way up the wide oak staircase to the upper floor and threw open a door.

Clotilde glanced appreciatively round the room. Very dainty it looked in the shaded glow of the electric lights which had been fitted in the antique silver sconces on the walls. The sombre effect of the dark oak panelling was relieved by the pale-green upholstery of the gilt Empire furniture; a carpet of the same delicate hue covered the floor.

"Does Madam find the room to her liking?"

There was an intonation in the maid's voice that was almost a sneer. But if the cinema star noticed it she made no sign of having done so as she slowly crossed the room.

"Yes, everything is quite satisfactory, Susan," she answered, and for the first time she looked directly at the other, who returned her look with an impudent stare.

"Ho, I'm glad of that, my lady Señorita Clotilde la Zorita," she said, mocking the actress's languid tone. "I expect this is more to your liking than some bedrooms that you knows of! What about Cell B55 at Aylesbury, hey? You didn't have no soft pillows or silk curtains, or hot and cold waters there, did yer?"

So unmoved was Clotilde by this outburst that one would have thought that she had not heard. It was only when the other girl had paused for breath that she made answer:

"Really, my good girl, the most charitable construction that I can put upon your extraordinary outburst is that you are temporarily insane." She stifled an elaborate yawn as she went on: "I am scarcely flattered by your mistaking me for one of your gaolbird acquaintances, of—let me see, where did you say?—Aylesbury?—"

"You know well enough what I said—you were there long enough to know the address, I reckon!" the maid interrupted. "But they didn't call you no Señorita Clotilde then. You were Maud Carter, alias Chicago Maud, alias 'Goldie'. Ho, I know you well enough, and you know me. And you'll know me better unless you let me in for a share of the pickings of the lay you're working here! Oh, for heaven's sake take that injured-innocent look off your face. It might go down with the old fool downstairs, but it's wasted on me. Come on, what's the big idea, Goldie? Spill it—quick!"

Clotilde did not answer immediately, or in words. There was a faint smile hovering about the corners of her rose-bud lips as she picked up her white leather handbag, took out a small object, and advanced to the other girl.

The maid's eyes were of a sudden filled with panic.

"Keep back!" she almost screamed. "Keep back, I tell you—or—Ah!"

Like a serpent striking, Clotilde's hand had shot out and landed on the girl's breast. But there was no deadly weapon in her grasp—merely a crimson lipstick.

"You want to know what the game is, Milly Sedley?" said Clotilde very softly. "It is—*this!*" And she slowly traced a large note of interrogation on the breast of the girl's white apron.

"The Crimson Query!"

Milly's trembling lips could scarcely form the words as she looked down at the dread symbol.

"You recognize the sign, it seems!" Clotilde's violet eyes were as merciless as a tigress's now. "Then beware! Next time it is traced on you it will not be in paint. Go!"

Milly recoiled as if from a blow. Then, pausing only to remove her apron with its tell-tale sign, she quitted the room without a word or backward glance.

CHAPTER XVI

FEAR RULES THE WORLD."
Count Ravangar sat in the cabin of his anchored yacht. His eyes were fixed upon the book, bound in red leather, which lay open on the table before him, slowly reading the words of the printed page.

Fortunate is the man of ambition who is able, himself unseen and unknown, to inspire terror in the hearts of his fellow men. For to inspire terror is to compel their obedience; to compel obedience is to gain power; and the man of power—providing he has the courage and determination to use that power ruthlessly—is Master of the World.

Slowly, almost reverently, he turned the page and continued:

Of all the fears to which the human mind is subject, that vague, intangible, instinctive dread of the unseen and unknown is the most potent and abiding. It is a subconscious, protective instinct which, like all such persisting instincts, was once a vital necessity to the individual existence of its possessors. Long before Man had reached that stage of development which led him to clothe himself in skins and arm himself with roughly chipped flints, the instinct of Fear had struck its roots deep down in his as yet unreasoning mind. An instinctive dread of the lurking danger was his only protection during those ages before the increasing development of the brain of Man gave him mastery over the lower animals. Those individuals who possessed it lived to pass on the trait to successive generations; those who lacked it came to an untimely end under the claws of the great Cave-bear or the fangs of the Sabre-toothed Tiger. For in those ages Man was the most helpless of all the creatures of the earth. He was naked and defenceless amid a world of enemies. Other animals could save themselves either by their speed, their power of flight in the air, their bony protective armour, their teeth, or their claws; but Man had only his instinct of Fear—fear of the darkness, fear of what lurked beneath the waters, fear of what caused the swaying of the jungle grass—to warn and protect him. And even to this day, in the security of our policed and guarded towns and cities, the instinct of the primeval forests persists. Man cannot shake off the badges of his humble ancestry. Together with his pointed canines, his now useless muscles which moved his ears, his forearm with its converse-running hairs—*the fear of the Unknown* still lurks; unrecognized and dormant, maybe, but still ready to leap into being at the moment of suspected peril.

And as it was in the beginning, so will it be for all time: FEAR STILL RULES THE WORLD.

Coming to the end, Count Ravangar gently closed the book and, pushing back his chair, for a while remained motionless, apparently sunk in a reverie. Had anyone been observing him—a feat which was impossible owing to the fact that the cabin had neither skylight nor portholes—he might have speculated in vain as to the nature of his thoughts; for the handsome bearded face, which was the only aspect the world knew of the mysterious Count, remained as fixed and impassive as the mask it actually was. At long last he seemed to come to a decision.

"Yes, I think it had better be tonight," he muttered, as he rose to his feet, and pushing back the panels which concealed a transmitter connected with the yacht's wireless installation, he placed the mouthpiece near the large gramophone in the corner and set the machinery in motion. Scarcely had the opening bars of Schumann's *Symphony in B Flat Major* been broadcast, before three prolonged oscillations, sounding in the ear-phones clamped to his head, gave the intimation that his musical code-signal had been heard and understood.

Ravangar at once switched off the record and pressed a bell on his desk. In a few seconds a man appeared at the door.

"Tell them to lower the motor-dinghy, Rawlins," the Count ordered in his artificial, high-pitched voice. "'Thoady already has the signal. He will meet us with the car at the usual place."

"Very good, chief," answered Rawlins. On the way to the door he paused, then returned, nervously rubbing his hands together. "Beg pardon, chief, but . . . is it another job on the moor?"

For a moment Ravangar looked at him in silence; then he shook his head sadly.

"I think you know me well enough by this time to know that curiosity is a trait which I do not admire—or tolerate," he said gently, but the eyes which glared through his mask held a menace which made the other cringe before him.

"I know, I know," Rawlins hastened to assure him. "I wasn't asking out of curiosity—I know better than that, as you say. But there's another matter—about O'Connor—"

"That incident is closed," returned the masked man in a tone of finality.

But Rawlins, though the beads of moisture glistened on his forehead, still stood his ground.

"It may be closed for you, Count," he said doggedly, "but it's far from being closed for me! Maybe you've forgotten that letter I wrote to O'Connor, asking him to meet me near the aerodrome? After I'd 'coshed' him, I searched his pockets, but there was no letter there."

"He may have destroyed it," said the Count with a shrug.

"And he may have given it to the girl he met at the gap in the fence of Abbot's Towers just before he kept his appointment with me!"

There was a gleam of interest in Ravangar's eyes as he looked up.

"So, that soldier had friends hereabouts, eh? That is certainly news to me," he said thoughtfully. "But I do not see how it concerns you in any way."

Rawlins shook his head sullenly.

"If the 'busies' get hold of that letter connecting me with the murder, then it'll be all up with me. They've got my record at the Yard, and they've got specimens of my handwriting. If that girl at the Towers takes it into her head to show the letter to Lee Norton—"

"He would see nothing more than a blank sheet of paper, my jumpy friend!" laughed Ravangar. "The fountain-pen with which you wrote that letter was filled with a special ink of my own invention, which has the useful property of totally disappearing three hours after the words have been written. Have no fear, my good Rawlins; I have at least the virtue of safeguarding those who serve me well. It is only those who try to serve me ill who find their necks in danger. But we waste time. See that the boat is prepared; then you may turn in. Tonight I go to Abbotsmoor alone."

The early twilight had fallen, and the distant lights of Cowes were twinkling out one by one as the dinghy pushed off from the

Lapwing's side and headed westwards along the calm waters of the Solent, towards the sunken sand-pit which guards the mouth of the Beaulieu River. By the time they had gained the upper reach, where the car awaited the coming of Count Ravangar, the last vestige of daylight had vanished and the moor stretched dark and desolate before them.

Carefully avoiding the main gates of Abbot's Towers, the car, its headlights now extinguished, glided silently up the narrow road which skirted the Abbey ruins. Halfway along, the driver slackened speed and looked inquiringly at his passenger.

"The gap?" he asked.

Ravangar shook his head with emphasis.

"Certainly not. There is a possibility of that very convenient mode of entry being watched, and I should be somewhat at a loss to account for my presence if I were to be confronted by that extremely astute Mr. Lee Norton. I might be compelled to terminate his career with some abruptness, and I have no desire to do that— yet. The members of the detective force may possibly have their petty jealousies, but they have a reputation for getting their man when one of their own number is killed. Drive on about a hundred yards; then run the car close alongside the fence. I'll mount to the roof and drop over. Here we are! Drive on the moment you see me drop. You can pick me up somewhere along this road in two hours' time."

Ravangar was already crouching on the roof as the car swerved across the strip of grass which bordered the road, and scarcely had it come to a stand alongside the fence before he had swung himself over and dropped lightly on the other side. Gathering speed again, the car regained the road, and in a few seconds disappeared in the darkness. Apparently the intruder was well acquainted with his surroundings, for he set off through the trees without hesitation, and in a few minutes emerged into the clearing in which the ruins of the Abbey stood. Entering the main door, he turned sharply to his left and ascended a narrow winding staircase which brought him to a narrow gallery overlooking the place where the altar had formerly stood. Here for the first time he brought his electric torch into use, counting, by its light; the large square slabs of stone which formed its floor. At the seventh stone he paused, and brushing away the dust with his gloved hand, found what appeared to be a circle of about three inches diameter chiselled on its surface.

To the ordinary observer it would have appeared to be merely a mason's mark chiselled on the slab, but Ravangar knew different.

He placed his fingers in the centre of the ring and pressed sharply downwards, forcing it inwards until his groping fingers could feel and raise a loop of bronze concealed in the cavity. The raising of this must have released some hidden fastening; for the slab, previously firm and immovable, now tilted upwards at a touch, revealing another winding staircase running down the centre of one of the massive pillars which supported the bell-tower. Without hesitation, he stepped into this well-like shaft and began to descend.

Down and yet down went that dizzy, corkscrew-like descent, and when at last the stairs gave place to a narrow vaulted tunnel, it was clear that he was many feet below the level of the ground. The walls were wet with slime; huge masses of yellowish fungus growths splotched the surface of the masonry, the atmosphere was damp and rilled with a death-like chill. But, probably owing to the height of the chimney-like shaft at the entrance, the air of the tunnel was breathable—he could even feel a slight breeze playing on his face as he pressed onwards.

After a few minutes' walking, it was obvious that the tunnel was running beneath a belt of wooded country. Great roots of trees had pushed their way through the crevices of the stones, in some places almost blocking the path. Here, at least, some concealed shafts must have communicated with the outer air; a bat, dazzled by the glare of his electric torch, blundered past him with a frightened cry; at a place where the moisture had collected in puddles on the ground, the hoarse croaking of frogs was suddenly stilled at his approach.

At last the velvety blackness ahead gave place to a faint gleam of light. It was the light of his torch reflected in the moisture on the wall of masonry which marked the end of the tunnel. Another long flight of steps, straight this time, and set at right angles to the tunnel, led to a long, narrow passage, and here for the first time Ravangar showed some caution in his movements. He trod more carefully over the floor, which was now of wood, and finally he switched off his torch and guided himself by his sense of touch on the rough oaken boards which formed the right-hand wall.

Half-way along, he halted, and applying his eyes to two tiny holes in the woodwork, which were concealed from view on the other side by the carved frieze of the panelling, he looked through. A faint sound of disappointment came from his bearded lips as he saw that the Great Hall of Abbot's Towers was silent and deserted, illuminated only by the faint glow which came from the dying embers on the wide, open fire-place. Turning abruptly, he passed on until he came to another passage running at right angles to the first. Again he looked through the ancient Judas-hole in the wall, and this time he was better rewarded. It was the library, and three men lounged in the great leather-covered chairs.

"I suppose you won't be sorry to pack up and leave the case for somebody else to solve, Mr. Norton?" Sir Raymond was saying. "Three murders without a single arrest is rather a bad record for the police, is it not? I notice that the Press are beginning to get rather sarcastic over the matter. There was a leading article in this morning's *Wire* that said—"

"Yes, I saw it, Sir Raymond," Lee answered quietly. "The writer evidently looks upon Scotland Yard as the last refuge for the weak-minded. But I noticed," he added with a smile, "that he was adroit enough to refrain from recording his own theory about the identity of the assassin whose trade-mark is the Crimson Query."

The baronet laughed.

"Truly we live in a commercial age! Why, even the crooks are beginning to brand their work—presumably so that the public shall not be put off with an inferior article! But, seriously, doesn't it strike you that the man who is responsible for the murders is at the same time *not* responsible for his actions? Such a senseless series of crimes can be but the work of a homicidal maniac."

"If he is mad, then there's much method in his madness," said Lee. "Although at first glance the crimes may seem to be unconnected with any definite aim, a little calm thought will show that they were all part of a vast, deeply laid plan."

Amos Aintree looked up from the depths of his armchair, a shrewd look in his pale-blue eyes.

"There's only one class of crooks who advertise their work, and that is a secret society," he suggested in his slow, drawling voice.

"Secret societies don't flourish in the English climate, sir," Lee answered shortly.

"And I've got a hunch that's the very reason why you're leaving this country," laughed the American. "And I must allow that you're wise. A little chat with the chief of police of, let us say, Naples or Brindisi might go a long way towards an arrest. And I wouldn't mind betting that's where you're bound for."

"I never bet on matters which I am not allowed to discuss," was Lee's answer. In his own heart he knew that the solution of the mystery would be found nearer home than the seaports suggested by the American. He glanced at the clock and rose to his feet.

"It's getting late, and I have some packing to do before I turn in."

Sir Raymond Chalmers reached towards the bell. "I'll order the car for you."

"Pray do not trouble," Lee protested. "I know my way across the moor, and a little exercise will do me good."

Aintree looked up as Lee crossed to the door.

"Which way do you take across the moor, Mr. Norton?" he asked carelessly, and like a flash the memory of "Swab" Simson's last words returned to Lee's mind.

He gave a laughing shrug, as he called back:

"Oh, any old way suits me—so long as it's not through Abbot's Mire!"

And the unseen watcher behind the wainscot made a mental note of the fact that Lee Norton had suspected the American's motive in asking the question. He seemed to have no further interest in what took place after the detective had quitted the room, but immediately made his way along one of the other secret passages which honeycombed the ancient walls, and, ascending another short flight of steps, reached the upper floor, and when again he stopped it was to peer through the wall of the room which had been allotted to Señorita Clotilde.

The girl was sitting on one of the great gilt arm-chairs, which she had drawn up close to the tall shaded lamp beside the bed; she wore a wrapper of filmy lace, over which the masses of her unbound hair flowed like a cascade of gold. She looked up with a start as there fluttered down on the page of the book she was reading a fragment of tightly rolled paper. Slowly, almost indifferently, she took it in her slender fingers and unrolled it, noting without surprise that it bore a query drawn in crimson ink.

It seemed as if the sign had been expected, for she looked up, waiting, neither astonishment nor fear showing on her saint-like features.

"Clotilde!" The whisper, low and sibilant, came from the wall above her head. The girl drew nearer the spot whence it came, raising her head, listening. "I see that you have succeeded in entering this house according to plan. Do you think anyone suspects you?"

She nodded her head, and her eyes were no longer saint-like.

"Hilda Maune—the old man's secretary—I think she suspects."

"I will attend to her—later," said the whisper in a tone of cold menace. "The men?"

She did not speak, but the contemptuous smile which curved her heart-shaped lips was sufficient answer.

"Good," whispered Ravangar. "First burn that paper, then listen carefully to the orders I am about to give . . ."

Five minutes later Count Ravangar descended and made his way through the secret tunnel, carefully replacing the slab which covered the staircase in the pillar of the Abbey chapel.

Two hours later he was aboard the s.y. *Lapwing*, steaming past the Needles Light on the way to the open sea.

CHAPTER XVII

LEE NORTON REACHED LONDON by an early train, and drove straight to Portman Square, where he found Sir John Lambert and Captain St. Quentin eagerly awaiting his coming.

The airman proved to be a tall, dark man of about the same age and build as Lee himself, and it did not need a second look to convince the detective that it would be an easy task for him to assume his outward appearance. The strip of sticking-plaster which decorated one of the airman's cheeks, and the sling which supported his right arm, bore witness to his recent narrow escape.

"Pleased to meet you," said St. Quentin, when the Chief Commissioner had introduced him to his prospective double. "Excuse my not offering you my hand, but that confounded motor-bandit has put it out of action for the time being. Yes," he added with a reminiscent laugh," and he very nearly succeeded in putting me out of action for good!"

"Have you no suspicion who these people are?" asked Lee.

"I haven't the foggiest notion," answered the other, with a shake of his head. "So far as I am aware, I haven't an enemy in the world, and it's a mystery to me why they should evolve all this elaborate stunt stuff to put my light out. I am forced to agree with Sir John here, that the gang are out to prevent my new aeroplane becoming an accomplished fact."

"Is your invention of such importance, then?"

"Well, I hope you won't think I am suffering from swelled head when I say that candour compels me to tell you that whichever Power holds the secret of my 'plane will hold the mastery of the air. Possibly you may have heard that expression used before, in newspapers and elsewhere; but I can assure you that in this case it is nothing more than the sober truth."

Sir John Lambert stepped forward.

"In my own mind, I think there can be no other explanation," he said. "The very ruthlessness with which this unknown body of men are conducting their operations can admit of no other theory. What are three lives—or a dozen—or a score—compared with the thousands of lives which may be sacrificed when, in the next war, the new aeroplane comes into action?"

The gravity of his words gave Lee the opening that he had been awaiting.

"If the issues at stake are so vital to the welfare of Britain, do you think you are still justified in refusing to put the details of your invention on paper, Captain St. Quentin?" he asked seriously. "I would earnestly advise you to do so, especially now that circumstances have arisen which will show that your motive for doing so is not personal fear."

The captain looked at Lee keenly.

"Yes, I think you are right," he said at last. "As you are taking my danger at the same time as you take my identity, it is only due to you—"

The detective held up his hand abruptly, and the other stopped.

"That aspect does not affect the issue at all, sir," he said a trifle stiffly, for the tone of thinly veiled contempt in the other's voice had stung him like a whiplash. "If you put the details of your 'plane into writing, the only persons who will be aware of your having done so will be we three. What would be the use of my taking your place in order to trap the crooks at their next attempt if we were to remove the inducement for such an attempt being made? It was in the interests of Britain that I made the suggestion—not to protect my own skin."

"I'm sure of that," agreed Sir John heartily; none knew better than he that the young detective had proved his courage again and again. "But I would advise that you draw out the plans, Captain, and deposit them at the War Office before you leave London. We are fighting against a very well-organized and extensive gang, and the less risks we take, the better for all of us."

The sudden whirr of an electric bell sounded from below.

"That, unless I'm mistaken, is Monsieur Pecontier."

The diminutive Frenchman who made his appearance a few seconds later was the head of a famous firm of theatrical costumiers who, although the fact was not advertised by them, had a standing appointment at Scotland Yard. He already knew what was required of him, and lost no time in getting out the rather surprising contents of the brown leather case which he had carried in.

"Do you think that you will be able to make up this gentleman so that he can pass as the other?" asked the Commissioner.

Monsieur Pecontier gazed from one to the other, then nodded his head vigorously.

"Mais certainment, Sir John," he answered eagerly. "Observe, there is already a *soupçon* of resemblance in the features. A little darkening of the hair and eyebrows, a few hairs shaved close at the temples and—" He broke off suddenly and eyed Lee's upper lip wistfully. "I suppose there would be not time for Monsieur to grow a moustache, so that I could dye it and trim it like the one worn by *Monsieur le Capitan?"*

"Scarcely," laughed Lee.

"Pardieu, that is unfortunate—it would have saved Monsieur the inconvenience of having to wear a false one. But have no fear, messieur, I will render you *comme deux gouttes d'eau."*

For over an hour Lee submitted patiently to the manipulation of the Frenchman's deft fingers, and when at last the cloth was whisked away from his neck with a triumphant *"Voila!"* he was compelled to admit that Pecontier's boast to make him as like the captain "as two drops of water" had been no idle one.

He quickly donned the blue-grey uniform, placed his right arm in a sling which had been already procured in readiness, and took his place by the side of the real captain in front of the long looking-glass. The roar of surprised laughter which burst from their lips was a tribute to the skill of the little Frenchman.

"By the Lord Harry, it's twins you are!" spluttered Sir John as he looked from one to the other.

"Monsieur is satisfied?" asked the beaming Frenchman.

"More than satisfied," cried Lee. "You're a perfect marvel at make-up."

"Bien! Then I will take my leave. *Bon soir, messieurs, et bonne chance."*

It was with a tingling feeling of expectancy that Lee Norton descended the front steps of the house to make his first public appearance in his assumed role. It was no new thing for him to go about disguised; neither was it a novelty for him to go in danger of his life. But the fact that he was now to all outward appearances the man whose murder had been attempted on two occasions, in a coldblooded and most business-like manner, was sufficient to keep him very alert during his walk to Waterloo. Concealed in the black silk sling which supported his seemingly useless right arm, ready to his hand for instant use should it be required, was a small but thoroughly effective automatic pistol.

Having plenty of time on his hands, he purposely took a round-about way, availing himself of all the dodges which experience had taught him were likely to reveal the presence of a "shadow". But by the time he reached the terminus he was convinced that his movements were not being watched—a fact which caused him to be somewhat depressed. Considering that he was the "red herring" that was to draw the crooks off the trail of the real Captain St. Quentin, Lee would have felt much more happy had he seen a couple of suspicious-looking characters dogging his steps.

The train was far from crowded, and Lee had no difficulty in finding an empty compartment. But just as the whistle was being blown, and the train already on the move, a grey-haired old man sprinted nimbly down the platform and entered.

"Near shave, that, Captain St. Quentin," he remarked genially as he deposited a large black bag on the seat before him and mopped his streaming forehead.

Lee started as the other addressed him by the name of his assumed character, and hastened to murmur a few words of agreement, at the same time keenly examining the appearance of the new-comer. St. Quentin had gone to a lot of trouble to explain to him the people whom he would be expected to know, but he racked his brain in vain to remember hearing of a wizened, carelessly dressed old man with unkempt grey hair and an old-fashioned goatee beard. So he added the non-committal remark that it was a fine day and waited for the unknown to give him a lead.

"Yes, I ran things rather close," the other went on. "I came up to Town to see about the illustrations of my forthcoming book, and I was detained rather longer than I expected. The firm of photographers to whom I have entrusted the work of taking the initial pictures would have liked me to have left my specimens in their charge for a day or two, but I value them far too much to allow them out of my own hands."

"Quite right too," agreed Lee, who had not the slightest idea to what he was referring.

The old man beamed.

"Ah, you agree with me? I thought you would. My collection is absolutely unique, and my latest find—" He broke off abruptly and began to unfasten the straps of his bag. "You remember the occasion when you met me on the moor?"

"Oh, perfectly," said Lee, secretly wondering what the other was driving at.

"I was excavating that big tumulus near your aerodrome—"

"Of course you were," agreed the very relieved detective.

"And the moment you had gone I—But you shall see for your-self. There!" And to Lee's unbounded amazement, he placed in his hand a human skull.

The expression which mounted to the detective's face when he found himself holding the grim object might have betrayed him on the spot, but fortunately the old man was gazing so affectionately at the relic that he had eyes for nothing else.

"That was what I found, sir, together with a bronze sword, a spearhead, a socketed celt, a brooch, and a pair of the usual so-called 'food vessels'. The skull, you will notice, is decidedly doli-chocephalic."

"Oh, decidedly—decidedly. Anybody can see that!" agreed Lee, secretly wondering how on earth he had managed to find out the names of the deceased. "And how long ago do you think it is since this lady—"

A shout from his companion caused Lee to stop.

"Lady?" the old fellow almost shrieked. "Lady, sir? Why, the skull is that of a full-grown man!"

"But," protested Lee, "you said a moment ago that her name was Dolly Chocephalic."

The other regarded him with withering scorn.

"It seems that you are pleased to make a jest of what is to me, at any rate, a serious and important matter," he said stiffly. "Had not our previous conversations convinced me that you were a man well versed in at least the rudiments of archaeological nomenclature, I should have put down your last remark to ignorance. Surely you must be aware that 'dolichocephalic' is merely the Greek term for 'long-headed', just as, conversely, 'brachycephalic' stands for 'short-headed'?"

Lee saw that he had blundered badly.

"Of course," he hastened to say. "I'd forgotten for the moment. You see"—he indicated his bandaged right arm—"I've met with a rather nasty accident lately."

"It must have been a terrible accident to make you confuse a scientific term with a lady's name!" The old man favoured Lee with a long, suspicious stare as he replaced the skull in his bag, which, judging from its general outline, seemed to contain several other objects of a like nature.

Lee smiled and hastened to turn the conversation into less dangerous channels. But he found it impossible to keep his companion away from the subject of the ancient remains which he had from time to time unearthed on Abbotsmoor. He produced a copy of a monograph, of which he proudly informed Lee that he was the author. It bore the imposing title: *A Treatise on the Confirmation of the Aryan Origin of the Ancient Britons as indicated by the Exhumed Tumuli of Abbotsmoor*. A glance at the title-page of this formidable-sounding work told the detective that his fellow-traveller was no less a personage than Professor Gideon Wilfer, F.S.A. Fortunately for Lee, the professor was so engrossed in the explanation of his pet theory that he was content to do most of the talking. All the impression that his hearer retained of the subsequent monologue was a chaotic memory of a much-repeated insistence that the fact of ancient skeletons being burnt or unburnt, and their bronze axe-heads being fastened to their handles by flanges or sockets, and the fact that the Latin name for the beech-tree is the same as the Greek for the oak, had a bearing on the contention that the prehistoric inhabitants of the British Isles originally came from somewhere in Central Asia. It was not until the train was nearing Southampton that there emerged from the professor's torrent of statistics and theories a fact that concerned somebody not living in some undetermined date B.C.

"I suppose you have not come across any traces of the old buried treasure of the Abbey in your excavations?" Lee asked in one of the rare pauses.

Gideon Wilfer shook his head.

"There's small chance of that," he replied. "To my mind there is no doubt that the treasure of St. Nicholas was hidden in the same way as that of Ramsey Abbey."

"And how was that hidden?" asked Lee with the first gleam of real interest.

"Somewhere about 1850 Ramsey Marsh was drained, and shortly afterwards a farm labourer unearthed a gold censer, an incense-box, a monstrance, and a reliquary which had belonged to the old Abbey near by. If you are interested in the subject, you may see the objects displayed in a glass case at the South Kensington Museum, still bearing a rebus of the name of the abbey in the shape of a ram's head rising from the sea. It's my belief that the treasures of St. Nicholas were hidden in the same way. At any rate, it is certain that every head of the House of Chalmers has searched in vain for them." Professor Wilfer smiled rather strangely as he added: "It might be very convenient for the present holder of the title to find the great diamond at this moment."

There was a tone of such hidden meaning in the old man's voice that Lee looked up sharply.

"What do you mean, Professor?"

Gideon Wilfer laid his hand on the other's knee and leant forward impressively.

"I happen to know for a fact that Sir Raymond Chalmers is very pushed for ready money—indeed, I am not overstating the case when I say that he is on the verge of ruin!"

CHAPTER XVIII

I T SEEMS AT FIRST SIGHT a long cry from a bottle of champagne consumed in the *presidéncia* of a tiny South American republic to the threatened insolvency of an English baronet, yet one event undoubtedly set into motion the long train of cause and effect which ultimately resulted in the other. For had not Señor Ezequias Rasparteo, President of the Republic of San Severino, opened that final magnum with which to celebrate the capture of the notorious bandit, "Malvado Miguel", he might have reached for his gun a trifle quicker than was actually the case when the faithful followers of that enterprising freebooter entered the president's bedroom and there and then effected a change in the constitution by the simple expedient of shooting Señor Rasparteo dead; and before the smoke of the fatal shots had dispersed, they had filled the vacancy thus created by electing Malvado Miguel president in his place.

To those unacquainted with the very direct methods which prevail in the politics of San Severino, it may be something of a surprise that the inhabitants of that country should be content to be ruled by a man of Malvado Miguel's reputation and antecedents; but the man who holds the gun is apt to prove a very persuasive person, possessed of arguments well calculated to silence all objectors—for ever, if needs be. So Malvado Miguel was conducted from the condemned cell to the *presidéncia,* and at once started to rule his new domain, with disastrous results to San Severino and all who had financial dealings therewith. For the sole difference in the tactics employed by Miguel the brigand and Miguel the president was, that whereas he had been perforce content to confine his depredations to a few lonely mountain roads, now he had the whole of the country at his mercy. How nobly he rose to the occasion may be gathered by the fact that he had not been in power a week before the shares of the various mining companies situated in his territory were worth a trifle less than the value of the paper and ink of their certificates.

Wise speculators in San Severino stock unloaded the moment they heard of the assassination. But Sir Raymond Chalmers was not wise, and by the time he had made up his mind to sell, there were no buyers at any price. Sir Raymond's entire fortune had vanished as quickly as had the evanescent bubbles in the unlucky Rasparteo's last glass of champagne.

Hoping against hope that the set-back was but temporary, he made a hurried journey to London. But he found his brokers cautious and far from comforting. They shook their heads dubiously when he mentioned the possibility of foreign intervention.

"If this new president had only taken it into his head to shoot a few American subjects, he would have Uncle Sam shaking his big stick on his door-step by now," they told him in effect. "But up to the present, the wily Miguel has confined his attentions to his own citizens. Still, you never can tell what may happen in a place like San Severino. The presence of a few U.S.A. battleships would make a whole lot of difference to the value of your shares, Sir Raymond. We can only advise you to sit tight and await developments."

It was a very worried Sir Raymond who journeyed back to Abbot's Towers. The advice of the broker had fallen like lead on the heart of its recipient. It was all very well being told to "sit tight", but for a man of Sir Raymond's position to do so meant the expenditure of ready money, and at that moment less than £500 lay to his credit at the bank. Too late he realized the truth of the proverb which warns against putting all one's eggs in one basket. Too well he knew that until the ex-bandit was deposed there would be no dividends forthcoming from the mine in which the whole of his fortune had been invested.

As he lay back on the cushions of the car which had met him at Southampton, his mind was busy evolving schemes for raising the money necessary to tide him over the period that must elapse before San Severino would be restored to law and order. A dozen ideas occurred to him, only to be rejected one by one. There was a strict entail on the Towers estate, which precluded the possibility of a mortgage on the property. Pride forbade an appeal to his friends for a loan. Money-lenders would require a greater security than he was able to offer. A wealthy marriage . . .?

He toyed with the idea between the slow puffs of smoke from his cigar. He was but forty-five years of age; still hale and hearty. He knew that he was not bad-looking, and the title and social position which he would be able to offer made him an attractive proposition in the modern matrimonial market. Yes, the idea was worth considering—as a last resource. Meanwhile, he might be able to carry on at his present rate of expenditure for, say, a month.

But all through his musings an ugly black shape had been persistently rearing its head—a lurking temptation that, try as he might, he could not entirely banish from his mind: Beryl's fortune—the £150,000 that had been left in trust for her under the will of her uncle. Sir Raymond was the sole trustee, and no difficulties would arise if he were to use a part of the money—"

"No!" he cried aloud. "I'd sooner go through the bankruptcy court than touch her money. Thank God, she, at least, will be provided for. I suppose she'll be marrying Captain St. Quentin soon . . ." His eyes lit up as a sudden thought came to him. "By George! Wouldn't that diamond, the 'Child of Light', come in useful just now if I could only lay my hands on it? I wonder if that beautiful Spanish girl is really psychic? If so, she might be the means of revealing its hiding-place."

The recollection of the golden-haired cinema star seemed to open up a pleasing train of thought in his mind, for there was a smile on his lips when he alighted at the entrance to the Towers. Dim and nebulous as it was, an idea had come to him which seemed to promise a way out of his difficulties.

Clotilde la Zorita had spoken no more than the truth when she told Count Ravangar that the only person who suspected her real motives for visiting Abbot's Towers was Hilda Maune. It was true that the dark-haired, keen-eyed girl had allowed no spoken word to betray her suspicions, but Clotilde was clever enough to draw her conclusions without such obvious signs. Whenever they came face to face she was conscious of those dark eyes watching her, weighing her every look and action, seeking to probe beneath her saint-like mask of innocence, and guess the secret of the cunning brain beneath. But each girl was far too clever to openly betray her feelings towards the other, and Amos Aintree, the only person who suspected the real state of affairs, found the situation not without its humour.

"They remind me of two pretty pussy-cats," he mused to himself as he watched them one day. "Walking round each other purring, but only waiting the chance to give each other a sly scratch. And won't the fur begin to fly when their claws are out in earnest!" It was not long before his amusement was changed to a deeper and more dangerous emotion.

Clotilde had chosen her moment unerringly. Sir Raymond had dined well, as was his custom, and afterwards Aintree had suggested a turn or two on the terrace as they smoked their cigars. There they had been joined by the Spanish girl, looking like some beautiful, ethereal spirit in the gauzy white wrap which she had thrown over her gleaming hair. It was a perfect night in autumn, with the thin silver sickle of the young moon peeping above the distant beech woods, tempering the night's ebony pall with its soft, translucent rays.

"How beautiful it all is!" She breathed the words rather than spoke them. "How I envy you, Sir Raymond, living here in the house which has been hallowed by the presence of generations upon generations of your ancestors. I know that envy is a passion which we should banish from our souls"—she lifted her slim white shoulders in a tiny shrug—"but I really cannot help it when I think of the treasures you possess—the old armour, the wonderful pictures, the tapestries, the ancient books . . ."

This was the cue that Amos had been waiting for.

"Talking of old books, Sir Raymond," he interposed briskly, "you have one in your possession that I should very much like to see. I refer to an old copy of the mystery-play that used to be acted by the monks of the Abbey. It is entitled *St. Nicholas and the Three Poor Maidens."*

The baronet shook his head.

"I do not recollect having a book of that title in my library."

"I'm surprised to hear you say that," returned the other. "I found a copy of the report of the Royal Commissioners which gave a list of the Abbey property which was handed over to your ancestor, Sir Randolph, and that manuscript was specifically mentioned."

"In that case you had better consult my secretary, Miss Maune; she takes an interest in the old musty parchments relating to the house." He turned and looked curiously at the film producer as he went on: "Have you any particular reason for wishing to see that old play?"

"Yes, sir, I don't mind admitting that I have," answered the other without hesitation. "I'm writing a film scenario based on that very play, and as there is no copy in existence, I should like to have a look at the original. That is, of course, if you have no objection."

"Oh, you are quite welcome," shrugged the baronet. "My secretary keeps the keys of the old muniment-chest. I'll ring for her."

Sir Raymond led the way into his study, and a few minutes later they were joined by Hilda Maune.

"The old play-book?" she said in answer to Aintree's request. "Oh yes, I anticipated that you would wish to see a copy, so I have already typed one out."

The film magnate did not seem very pleased to find his wishes so unerringly anticipated. A sour look mounted to his face as he shook his head.

"I'd sooner see the original, if it's all the same to you, Sir Raymond," he said, turning to his host.

A faint smile curved Hilda's red lips.

"But I assure you that my copy is quite accurate, Mr. Aintree, and it will be far less trouble to decipher than the crabbed black-letter script of the original," she told him.

Aintree turned on her swiftly, and it seemed as if he were on the point of making an angry reply, when Clotilde stepped forward.

"How perfectly sweet of you to take all that trouble to copy out the play, Miss Maune!" she murmured, her words falling like honey from her lips. "Some day I trust to be able to repay you for so charmingly forestalling our desire! But in the meantime I myself would like to see the queer old parchment that the monks wrote so patiently. Although your copy will be of the greatest use to Mr. Aintree in compiling his film, I—purely out of curiosity—would like to read the original. May I, Sir Raymond?" she added, turning with a winning smile to the somewhat bewildered baronet.

"Certainly, certainly, my dear Senorita. Please bring the original manuscript down at once, Miss Maune."

It was an order which left no loophole of escape; yet, for one hesitating second, it seemed as if Hilda were about to refuse to comply with it. Then she shrugged slightly and an odd look came into her eyes as she bowed her head.

"Very good, if you wish it, Sir Raymond," she murmured as she quitted the room.

The moment the door had closed Amos turned to his host.

"I don't trust that woman, Sir Raymond," he said in a low voice.

The other man was palpably startled.

"Indeed? Why not?"

"Well, there seems to be something underhand and sly about her. Did you notice how confused she looked when I asked to see the old manuscript? It's my belief—"

He paused suddenly as the door was thrown open and Hilda Maune appeared. For a moment she stood there, trembling from head to foot.

"The manuscript of the play—it's not in the chest—it's gone!"

"What!" The American almost shouted the word. Rage, suspicion, baffled greed, showed in every line of his working features.

In two strides Sir Raymond was by the side of the shaking girl.

"Come, Miss Maune, pull yourself together," he said, laying his hand with a not unkindly gesture on her shoulder. "What exactly do you mean? Have you mislaid it after making the copy you were telling us about just now?"

Hilda shook her head vehemently.

"I am certain that I replaced it last night. It's been stolen!"

Sir Raymond laughed. "Nonsense, my good girl. Who would want to steal an old musty manuscript? We must make a search—"

"You're right there!" came from Amos, with a harsh laugh. "And I guess that it'd pay you to begin that same search by turning out the boxes of this young lady herself!"

Sir Raymond Chalmers stared.

"You suggest that Miss Maune has stolen it herself?" he gasped. "The idea is absurd! Why should she risk her liberty and reputation by such an action?"

"Why?" There was a note of sneering triumph in Aintree's voice now. "I'll tell you why. It's because she has already offered to let me have the manuscript of *St. Nicholas and the Three Poor Maidens* for the sum of"—he paused and fixed the shrinking girl with his eye as he concluded, letting each word fall with icy precision—"a quarter of a million sterling!"

For the first time the old baronet turned and looked full at Hilda, noting as he did so her bloodless features and downcast eyes. There was no tenderness in his grasp as he caught her by the wrist.

"Is this true?" he thundered.

She raised her head and threw it back with a quick, defiant gesture.

"It is quite true, Sir Raymond," she said in a voice that did not shake.

"Then—you stole the play?" He spoke the words like a man in a dream.

"That is a question that I will only answer when we are alone, Sir Raymond," she said firmly.

The baronet turned to his two guests with a request that they would leave the room. When they had gone he turned again to the girl.

"Well? Now will you tell me why you stole that play?"

"Gladly, and when you know the truth, the contempt that you now feel for me will be turned to gratitude. I took the play to save you from ruin, Sir Raymond. Contained in the play is the clue to the hiding-place of the Abbey treasure. Aintree had gained an inkling of this fact, and sought to get the manuscript into his hands to forestall you and secure it for himself. That was why he came down here—the story of his film was a mere blind to enable him to get the book into his hands. I knew that, and pretended that it was stolen when you asked me to get it."

Surprise, incredulity, and finally boundless delight had possessed the heart of the old man as she made the explanation. At the conclusion he came forward, his hands outstretched, as though he would hug her in his delight.

"This is good news indeed!" he cried. "Come, let me have the manuscript and we will look for the treasure without delay."

Hilda Maune drew back, a slow, enigmatical smile hovering about her lips.

"And how about my reward?" she said gently.

He drew suddenly back as though from a blow.

"Reward?" he repeated. "Can you not trust me to see that you are suitably recompensed? If the treasure indeed exists, and is as great as tradition says it is, I can promise you the sum of a thousand pounds the moment it is in my hands."

She shook her head slowly.

"My price is higher than that," she said.

He looked at her for a moment steadily.

"You certainly do not lack nerve, Miss Maune. You have the effrontery first to steal my book, and then to dictate terms to my face! Do you not realize that I have but to lift that 'phone and in less than an hour you would be in the hands of the police, and the book would be in mine?"

Again she shook her head, and this time she was smiling openly.

"You forget that the book would tell you nothing unless you knew the secret of the cypher which tells of the ancient treasure. And that secret I alone possess."

"Well, you are at least frank," he said with grudging admiration. "I, also, will be frank with you. What are your terms?"

She looked him full in the face.

"That you make me your wife."

Had the earth suddenly opened at his feet, Sir Raymond could not have been more startled than he was by the announcement that fell so calmly from the lips of the girl before him. His ruddy face grew purple; his eyes bulged until they threatened to start from his head; his mouth opened to emit a shout of outraged indignation. But it was never uttered, for, suddenly, as though he were beholding her for the first time, it occurred to him that she was a very pretty and presentable girl.

There was a long silence, during which he slowly crossed to the table, selected a cigar from the box that lay there, lit it, and began to watch the smoke-spirals as they rose ceilingwards. Sir Raymond Chalmers was a gambler, otherwise he would not have been so deeply involved in the San Severino crash, and to him the project offered appealed vastly to his sporting instinct. He had been contemplating making a rich marriage—here was a bride who would bring as her dowry a diamond unparalleled in the history of the world, not to mention a treasure whose value besides would probably run well into six figures.

He threw his half-smoked cigar into the fire-place with the air of one who takes a plunge.

"Done!" he said, and held out his hand to his future bride.

"Let me be the first to offer my congratulations!" said a quiet voice from the door-way.

Looking round, the pair who had been thus strangely engaged turned to meet the scornful eyes of Beryl Chalmers.

CHAPTER XIX

G REAT AS WAS LEE NORTON'S FAITH in the completeness
of the disguise with which the deft fingers of Monsieur
Pecontier had endowed him, his estimation of that artist's
skill went up several points when he saw the unquestioning manner
in which the officials of the Westdown Aerodrome accepted him as
Captain St. Quentin. Even Jim Mapes, the captain's batman, took
his coming as a matter of course, and after that Lee had not the
slightest fear of failing to keep up the borrowed identity which his
duties had thrust upon him. The very minute instructions which St.
Quentin had given him enabled him to fall into the routine of the
establishment—a task which was rendered easier by reason of his
previous military service. And the fact that his arm was supposed
to be injured ruled out the possibility of his being detected through
the difference between his own handwriting and that of his assumed character.

So far he was very satisfied, but whether Beryl Chalmers' eyes
would be so easily deceived was another matter, and, much as he
would have liked to have seen her, he resolved to put off a meeting
as long as he possibly could. But fate ruled otherwise. Scarcely had
he got settled in his new quarters than a ring at his telephone
caused him absent-mindedly to lift the receiver and place it to his
ear.

"I wish to speak with Captain St. Quentin," said a voice which
almost caused him to drop the instrument.

For a moment Lee did not answer. Mentally he was cursing his
stupidity in not leaving instructions at the orderly-room that all
calls for him were to be ignored.

Aided by his changed appearance, he might be able to pass as
the captain, but his voice alone was almost sure to betray him to
one as familiar with it as was Beryl Chalmers.

"Beg parding, miss," he called back, making his voice assume a
decided Cockney accent. "Sorry, miss," he went on when the girl
had repeated her request, "but the capting 'as ter attend a speshul
meeting of the delegates from the Hair Ministry."

There was a short pause; then:

"Who are you?" said the voice. "I seem to have heard your voice before somewhere."

"Very likely, miss," answered Lee in the same tone. "I'm Private James Mapes speakin', the capting's batman—servant, that is."

"Then will you please ask Captain St. Quentin to call at the Towers the moment he is free?"

"Very good, miss."

During the few moments that the conversation had lasted, his mind had been working at express speed. One moment he had been tempted to put off the dreaded interview by telling her of the "motor accident" in which he was supposed to have been involved. But, apart from a natural reluctance to needlessly alarm her, he had a shrewd suspicion that as she thought him to be seriously injured she would hasten to the bedside of her supposed fiancée, and thus precipitate the meeting he was so anxious to delay.

"May as well take the plunge and get it over," he muttered to himself. "After all, it will straighten matters out quite a lot if she tumbles to me straight away."

Swinging on his uniform cap, and placing his little automatic in a convenient position beneath the bandages of his right arm, he called out to Mapes not to wait up for him, and a few moments later had passed the main-guard, and was striding across the moor in the direction of Abbot's Towers.

Although it had happened but two hours since, it seemed to Beryl Chalmers that an eternity had passed since she had opened the study door and overheard Hilda Maune's cool proposal to her father. Every word of the stormy interview that had followed remained in her memory as though traced in letters of fire. With a bluntness that was almost brutal, her father had told her of his impending ruin. Gently but firmly waving aside her impulsive offer to let him use the money that he had in trust, he had emphasized that the discovery of the treasure was his sole hope of weathering the financial storm which the upheaval in San Severino had caused to beat upon the barque of his fortunes. He had, he told her, been seriously contemplating marrying again, and had not disguised from himself the fact that the possession of money would be a more potent factor in choosing his future bride than social eminence or personal beauty. Hilda's proposed *mariage de convenance* had come most opportunely. As for the girl herself, well, she was good-looking, well-educated, and undeniably clever.

"I will grant she is *that!*" Beryl had retorted with scornful emphasis as she had terminated the scene by taking her departure. "But she may find that there are cleverer people in the world than she!"

It would not be strictly true to say that she hated this dark-haired girl with the clever, inscrutable eyes; but Beryl had always looked upon the marriage tie as something so sacred as to be above all considerations of worldly expediency, and at that moment she would have been prepared to go to almost any lengths to prevent her father from falling a prey to this scheming adventuress. How she longed for the keen wits of the young detective to aid and advise her in this unexpected crisis! But Lee Norton was far away, and with a feeling of hopelessness she realized that she did not even know his address. It was only when she had seen that an appeal to Lee was impossible that she had telephoned to Captain St. Quentin, and a wave of self-reproach swept over her as she remembered the fact. Almost imperceptibly, she had come to regard Lee with feelings of that deep regard which, as she told herself with a sudden consciousness of disloyalty, should have been reserved for the man to whom she was engaged to be married. Married! The word threw her mind into a turmoil of fear and indecision. Three months ago she would not have dreaded that word, for then she had not met Lee Norton; but now . . .?

A discreet tap at the door and the announcement, "Captain St. Quentin to see you, miss," caused her to rise hastily from the bed on which she had thrown herself. As she slowly descended the wide oak staircase she felt in her heart that she was about to face the crisis of her fate.

The lights of the library had not been switched on, and against the soft grey twilight which illuminated the high mullioned window she saw a tall figure outlined as she entered. Instinctively she paused, and her hand fluttered to her throat. Was it the mere fact of the unconscious association of ideas, because Lee Norton had been so recently in her thoughts, that the figure before her reminded her so irresistibly of the man who now was far away? For one brief instant she was almost persuaded that the detective stood before her; then the figure turned at the sound of her footstep, and in a flash the illusion was dispelled. The face that looked into hers was that of Captain St. Quentin. But all else was forgotten as she saw the arm which rested limply in its sling, and the strip of plaster on his cheek.

"Stephen—you are injured!" she cried. "Those terrible people have attempted your life again?"

He shook his head, a reassuring smile showing beneath the short dark moustache which decorated his upper lip.

"It is nothing, Beryl," he returned, his heart giving a sudden bound as he addressed her for the first time by her name. "There was a car smash in London, and I happened to be involved to the extent of a fractured arm and a gashed cheek. Nothing serious, I assure you; but I shall not do any flying for some time to come."

"I'm glad you have returned!" she cried impulsively. "I want you to advise me—badly."

"That is probably how I shall advise you."

"How?" she asked in surprise.

"Badly. That is generally how I do advise people."

For the first time a faint smile broke the line of her set lips.

"It seems to me that you have lately been in the company of Inspector Lee Norton, of the C.I.D.," she said.

"I certainly know something of that gentleman," Lee replied cautiously. "Why do you ask?"

"Because you have caught some of his irresponsible humour, Stephen. When you answered me just now, I could almost have persuaded myself that I was listening to his light-hearted, bantering talk."

Lee Norton allowed himself to frown.

"I'm surprised to hear that. Such a flippant trait is very unseemly in a responsible official. But there, the fellow struck me as being a bit of a fool—"

"Surely not!" she cried quickly; and Lee noticed with delight that a flush of anger had mounted to her face. "He struck *me* as being a very capable and intelligent officer, who is doing his utmost to unravel a very complicated series of crimes."

"Well, he doesn't seem to have made much headway since he has been down here," commented Lee, with a disparaging shake of his head. "Perhaps it is as well that he has been taken off the case."

"I think you are very unjust towards him, Stephen," she returned with some warmth. "Your accident must have affected your power of judgment when you say things like that. I do not think you are quite yourself yet."

This remark was so near the truth that Lee hastened to turn the conversation into less dangerous channels. "I think you said something about asking my advice?" he suggested.

"Yes, Daddy is going to marry again," she burst out, "and who do you think is to be my future stepmother?"

Lee shook his head.

"Señorita Clotilde?" he suggested at a venture.

"Oh, I wouldn't have minded so much if it were she," Beryl replied. "She, at least, is far too well-bred to throw herself at poor Daddy's head in the barefaced manner that Miss Maune has!" And she plunged into a narrative of the scene which had taken place in the library that afternoon.

Lee's brain was working quickly as he listened. He had always regarded Hilda Maune as something of a mystery, and her meeting with the ill-fated O'Connor just before his death had never been satisfactorily explained. Now it appeared as if she were in possession of the answer to the riddle that had baffled the ingenuity of every successive head of the House of Chalmers to unravel. Had the solution come to her in a sudden flash of inspiration whilst examining the old manuscript? Or had she deliberately set herself to study in the hopes of obtaining the treasure for herself? For, clever though she might be, he argued, she would scarcely be able to anticipate the fact that Sir Raymond would find himself in sudden need of ready money just at the crucial moment.

The girl herself was of an unusual type of beauty; her raven hair and dark, flashing eyes seemed to hint of foreign blood, yet her English was as faultless as his own. Was she of Italian extraction; of Spanish; or—

Like a flash of lightning illuminating the midnight sky the answer rushed upon him, and with it came also the answer to other things that had puzzled him.

"By heaven! I see it all now!" he cried to Beryl. "Who were the stage-players of the olden times? Why, the gipsies, of course! It was only strolling vagrants who acted in plays in the days when every actor was by law and custom regarded as a rogue and vagabond. Doubtless a band of gipsies acted *St. Nicholas and the Three Poor Maidens,* and thus had access to the old manuscript. If they had discovered the hidden cipher, what is more likely than that the tradition should persist in the band to this day?"

Beryl looked bewildered.

"I do not see that your theory takes us very far," she objected. "It does not explain how Hilda Maune came to know about it."

"It explains itself when I tell you that Hilda Maune is herself a gipsy."

"Hilda a gipsy? Impossible!" gasped Beryl.

"Think for a moment. Consider her jet-black hair and eyes; consider her strange interest in this old parchment book; her secret study of it. Think of her interview with the soldier just before he met his death—"

"But surely O'Connor was an Irishman!" interrupted the girl.

Lee shook his head.

"That was only an assumed name," he told her. "I have found out—no matter how—that the man's real name was Juan Conreo, and that he altered it to O'Connor when he enlisted."

Suddenly he was aware that she was looking at him strangely.

"Why, Stephen, anyone would think that you were a detective yourself by the way you have been ferreting out information! You had better try your hand at unmasking the authors of the Crimson Query crimes!" she concluded with a laugh.

"I may do that yet," he muttered grimly. "In the meantime, I have something else to ferret out. I should like to have a look at the book of that old miracle-play; knowing what we do, we might secure the treasure for your father without the necessity of his marrying again."

"But Hilda has hidden it," she said, dismayed.

"She must be made to give it up," he returned firmly. "Even if she has solved its cipher, that does not make the book her own property."

Beryl Chalmers darted to the door, her face aglow with excitement.

"Come on, then. The sooner we get hold of it the better."

To say that the old baronet was amazed at the news they had to tell him would be but a faint description of his feelings. But Beryl waited in vain for the outburst of anger that she had expected. Instead, he seemed rather to admire the cleverness of Hilda.

"A gipsy, eh?" he said when he had heard all they had to say. "I thought there must be some explanation of her artfulness! But being a gipsy isn't a capital crime nowadays. However, if you're anxious to try your hand at solving the riddle, you're at perfect liberty to do so. I'll see that she gives up the book at once."

Somewhat to Lee's surprise, Hilda Maune appeared quite unmoved when Sir Raymond demanded the book.

"Certainly, Sir Raymond," she answered with a little shrug of indifference. "The book is your own property, and I will at once render it up to you. But," she went on, fixing her eyes on the fictitious Captain St. Quentin, "if this gentleman thinks he is able to read the cipher, he is very much mistaken. Believe me when I say, quoting the words of a couplet as old as the book itself:

> "While the Sun shines by day, or the Moon by night.
> Ne'er shall thine Eyes see the Child of Light,
> Unless first they read the Riddle aright."

Lee stared at the girl intently.

"Where did you learn that jingle?" he asked.

"It has been handed down in my family from generation to generation—ever since the time when my ancestors played their parts in *St. Nicholas and the Three Poor Maidens,*" she replied. "And those words of the rhyme are nothing more or less than the literal truth. Now come with me to the study and I will give up the book."

Switching on the light as she entered, Hilda Maune went straight to her desk and pulled open one of the drawers—only to stagger backwards with a stifled shriek on her ashy lips.

Amazed, the others drew near. There was no book inside the drawer—only a small square of cardboard bearing the now familiar symbol in blood-red ink.

"The book has been stolen!" cried Sir Raymond, snatching up the card.

His daughter gave a contemptuous laugh.

"Say, rather, that she has hidden it!" she cried.

With one accord they turned towards the gipsy girl. But a single glance at her fear-distorted features was enough to show that she was not dissembling.

"It is the Crimson Query!" The words came in an awe-stricken whisper, like those of one who pronounces her own doom. "They have marked me down at last!"

And before Lee could catch her, she had slipped to the floor in a dead faint.

CHAPTER XX

WHEN SERGEANT HATTERSLEY arrived at Abbot's Towers in response to Lee Norton's 'phone message, he was ushered straight into the study where his superior was awaiting his coming. Hattersley had not seen Lee since he had assumed the character of the absent Captain St. Quentin, and, such was the effectiveness of his disguise, for a moment the old sergeant failed to recognize him. Nor did his expression of mystification clear when Lee had informed him of the details of the disappearance of the ancient book containing the script of the old miracle-play.

"The more we go on the deeper we get, seemingly, sir," he said with an aggrieved air that made Lee secretly amused. "I thought the Crimson Query gang were out to get the secret 'plane, but now it seems that they've developed a sideline in the shape of the Abbey treasure—that is"—he added as though struck by a brilliant idea—"unless you think this latest crime is only a fake put up by the Maune girl."

Lee Norton shook his head decisively.

"The girl was almost crazed with fear," he told the other. "She is under the doctor's care at this present moment, utterly prostrated by the shock. No, no, I think you are wrong when you suggest that she may have stolen the book herself. I will grant that her previous actions were by no means free from self-interest, but I am convinced that she knows nothing of the actual theft. Then there is the question of the card bearing the Crimson Query."

Sergeant Hattersley smiled.

"If a girl was clever enough to fake a theft, she'd be quite capable of drawing a note of interrogation on a piece of card! Can I have a look at it, sir? I've got my finger-print outfit with me—"

"Good!" exclaimed Lee. "There it is, in the drawer. I have not disturbed it since it was first found."

Gingerly lifting out the square of pasteboard with a pair of forceps, the sergeant laid it on the table and lightly dusted its surface with a specially prepared black powder. A simultaneous exclamation of satisfaction broke from both men as a faint impression of a thumb appeared on one corner of the card.

"This will mean a quick run up to London for you, Sergeant," said the detective as he examined the tell-tale smudge. "And there's no time to lose, either. That print may be the first step towards running the gang to earth—and it's the first step that counts in a case like this. If you hurry along right now, you may be in time to catch the 7.15 from Southampton—that will be quicker than waiting for a local connection. I'll 'phone up the Yard to keep an official of the Record Department on the premises, so that there'll be no delay. I'll wait here until you ring me up to tell me if you have succeeded or not. And don't forget that my name is Captain St. Quentin for the time being."

Hattersley did not appear to be very hopeful of success.

"It looks like an inside job to me, sir, pulled off by someone in the house. It seems to me like waste of time to go rushing off to the Yard. The only records they've got there are those of crooks who have been through their hands—"

Lee turned on him swiftly.

"And wasn't 'Swab' Simson a crook? And Dippy Nolan? Though, to do him justice, I think he was more of a stool-pigeon than anything else. And now run along and don't ask questions. And you can drop a hint to your chauffeur not to worry about speed-traps between here and Southampton."

At the door the sergeant paused and looked curiously at Lee.

"How about you, sir? Are you going to cross the moor alone when you return to the aerodrome?"

"I certainly shall not 'phone for an armed escort, if that is what you mean," Lee laughed. "But don't you trouble about that. In all probability, when I leave this house I shall be accompanied by somebody wearing a pair of bracelets."

Lee heard the sound of his subordinate's heavy footsteps pass down the corridor; then came the purring hum of his car starting up outside and gradually dying away in the distance.

For a long time Lee sat silently pondering over the intricacies of the amazing case whose latest development had occurred almost under his very eyes. Without doubt the theft had been committed by one of the inmates of the Towers, or at least by one who was able to gain entry at will; but he knew that all further speculations were useless until he heard from the Record Department of Scotland Yard. Then, and only then, could he act.

At last he rose, and, crossing to the bookcase which occupied the whole of one wall of the room, ran his eye over the rows of volumes.

"No light reading here!" he smiled to himself as he read the titles of the fat, leather-bound tomes. The least indigestible morsel of that heavy literary feast appeared to be a comparatively thin volume bound in red morocco and bearing the title: *Diary of Dame Alice Chalmers during the investment of Abbot's Towers by the Parliamentary Army,* 1645. It would, at any rate, serve to pass the time; so, settling himself comfortably in an arm-chair, he opened the book and began to read.

But his expectation of being regaled with an account of stirring charges and sorties, hand-to-hand fighting, and desperate surprise assaults, was speedily dashed to the ground. The good Dame Alice seemed to have recorded only the driest details of the state of the larder during that epoch-making period. The so-called "Diary" was nothing but a list of provisions consumed each day by the garrison, and set against it was another column showing the amount of foodstuffs remaining. Lee was just about to replace the book in disgust, when a sentence caught his eye which sent him thinking.

On the face of it, it seemed but a bald entry on the credit side of the ledger, so to speak:

> *Thys 15th. Daye of November, and ye 47th Daye of ye Siege, came Robt. Falconer & Willm. Alward through ye Rebyl Lines with 3 Hogges, 2 Sheep and 1 Ox cut in small for passing beneath.*

Lee read and re-read the crabbed, faded writing, admiring the skill and daring of the two men in thus bearing six unwieldy carcases into a closely besieged castle. But the clue to the achievement seemed to lie in the words—

"1 *Ox cut in small for passing beneath.*"

Beneath what? The words could only mean that they passed beneath the Roundhead pickets, by means of a secret passage that was large enough to admit a man carrying a hog or a sheep, but not large enough to allow the passage of an ox unless "cut in small" for that purpose.

Further search of the pages brought to light many similar entries, and always, he noted, the more bulky articles had been divided. All this clearly pointed to the existence of an underground passage running from the interior of Abbot's Towers to some spot outside its walls. There was a peculiar expression of thought on Lee Norton's face as he carefully replaced the book on the shelf.

He was still deep in his ruminations when the butler entered the room.

"Hullo, Riggs," said Lee. "Have you heard how Miss Maune is getting on?"

The old man shook his head.

"She's very queer, they do say, sir. Susan and the other parlourmaid has put her to bed, and the doctor has been with her some time. Brain fever, sir, so I heard Miss Beryl tell Sir Raymond, brought on by a shock of some kind, maybe through her losing that old book that the master had entrusted to her care. Lord, what a fuss to make over an old book—just as though we hadn't got enough of 'em and to spare, lumbering up the place and gathering dust!"

And the old retainer jerked his grey head towards the orderly rows of volumes stacked on the shelves behind him.

"There be 'unnerds and 'unnerds of 'em, never opened from one year's end to t'other. What does one more or less signify?"

Lee smiled at the old man's aggrieved tone.

"Evidently you are not a lover of literature, Riggs," he said. But the old man seemed to resent this as an unmerited slur.

"Oh, but I am, sir," he protested vigorously. "I likes to sit down and have a read now and ag'in. But I likes something bright and excitin', or something a bit creepy-like to keep your nerves on edge."

Lee looked up quickly; here was an opening too good to be missed.

"But surely the mere fact of living in an old house like this ought to make you feel creepy enough, without having to resort to ghost-stories? I'll wager there are any amount of hidden panels and secret passages in the old place."

Riggs smoothed his scanty grey locks with a puzzled air.

"Well, sir, there was a 'priests' hole' above the library."

"Yes?" said Lee encouragingly.

"You can have a look at it if you like, sir. We use it for storing the lumber in."

This was hardly what Lee wanted.

"You've never heard a rumour of a passage running underground and leading somewhere outside the walls, have you?"

"Never, sir." The man's tone was positive. "I've been in service here for fifty years, as my father was afore me, and I've never

heerd tell o' such. Still, I shouldn't be surprised to hear of one being found. It were troubled times when this here house were built,
sir, and some dark deeds have been done within these walls, so
they say. There was one Sir Martin Chalmers stabbed to the heart
in this very room, with the doors locked and not a soul inside besides himself."

"That sounds interesting," remarked the detective, inwardly certain that he was about to hear something that would corroborate his
theory. "Tell me about it."

"Sir Martin was an officer in the army of the Duke o' Marlbor-
ough—you can see his portrait hangin' in the Great Hall, with his
three-cornered hat and big jack boots. He served through the war in
Spain, and while he was there he was captured by the Spanish ir-
regulars—the 'gorillas' I think they call 'em—"

"Guerrillas?" suggested Lee.

"That's what I said, sir. Well, these here gorillas tortured him to
make him give information, and they would have killed him, for
sure, if a cavalry patrol hadn't happened to come up in the nick of
time and rescue him. After that they say he never gave quarter to a
Spaniard. At the capture of Villa Viciosa he acted like a madman,
pistolling the prisoners until he was forcibly disarmed by his own
men. Nor was he much better when he came back to England.
'Mad Sir Martin' they used to call him, for the mere sight of anyone who appeared the least like a Spaniard was sufficient to send
him into a murderous rage. He nearly lashed a harmless Jew pedlar
to death with his hunting-crop just because he was dark-skinned
and foreign-looking. But the end came when he happened to light
on a band of Spanish gipsies who had encamped on the moor not
five hundred yards from the gates of Abbot's Towers."

The old man paused and seemed half inclined to leave the rest
of his tale untold. But the most interesting part, for Lee at any rate,
was still to come. Under his prompting he presently continued:

"Well, sir, it's not fitting for me to tell, nor you to listen to, an
account of all that occurred. The poor gentleman was crazed in his
mind, or he'd never have acted so brutally. Finally he caught up
one of the young girls—Sibyl Morona was her name—bound her
hand and foot with his stirrup-leathers, and carried her shrieking to
the Towers, brandishing his loaded pistol and vowing to scatter the
brains of the first man who stayed him. He took her to this very
room and locked the door, intending heaven alone knows what
devilry. And heaven alone knows how he met his fate. The trembling servants, gathered round the door, heard a sudden howl like

that of a fiend in torment, and when they had gathered courage to break in, Sir Martin lay weltering in his own blood, stabbed to the heart with a Spanish dagger that none of them had ever seen before."

"And the girl . . .?"

"She had vanished, none knew whither," said the old man in an awed whisper. "She was never seen by mortal eye again."

The moment Riggs had departed Lee Norton slapped his thigh.

"A secret passage—that proves it!" he muttered to himself. "It only remains to find out the entrance—"

The sudden shrilling of the telephone bell brought him across the room at the double. Lifting the receiver, he found it was the expected trunk-call from London.

"I've checked up on that finger-print," announced Hattersley. "It tallies with that of a man called Lal Thaxted, who received ten years for forgery in 1900."

"Good!" exclaimed Lee.

"But that only gets us deeper in the mire. Thaxted had served half of his sentence when he escaped from Parkhurst Prison. His movements were traced to the other side of the Isle of Wight, where he stole a boat and a suit of oilskins to cover up his convict-clothes. Then he must have rowed across the Solent and struck inland, for his boat was discovered scuttled in the Beaulieu River, and months afterwards the skeleton of Thaxted was found, still dressed in his convict-uniform, in one of the prehistoric stone barrows on Abbotsmoor."

Lee Norton's eyes narrowed as he listened.

"Seems queer," he commented.

"Well, there's no doubt that the man who made that print is dead and buried years ago," continued Hattersley, with something like a snigger in his voice. "You can't arrest a ghost, can you?"

"I can't," admitted Lee quietly. "But all I know is that a ghost that is substantial enough to hold a card in its fingers is substantial enough to have a pair of bracelets snapped on its wrists. Make up your mind to it, laddie, I'm going to get this Lal Thaxted."

"Then you'll have to go to the churchyard for him," laughed the voice from the other end.

"That's precisely where I intend to begin my search!" answered Lee Norton grimly.

CHAPTER XXI

M R. AMOS AINTREE was not usually an early riser, but the following morning he was up, dressed and shaved, at an hour when the only other inmates of the Towers that were astir were the staff of servants. He encountered Riggs the butler as he descended the broad staircase leading to the entrance-hall, and gave him a cheery "Good morning."

"It's a lovely morning, Riggs," he remarked genially.

"Last night's wireless Weather Forecast said rain, sir," said the practical Riggs.

Aintree paused in the act of snipping the end off his cigar.

"Oh, so you've got a wireless set here, then? I understood Sir Raymond to say that he detested listening-in."

"That's true, sir," agreed Riggs. "But the set I use is a little set o' my own, a private installation, so to speak, which my nevvy fitted up for me in my room, Made it all himself, he did, sir, and a very wunnerful little set it is. I've only got to connect the screws that's marked 'aerial' to the wire bed-mattress, and the one that's marked 'earth' to the water-pipe, and I can hear as plain as I can hear you now. Ah, 'tis a wunnerful age we lives in, sir. They do say in the papers as how we'll soon be able to see through brick walls as well as hear through 'em."

The film director seemed very interested in the butler's private installation.

"Your room must be fairly high up?" he suggested.

"Top storey, sir."

"How many stations can you get?" was his next question. But the old servant shook his head.

"My nevvy tunes it in to Daventry, and there I leaves it. I thought that summat had gone wrong with it last night, though," he added.

"Yes?" said Aintree encouragingly.

"I did, sir. There were a bit o' play-acting going on at the time—two chaps talking, you know, sir. Rare funny fellows they were, too. One of 'em was supposed to be—"

"Yes, but what happened to your set?" interrupted Amos Aintree.

"Well, as I were saying, these two fellows were talking, and right in the middle of it there came some music."

Riggs, when he saw the sudden start that his listener gave, decided that the American gentleman was an enthusiastic wireless fan.

"What sort of music?" he asked eagerly. "Can you remember the tune?"

Riggs gave a vague gesture with his hands.

"It weren't what you could rightly call a tune, sir. It were one o' these here what you may call 'classical' bits."

"Did it go anything like this?" And Aintree pursed up his lips and began to whistle the opening bars of Schumann's *Symphony in B Flat Major*.

A smile of recognition broke over the old man's features.

"That's it, sir!" he cried delightedly. "I wonder where it could have been coming from?"

"I shouldn't worry about that if I were you," Aintree answered eagerly. "Probably your set went off the proper wave-length for a moment—it often happens like that if you get your microfarads entangled with the ohmns from your filiment-resistance."

"Is that so, sir?" cried the impressed Riggs, to whom the inner workings of his set were as a sealed book. "I hope I have not been 'inoculating' by any chance?"

"No, I don't think so," returned the American gravely. "Still, you never know. If you should hear the music butting in again, you'd better let me know at once. I'm very interested—in broadcasting."

Which, in a sense, was true. But the fact which interested Amos Aintree at that moment was the unexpected intimation he had received, by the merest stroke of luck, that Count Ravangar's yacht had returned to home waters.

He lit his cigar as he passed through the arched doorway, puffing contentedly as he slowly strolled along the terrace, pausing now and again to admire the view which stretched beyond the stone balustrades, his manner seeming to indicate that the sole purpose of his early stroll was a desire to admire the panorama of autumn-tinted woodland which lay before him. Once out of sight of the windows of the house, however, he quickened his pace.

He was not the only one who had risen early that morning. On a carved stone seat, discreetly screened by tall hedges of neatly trimmed box, sat the girl who was known as Clotilde la Zorita. Clothed, as usual, in robes and cloak of spotless white, her long plaits of hair lying like two ingots of virgin gold upon her slender shoulders, at first sight she might have appeared like a picture of one of those Madonnas which the old Italian artists loved to paint. But the very modern note struck by the perfumed cigarette which dangled between her heart-shaped lips would have quickly dispelled the illusion. She glanced up expectantly as Aintree's footsteps approached.

"Well?" The sharp, metallic tone of the one word with which she greeted him was very much at variance with her usual melodious voice. But Aintree was too familiar with the real woman which lay beneath her carefully studied pose to be either surprised or disconcerted by the abrupt greeting. Without troubling to remove his cigar, he seated himself beside her and fixed his pale eyes on hers.

"The *Lapwing* is back again," he said shortly.

She slowly removed the cigarette from her lips and exhaled a languid cloud. "Then you haven't seen Count Ravangar?"

"Seen nothing," he snapped. "It was the merest fluke that I got to be put wise. The old fool of a butler is in the habit of filling in his spare time listening to the Daventry Station. Last night he heard the opening bars of the *Symphony in B Flat Major,* which is the code-signal for Thoady to have the car waiting on the road beside the Beaulieu River."

A look of interest came into Clotilde's sapphire eyes.

"That means the Count was here last night," she said thoughtfully.

"And it also means," he supplemented with a grim laugh, "that there will probably be a splash headline in this morning's paper. But I did not come here to discuss that—I guess Rawlins is able to do his little piece of gunning without any help from us. I wanted to speak to you about the girl who's ill upstairs—Hilda Maune."

"Ill?" The poppy lips curved in a sneer. "More likely shamming!"

"Then she has shammed good enough to deceive the doctor. But you can make up your mind that she's ill all right. I heard Sir Raymond discussing the advisability of calling in a trained nurse to look after her."

She flicked the ash from her cigarette with a gesture of studied indifference. "I'm afraid that the subject of the health of Miss Hilda Maune is one that does not interest me," she drawled.

"No? Well, I guess the sooner you get interested in it the better!" he retorted sharply.

She threw away her cigarette and turned and regarded him in undisguised amazement.

"Do you expect me to take her some flowers and hothouse grapes?" she inquired with elaborate sarcasm. "Or would it please you better if I were to offer to act as her nurse?"

He nodded curtly.

"I guess you've just about said it, Clo. That's just what you are about to go to Sir Raymond and offer to do right now."

"What!" she cried, starting to her feet.

"You're going to be a good, kind angel of mercy towards your poor afflicted sister, and sit up all night with her holding her hand and giving her her medicine."

There was but little of the merciful angel in her demeanour as she turned on him with a string of vituperation that could scarcely have been excelled by one of the denizens of St. Lazare. ". . . And I'll see my afflicted sister in the infernal regions first!" is a paraphrase of her concluding remark.

"That's just about the place where you will see her," observed the unmoved Amos. "But until that happy reunion takes place, you'll just take that look off your face and do as you're told. This Maune girl knows a sight too much for us to let any strange nurse listen to her delirious ravings. I've got that old book of the miracle-play hidden away in a safe place—"

"Where?" she asked, with a sudden gleam of interest lighting up her sulky countenance.

"In a safe place," he repeated slowly, "where you, for one, would never think of looking for it. But, though I've got the book, the secret of the cipher is as far off as ever. I spent most of last night trying out every dodge I knew, and all I found out was the fact that, unless we get the information from Hilda Maune, the treasure might as well be at the bottom of the sea for all the chance we'll have of fingering it. And that's where you come in, Clo. You're going to play the ministering angel for all you're worth. You're going to smooth her little pillow, cool her fevered brow— and all the rest of the dope that you know so well—and when you've won her confidence, you'll ask for the secret of that old book as her dying bequest—"

"But she might get better," put in the girl.

Aintree shook his head, and into his pale eyes there came a cold gleam which made them appear like burnished pewter.

"She ain't going to get well—*with you as her nurse,*" he said slowly.

She craned forward, peering into his eyes, and in their depths she read the ghastly truth.

"My God! You mean—"

"I mean that you've got to go the limit this time, Clotilde, my dear. And don't be too inquisitive about the why and wherefore. The only person that Count Ravangar allows to ask questions is himself. And he asks them in . . . crimson!"

And Amos Aintree rose from the stone seat and slowly sauntered back to the house, puffing his cigar as he went. Re-entering the hall, he paused opposite the oak table on which lay the morning's papers, running his eye over the headlines. But there was no sign of the words that he had so confidently expected to see there.

"H'm—strange," he muttered. "Surely Rawlins has not bungled a third time?"

He turned to the inner pages, with the same negative result. Then he carefully folded the paper, replaced it on the table, and crossed the hall towards the breakfast-room—only to stop dead in his stride as his eyes met the smiling gaze of the very man of whose death he had been expecting to read.

"Captain St. Quentin!" The cigar fell from between his jaws as he gasped out the name. "You are an early visitor, it seems!"

The smile which accompanied Lee's pleasant nod was not forced. It was the first time he had encountered the American while in his assumed guise of the airman, and it gratified him to see the unhesitating manner in which the other took his identity for granted.

"Not so early as you may think," he returned carelessly. "I felt too lazy to tramp back to my quarters last night, so I accepted Sir Raymond's offer to stay here. I thought it would save me a journey across that depressing moor."

Amos Aintree knew well enough that the decision had saved the man in the blue-grey uniform from something more than that; but he merely made a commonplace rejoinder and turned the talk into other matters.

An inquiry as to the condition of the invalid gave Clotilde her opening to make an offer to act as sick-nurse. Not wholly to her disappointment, she found Sir Raymond rather inclined to pooh-pooh the idea.

"It is very good and sympathetic of you to make the offer, Señorita," he said, "but it would be hardly fair for me to allow you to be put to so much trouble."

Clotilde shook her head, and into her golden-fringed eyes came an expression of one yearning to do good.

"Trouble, Sir Raymond?" Her very tone seemed to reproach the baronet. "How can you talk of such a petty thing as mere trouble to me when there is an opportunity of doing good to one lying ill and afflicted? Heaven knows, it is but little good that we poor butterfly creatures—as the world doubtless regards us actresses—can do to alleviate the suffering of others; but if you only knew how I sometimes long to be able to feel that I am of real service to others, you would not now deny me the work which my conscience tells me that I ought to do. Please, please, Sir Raymond, do not deprive me of the joy that I shall feel in knowing that I am helping poor dear Miss Maune in gaining health and strength."

Like a very angel of pity, she clasped her hands in sweet entreaty and looked up at him with eyes in which the tender tears seemed ready to start. As he looked at her, Sir Raymond felt himself almost wishing that he were taken with some interesting and not too painful illness that he might evoke the same feelings in this angelic creature.

"Well—if you really wish it—"

The long fringes of her eyes dropped with an air of saintly devotion.

"It is my duty, Sir Raymond," she said firmly, and within the hour she was installed in the post that she so ardently desired.

Her knowledge of nursing was so small as to be almost negligible. But she was an accomplished actress, whose studio experience had taught her to appear natural and convincing in such diversified characters, that she had no difficulty in impressing those around her that she was eminently capable of carrying out the necessary duties. And added to her apparent quiet efficiency was an air of tender sympathy for her charge that won all hearts. Even the detective, accustomed as he was to discount all outward show, felt that here was one who, in the midst of the grim and dark schemes of the unknown Crimson Query, was good and pure. Beryl Chalmers, however, was not so sure.

In the course of the morning Dr. Rollinson paid his usual visit. He was a young man who had taken over the practice of another doctor who had recently died. He expressed himself satisfied with the arrangements of the sick-room, and was visibly impressed with the appearance of the new nurse. But he frowned thoughtfully as he noted the condition of the patient.

"Still running a temperature, I see. . . . H'm. . . ." He glanced down at the thin, flushed face on the pillow and noted the vacant look in the wide-open eyes. "Has she been delirious, Nurse?"

Clotilde nodded her white-coifed head. "A little, Doctor."

"H'm . . . it's fairly evident that there is something preying on the patient's mind. Try to keep her cheerful and bright. Should she become light-headed, do your best to compose her. I will send a sedative over, so that you can administer it if necessary." He stopped speaking as he noted that Hilda's lips were moving. "Well, and how are you feeling this morning?" he asked in his best bed-side manner.

A wide-eyed, unseeing stare from the girl on the bed greeted his question; but her lips continued to move. He bent over the bed to catch the faintly uttered words.

"She muttered something about a 'crimson sign'," he said, turning to Clotilde with a puzzled look. "Have you any idea what she means?"

"I'm afraid I have not, Doctor." Her answer was accompanied by a sad sigh. Then she gave a studied start. "Unless—yes, that must be it—her mind is running on that series of tragedies which have taken place in the neighbourhood. The poor girl was always weak and hysterical," she lied glibly, "and you know the morbid interest which such people take in the more sensational items of the daily Press."

"Of course, of course," he agreed. "Well, well, keep her bright and cheerful, and don't on any account allow anyone to bring up the subject of those murders in her hearing."

"Very good, Doctor," said Clotilde dutifully; and the young medico took his departure mentally congratulating himself on having such a paragon in charge of his patient.

But he might have seen reason to revise his opinion had he witnessed what was taking place in that room soon after he had gone. Hilda was sleeping peacefully for the first time, when Clotilde, crossing quietly to her side, bent over her and whispered three words in her ear.

"The Crimson Query!"

Instantly a shudder passed through the frame of the sick girl, and her eyes, terror-haunted with a nameless dread, opened and looked fearfully around.

"Yes—yes—always the Crimson Query," she muttered in a faint but hoarse whisper. "Always the sign in crimson—the question that is never answered. . . . Never answered—never—never . . . and never will be, unless I choose to speak!"

The beautiful limbs of the listener had suddenly gone rigid as she stood.

"What can you tell of the Crimson Query?" she asked presently.

A faint smile parted Hilda's lips.

"I have the letter . . . given me by the Romany *chal*—the letter that he wrote to O'Connor, asking him to meet Rawlins on the moor the night he was killed."

A long breath of relief escaped Clotilde's lips. That letter, she well knew, had been written in an ink that would cause the writing to entirely disappear three hours after it had been penned. So *that* was the evidence that this fool was raving about! She had half turned away when a few disjointed words in the girl's feverish mutterings caused her to swiftly return to her side.

"Clever—yes, clever they thought themselves, but they could not trick me! . . . Disappearing ink—I saw it begin to fade before my eyes. But, letter for letter, word for word, I traced the writing before it faded. Clever—clever . . . but I was cleverer still!"

Clotilde eagerly grasped the girl's shoulder, shaking her to and fro in her excitement.

"Where is this letter—where have you put it?" she demanded.

Hilda smiled feebly.

"It is hidden . . . yes, hidden. . . ."

"Where?" cried her nurse in a strident, metallic voice, so urgent and menacing that it appeared to pierce the veil of the clouded mind of the invalid.

Slowly and painfully the sick girl raised herself on one elbow. There was dawning consciousness in the eyes which looked up at her questioner.

"I have hidden the letter . . . hidden it. . . ."

"Where . . . where?"

"Where you or your gang will never find it!"

And with a shrill laugh of triumph Hilda Maune sank back on the bed and lay motionless.

Two hours later her words were being repeated to Count Ravangar by Amos Aintree in the cabin of the *Lapwing*. The lifelike but impassive mask-face of the Count allowed no sign to appear of the expression of the real countenance beneath; nor did his voice, shrill and articulate as it always was, betray what feelings had been evoked by the unexpected revelation.

"It is well," was all he said. "We can attend to Hilda Maune later. There is more pressing work to do this night. Captain St. Quentin did not pass across the moor last night. Do you know why?"

"He stayed the night at Abbot's Towers," replied Amos.

"And so we waited for him in vain," nodded Ravangar. "Does he return tonight?"

"Yes." The American spoke with confidence, for he had overheard Lee, in his assumed character, announce that intention.

"Good! When he sets out, you will follow him at a safe distance, yet near enough to render help if it should be required."

Aintree's sandy eyebrows shot upwards with a questioning look as he placed his hand behind him and significantly tapped something which reposed in his hip-pocket.

The Count shook his head.

"No shooting this time," he ordered sharply. "I'm going to get Captain St. Quentin alive, bring him to the yacht, and . . . *make him talk!*"

In spite of the warmth of the day, Amos Aintree shivered slightly as he made his way on deck to return to the shore.

CHAPTER XXII

LEE NORTON WAS STRIDING ALONE along one of the winding paths which led through the densely wooded grounds of Abbot's Towers. It was a perfect afternoon, with the warm sunshine glancing through the yellowing leaves of the close ranks of trees, falling like spears of living gold on the leaves which, first fruits of winter's coming harvest, strewed the narrow way. Around him on every side the pageantry of the dying year flaunted its vivid hues: the golden-brown of the hoary oaks, the warmer copper-red of the giant beeches, tempered with the paler yellow of the silver birch, whose slender white stems stood out among the gnarled and moss-hung boles like pale, graceful ghosts.

But at that moment the solitary walker had no eyes for the surrounding scenery. His brows were drawn down in an unseeing, thoughtful frown; his strong white teeth were clenched on the stem of his pipe in a savage grip. Lee Norton was thinking hard, and his thoughts were not pleasant ones.

In his ruthless summing-up of the situation, he had not sought to disguise from himself the fact that, so far as unmasking the sinister association of the Crimson Query was concerned, he had accomplished nothing. It is true that Captain St. Quentin had not fallen a victim; but he regarded his success in this part of his duties as a merely negative result. His real triumph would be in the exposure of the diabolically clever crime-genius who, he had always felt, was the real instigator of the crimes.

Earlier in the day he had gone over to Westdown and had a long talk with Detective-Sergeant Hattersley, and from him he had obtained a detailed account of the circumstances surrounding the escape of Lal Thaxted from Parkhurst, and the subsequent discovery of his skeleton in one of the prehistoric subterranean stone burying-places with which Abbotsmoor was dotted. There were many points in the narrative which gave him food for thought.

Following his usual custom when endeavouring to fathom the motives of others, he had mentally placed himself in the position of the escaped convict. Lal Thaxted had immediately made for the coast, where, breaking open one of the boat-houses on the waterfront, he had secured a suit of oilskins and a sailing-boat. So far his actions were understandable; were, in fact, exactly what he himself would have done had he been placed in the same circumstances. It was what had happened afterwards that seemed to strike a jarring note. Why on earth had not the hunted man headed down-Channel and boarded an outward-bound ship? Or why had he not landed on some deserted stretch of coast where he might have laid low until he could get clear away? Why had he sailed up the Beaulieu River? True, he might have reached Southampton that way, by striking across country, but a big port like that was one of the first places which would be watched immediately the news of the escape was flashed round the country. Evidently he must have been making for somewhere where he knew that he could count on obtaining shelter or assistance. Somebody must have been living in the district at the time on whom he could have relied. It must have been some person well known to him, a friend, a relative, a fellow-crook. The question was—who was it?

A study of the papers relating to the trial had shown that Lal Thaxted belonged to the upper classes. In point of fact, he had been an undergraduate at Oxford when the discovery of his huge series of frauds had brought about his arrest and subsequent trial and imprisonment; and it was only to be surmised that the unknown refuge that he had been making for when death overtook him was the house of a man in the same station of life. Oxford! . . . The very name suggested a fresh train of thought. He remembered hearing that Sir Raymond Chalmers had been at the University when the sudden death of his father in the hunting-field had raised him to the title. A hasty calculation of dates suggested the possibility that the baronet might have been at Oxford at the same time as Lal Thaxted; in which case he might be able to give some valuable information respecting his friends and associates. At any rate, it was worthwhile making a tentative inquiry at the first convenient opportunity.

No sooner had he arrived at this resolution than his thoughts were interrupted by the sudden barking of a dog, and an instant later the redoubtable Brutus came into sight, and after standing for a moment at gaze, with quivering nostrils and pricked ears, made towards Lee at a run.

"Brutus! Brutus!" Beryl's voice was filled with apprehension as she vainly called to the dog. And the detective's mind was by no means free from the same emotion as he watched the dog's eager approach. For, though his elaborate disguise might deceive the eyes of his fellow creatures, it was powerless to hide his identity from the animal instinct of the dog. Only too well did Brutus recognize his late enemy, and by the way that his outstretched legs covered the ground between them it seemed as though he was only too eager to renew his acquaintance.

But this time Lee did not seek to evade the dog. Although every dictate of his reason bade him repeat his former tree-climbing exploit, he calmly stood his ground. Nor was his coolness without result. The dog paused, undecided, yet wary. Lee took a pace forward.

"Hullo, Brutus! Good dog . . . good old boy!"

The dog leapt forward at the sound of his voice; but it was the leap of delighted greeting. The next moment he was fawning on his late enemy as he stroked his sleek sides and playfully pulled his great, upstanding ears.

When Beryl came up a few seconds later, she gave an exclamation of relief.

"Thank goodness that he's taken a fancy to you, Stephen!" she cried. "By the way he dashed off, I thought he was about to serve you the same as he did Mr. Lee Norton, the detective."

For the life of him Lee could not repress a smile.

"So Brutus has been getting himself known to the police, eh?" he laughed. "But he seems quite a reformed character now!"

He turned and fell into step by her side as he spoke, and for a while they traversed the woodland path in a rather strained silence. With a sidelong glance he noted the neatness of her slim, tweed-clad figure; the perfect profile; the clear, natural complexion, ripened and sun-toned by long hours in the open air; the tender, sensitive mouth and the laughing blue eyes. And as he looked he found it in his heart to curse the fates that he was not in very truth the man he purported to be—the real Captain St. Quentin who was betrothed to the girl who now walked by his side. But his futile envy was destined to be shortlived. They had not proceeded far before she suddenly halted and faced him.

"Stephen . . . Captain St. Quentin . . . I hardly know how to begin . . ." The colour had deepened in her cheeks; then as suddenly had drained away. She was labouring under an emotion so strong and poignant that her breath came quick between her parted lips. "I—I must speak, now, at once. You'll think me heartless— fickle—but I simply can't go on pretending any longer."

"Pretending?" He echoed the word more for the purpose of gaining time than because her words had taken him by surprise. Of course, she had discovered his impersonation and was about to reproach him with it. But her next words showed that he was wrong.

"Stephen," she faltered, "I feel as though our engagement was a mistake. I thought I loved you—thought I could be happy as your wife—but now—"

He waited, his face as set and expressionless as a granite mask.

"Now I realize that it would be unfair to pretend any longer that I love you." And she slipped the hoop of diamonds from her finger and held it out towards him.

Lee Norton's head was in a whirl. Was ever a man confronted with such a baffling predicament as he now found himself? But one fact stood out clear and distinct amid the welter of conflicting emotions which beset his mind. Common justice to Beryl, to St. Quentin, and no less to himself, demanded that he should reveal his own identity without delay. Yet he could not resist asking one question before he made the declaration.

"Your words, Miss Chalmers, have scarcely taken me by surprise, and in a moment or two I will explain why. But first I have a question to ask. Did the change in your feelings towards me take place during my present visit?"

She shook her head.

"It dates from long before that," she answered, and at her words a great load seemed to lift from Lee's heart.

"Thank God for that!" he cried fervently. "Now I know that I have not been a traitor to the man whose identity I have assumed."

"Identity . . . assumed?"

Her eyes were full upon his now, glowing with suppressed excitement as the cry broke from her. Almost it seemed as though she had already sensed the mad, bewildering confession that was to come. She caught his arm, impulsively, urgently.

"Who are you?" she whispered fiercely.

"I am Lee Norton, the Detective-Inspector from Scotland Yard." He, too, sank his voice as he uttered the words. "I could not tell you before—indeed, it is a breach of my orders to do so now, but I could not allow you to go on thinking that I was the man to whom you were betrothed."

"Where is Captain St. Quentin now?" she asked.

"I may tell you, in strict confidence, that he has left England," Lee answered.

"And you have assumed his place—and his peril?" Her eyes were glistening strangely now.

Lee Norton shrugged.

"All in the day's work," he returned carelessly. "We—wanted the gang of criminals who have marked him down to show their hand by attacking me. So far they have failed to do so, but I'm still living in hopes," he added cheerfully. "You are the only person, outside official circles, who knows of my masquerade, and I suppose it is scarcely necessary for me to ask you not to breathe a word of what I have told you—not even to your dearest friend."

She smiled faintly, then drew herself up to attention and gravely saluted him in military fashion.

"Very good, Captain," she said. "But if I carry out your orders you ought at least to reward me by telling me your future plans. I'd simply love to do my little bit towards the good cause."

Lee gave a wry smile.

"I'm afraid that my future plans are conspicuous by their absence just at present," he confessed gloomily. "Of the person, or persons, who are the back of this mysterious murder organization we have not the least idea. One thing alone we are certain of: sooner or later an attempt will be made either to gain possession of the secret 'plane, or else to silence the supposed Captain St. Quentin. Then, and then only, can we act."

"In short, you are the decoy?" Her heart gave a quick, sharp throb as she realized the peril in which he stood.

Lee shrugged slightly.

"Yes, you may put it that way if you like, Miss Chalmers. But please don't run away with the impression that I'm doing more than an ordinary constable may be called upon to do at any moment. My strong card is the fact that I appear to be a half-disabled man. Whoever is sent to tackle me will think he has such an easy task before him that his over-confidence may well prove his own undoing. Anyway, I am only taking the same risk that the captain would have to face were he here now. Really," he wound up as they came in sight of the house, "the only thing you can do to help me is to carry on the same as usual."

"Is that really all?" she asked wistfully.

"I fear it is."

Suddenly a peal of rippling laughter broke from her lips.

"Then I'd better begin now," she said. "In order to assist in your impersonation, I must play the part of a young lady saying good-bye to her affianced lover . . ."

And before the bewildered detective had realized her intention, she had flung her arms round his neck and kissed him full on the lips.

"Good-bye . . . and God keep you," she whispered. Then, while Lee was still striving to put into words the rapturous amazement which filled his heart, she sprang lightly up the steps of the terrace and disappeared within.

"Brutus, old boy," said the detective, looking down at the Alsatian who stood registering his approval with a frantically wagging tail, "this is decidedly my lucky day!"

CHAPTER XXIII

ITT WAS NEARLY TEN O'CLOCK when Lee Norton left the Towers to return to his quarters at the aerodrome. Overhead the night was clear and windless, the stars twinkling in the moonless sky with an almost wintry brilliance; only over the treacherous expanse of Abbot's Mire a thin veil of mist lay like a ghostly shroud.

Passing between the two massive stone pillars which flanked the gate of the park, Lee turned into, and for a short space followed, the high-road which led to the village of Westdown. Arriving at the spot where a rough moorland track branched off, he was aware of a quick patter of footsteps behind him, and, almost before he could turn, a soft furry body hurled itself upon him with a whine of delighted recognition.

"What, Brutus, old boy!" said Lee, leaning down and covering the sleek, muscular body with caresses dear to the doggy heart. "You want to see me safely home, do you, old chap? But you've got your own little job to look after. Home, Brutus, home!"

The great Alsatian drew back on its haunches and looked appealingly up at Lee, while from its mouth there issued a low whine of protest. It seemed as if some subtle instinct had warned the dog that its presence was necessary, and he was trying to pass on the information to the man. Not until Lee had repeated the order in a sharper voice did Brutus attempt to obey; and then he moved only to retreat a few paces and give vent to another long whine of protest. The instinct of obedience was for the time being overruled by another which warned him not to leave his new-found friend alone on the moor. So strange and unusual was the dog's manner that for a moment Lee hesitated whether he should let him accompany him back to the aerodrome, whence he knew the dog would easily be able to find his way back to Abbot's Towers. But there was the safety of another to be thought of—the sweet-faced girl who had earlier that night confessed her love for him in his real identity. What if the absence of her faithful watch-dog should expose her to the dangers which Lee knew but too well to cluster about the ancient house and its inmates? He shook his head at the dog and pointed backwards to the road they had come.

"Not this time, Brutus. Home, boy, home!"

And the Alsatian, with a last protesting whine, turned tail and pattered off into the darkness.

The track into which Lee had turned traversed a stretch of open moor, dead level except where the rounded mounds, which marked the burial-places of a forgotten, prehistoric race, rose here and there on its grassy surface. Although any of these hummocks might have afforded excellent cover for a hidden marksman, Lee did not pause or falter for an instant. Indeed, his actions and behaviour seemed to be those of a man desirous of advertising his presence rather than of concealing it. His footsteps would have been noise-less had he walked on the turf which bordered the road, instead of on the scrunching gravel of the road itself. But he tramped on with cheerful and noisy indifference, and presently, as he neared a dense clump of bushes which intersected his path, began to whistle the strains of an old Army marching-tune.

A hoarse chuckle broke from one of the dark figures which crouched low in the undergrowth near the spot where Lee must pass.

"The captain seems in a merry mood," he whispered to his fel-lows.

"He'll change his tune before the Count has finished with him!" jeered another grimly.

"Ssh! No talking!" warned the third. "Here he comes. Don't forget, I want him *alive.* You, Rawlins, hold him up in front while Thoady and I creep up behind. Watch his left hand—if he's armed he'll have to shoot with that, for his right hand is useless." And Count Ravangar took a cloth from his pocket and saturated it with the contents of a small green phial.

On came Lee Norton, whistling blithely as though he had not a care in the world. Twenty yards now separated him from the crouching thugs . . . ten yards . . .

Rawlins grinned in the darkness as he drew a murderous-looking dagger from its sheath on his hip. "It's too easy!" he thought as he rose noiselessly to his feet. Lee saw the black shape against the distant stars, but still he gave no sign. Not until his next step would have brought him into collision with the man who barred his path did he seem to be aware of the man's presence. Then his whistling gave place to speech.

"Good evening, stranger," he said affably. "It's a fine night for the time of the—"

His left arm was suddenly seized in an iron grip and a long blade glittered menacingly in the faint starlight.

"Don't move, Captain," growled a gruff voice. "We want to have a little talk with you."

"Delighted," said Lee, and a thin pencil of flame licked from the end of his bandaged right arm as he pressed the trigger of his automatic and sent a bullet through the shoulder of his attacker. At such short range it would have been a simple matter to have killed the man outright, but such was not Lee's intention; a living witness was worth a hundred dead ones if he was going to solve the mystery of the crimson symbol of death.

Uttering a curse that was half a groan, Rawlins went down headlong among the furze, and at the same moment two pair of hands seized the detective from behind.

The flash of the discharge scorched Lee's ear as he fired at random over his shoulder, and though the whine of the bullet told him that his blind shot had missed the men behind, the shot at least had the effect of making one of his assailants loose his hold. Desperately he sought to shake off the remaining man; but he stuck to him like a leech, and presently the other, gaining courage, dashed suddenly forward and wrenched the pistol from the detective's grasp.

"Swipe him, Thoady," said a shrill, unnatural voice.

For a moment it seemed as if the man in his blind fury would shoot him there and then. But the discipline ingrained on his satellites by Count Ravangar was such that, though Thoady's finger caressed the trigger lovingly, the bullet which would have terminated Lee Norton's career was not fired. Instead, pocketing the pistol, the man drew a heavy "cosh" from some handy pocket and raised it to strike him down.

In vain the detective threw his head from side to side in the hope of evading that downward stroke. Coolly dwelling on his aim, the man deliberately brought down the weapon with a sickening crash.

"That's fixed him!" laughed Thoady, as he saw the detective's body sag limply forward.

But the next moment the laugh froze on his lips. With the force and suddenness of a living thunderbolt, the Alsatian had launched itself at him. Under the impact of the hundred and fifty pounds of muscle, bone, and sinew the man went down, and with a long-

drawn growl of hatred the terrible fangs sought and seized the ruf-
fian's throat.

Dazed, yet not wholly unconscious, Lee heard the sound, and
with it hope returned. Swaying dizzily, he staggered to his feet,
determined at least to make a fight for life. But the third man had
not thought it prudent to await the outcome of the struggle, for he
had already glided silently away in the darkness.

"Loose him, Brutus—loose him!" cried Lee, laying hold of the
dog's collar with one hand and with the other endeavouring to
break the grip of the strong teeth. But the dog seemed unwilling to
loose his hold while his human enemy still showed signs of life.
When at last Lee succeeded in releasing the man it was clear that
he had been only just in time, He was panting heavily and half-
conscious, and the man whom Lee had wounded was in an even
worse plight.

For a moment Lee stood considering the situation. His prisoners
were clearly incapable of walking, and it was folly to think of attempting to carry even one of them to the aerodrome, where the
nearest help lay. Yet he was too well aware of the value of his capture to take any chances of their escaping. He dared not leave
Brutus to guard them, for in the dog's excited state he might have
renewed his attack. Added to the complications of the situation
was the possible chance that the third man might be lurking in the
darkness, ready to shoot him down the moment he flashed a light
or fired his automatic as a signal for help from the camp.

Finally he took a pair of handcuffs from his pocket and snapped
one steel bracelet on the wrist of the wounded man and the other
on that of Brutus' late antagonist, so that if one recovered he would
be forced to take the other with him in his flight. Then, passing his
handkerchief through the dog's collar, he set off along the path that
led to the aerodrome.

He had traversed half the distance when a warning growl from
the dog caused him to halt. Pistol in hand, Lee peered into the
shadow of the trees which bordered the path and thought he could
discern a lurking figure.

"Advance, whoever you are!" he shouted. "I've got you covered!"

"Thank God it's you, Lee," came the answer in a voice of unfeigned relief, and Sergeant Hattersley stepped forward and
grasped Lee by the hand. "I've been waiting here since dusk, and
when you failed to come I thought those devils had got you."

"They nearly did get me," returned the other a little dryly. "I was in a bad way when Brutus made his spectacular entry. But I fear that you misunderstood my directions, Sergeant. I meant you to await me at the first clump of trees—not the second."

Hattersley scratched his head.

"But this *is* the first," he protested indignantly.

"Yes—coming from the aerodrome! I meant the first coming from Abbot's Towers. However, it's too late to start arguing now. Two of the gang are lying neatly handcuffed over there."

"Prisoners? Good!" The sergeant rubbed his hands delightedly. "If we can get them to talk, we'll soon learn the identity of the Crimson Query. It's only a matter of time now before we get the lot."

"Things certainly look that way," admitted Lee in a tone of satisfaction. "Speaking personally, I shall feel more in the mood to congratulate myself when I have those two crooks safe under lock and key. I'll go back and mount guard over them while you push on to the camp, rouse the guard, and take a party—"

"My God! What's that?" Hattersley grasped Lee's arm and pointed back across the moor. In that sea of darkness a great pillar of flame had suddenly shot upwards.

A cry of bitter disappointment broke from Lee as he turned.

"It's the plantation where I left those crooks!" he gasped. "That red devil has fired the bushes! Come on!"

Unleashing the dog, Lee ran towards the leaping glare which shone like a beacon before him. At his heels pounded the heavier detective-sergeant. As they progressed, a familiar odour was wafted to their nostrils.

"Petrol!" gasped Lee. "I knew it was no accident!"

Dashing through the outer fringe of bushes of the little plantation, Lee saw that his worst fears were realized. The inferno was worthy of the human fiend who had called it into being. Nothing could have lived for an instant in that fierce blaze.

Hattersley arrived breathless and pointed to the blazing pyre.

"The prisoners are . . . there?"

Lee, his face a shade paler than the sergeant had ever seen it, nodded his head.

"The third man must have returned, thrown a couple of tins of petrol on the surrounding furze, thrown a lighted match, and . . . *this!*"

Hattersley passed a hand across a brow which had suddenly become moist.

"He burnt his pals alive so that they should not give evidence against him!" he cried huskily.

"And destroyed their bodies so that their fingerprints should not be traced," added Lee grimly.

"What an inhuman devil!" muttered the other. "The fact that he had petrol handy indicates the presence of a motor—"

"And there it goes—Listen!"

Far away, on the road that led to the Beaulieu River, the purring of a high-powered car was rapidly fading away in the distance.

CHAPTER XXIV

WHEN LEE NORTON HAD QUITTED ABBOT'S TOWERS to make the homeward journey that was destined to end so tragically for Ravangar's two satellites, Amos Aintree, mindful of the orders he had received from the Count, at once did his best to slip away unperceived in order to follow him and render such assistance to his fellow-crooks as might be required.

Under ordinary circumstances this might have been a simple matter; but Lee had already placed Beryl Chalmers in possession of enough facts of the case to make her highly suspicious of this American film director. She had noticed his quick, furtive look of interest as Lee had risen to take his departure, and when he rose a few seconds later, and sauntered with rather over-done carelessness towards a side entrance, her suspicions were sufficiently confirmed to induce her to follow him.

She did not tell anyone of her intention; for, after all, Aintree might only wish to have a few words of private conversation with the man whom he thought to be Captain St. Quentin—though that was not a very probable theory in view of the numerous opportunities he had had to speak with him during the day. The more she thought of it, the more she was convinced that some sinister purpose lay behind the American's movements.

Quickly slipping a wrap over her dinner-frock, she quietly unfastened the bolts of the great door, confident that her intimate knowledge of the grounds would enable her to take a short cut and arrive at the gates before Aintree reached them. She had passed through the door-way, and was just about to close the great nail-studded door behind her, when Brutus, with a sudden eager rush, slipped out and stood looking up at her with an expression of dumb appeal in his great brown eyes.

"Back, sir! Back!" she ordered, pointing indoors.

The dog wagged his tail and whined; but he did not move. Surprised—for it was the first time he had refused to obey her, she repeated the order, and stepped forward to seize his collar. Whereupon he immediately made off at full speed down the drive in the direction that Lee Norton had taken a few minutes previously.

With an exclamation of annoyance—which would have been changed to one of gratitude had she anticipated the momentous issues which were destined to hang upon the dog's subsequent actions—she softly closed the door and hurried down the shadowy alley between high borders of clipped yew, which would, she knew, be a much shorter route to the entrance gates than the broad, winding drive. A short walk brought her to the farther end of the alley, where, drawing back in the shadow of the tall hedges, she waited.

Doubly thankful for her sudden impulse was she when she noted the stealthy, yet swift, movements of Aintree when he presently came into sight. Had anything else been needed to confirm her suspicions of the man, the guilty start which he gave when she stepped forward would have done so.

"Why, if it isn't Miss Chalmers!" he cried, affecting an exaggerated surprise to cover his confusion. "Whoever would have expected to meet you here at this time?"

"I was just about to make the same remark," Beryl returned with a smile.

He hesitated, torn between his eagerness to hurry after his quarry and a desire to allay her suspicions by a specious excuse.

"Yes, I had a headache, and I thought a walk in the open would relieve it some," he explained glibly.

He turned to go, and, uninvited, she calmly fell into step beside him.

"Curiously enough, I too had a headache, Mr. Aintree. I wonder if your prescription would cure me?"

"Prescription?" He looked puzzled.

"A walk in the open air, you know."

"Of course, of course." He forced a laugh. "How stupid of me to forget. I fear that my thoughts were wandering, Miss Chalmers. But, as I was saying, there is nothing like a good fast walk in the open to cure a headache. By fast, of course, I mean *really* fast. That is to say, if my walk is to do me any good, I fear that you would not be able to keep up with me."

Beryl smiled to herself in the darkness. His obvious anxiety to get rid of her made her all the more determined not to leave him for an instant. Meanwhile Amos, as though desirous of demonstrating the energy with which it was essential for his exercise to be performed, had set off at a good pace along the road. Beryl's smile deepened as she noted his tactics. If he thought to shake her off in that manner, he would soon have his mistake pointed out to him!

"Are you feeling any better, Mr. Aintree?" she inquired sweetly, after he had progressed about a quarter of a mile at his fastest pace.

"Not much," he gasped, breathless with the unaccustomed exertion.

She gave a little rippling laugh.

"That's because you are not walking near fast enough to do you any good," she told him gaily. "If you really wish to get rid of your headache you should walk like this—" and she suddenly broke into a pace which left her companion hopelessly in the rear.

Amos Aintree pulled up and stood mopping his streaming brow.

"You've won, miss," he said; and there was a grim undercurrent of meaning in the seemingly good-humoured admission. "I guess I'm willing to give you best right now. May I have the pleasure of escorting you back to the house?"

"Thank you so much, Mr. Aintree," she beamed upon him. "If that means that your poor head is better, I'm so glad."

Even as she spoke the words, the sound of a faint pistol-shot echoed over the moor. The American swung round and made a step forward.

"Somebody's getting his 'gat' to work over yonder," he snapped. "I'd better see what's happening—"

"Don't move!" said Beryl quickly. He started at the change in her voice. Gone was the tone of laughing banter; in its place sounded a note of crisp command. He turned on her with a snarl of fury.

"I guess the moor's public property, miss. Stand aside—this funny stuff has gone far enough!"

"And so it's high time for the serious business to begin," she added coolly as she surveyed him, one hand resting carelessly in the side pocket of her wrap.

"My help might be needed over there—" he spluttered.

She sidled close to him with a movement which he might, at any other time, have considered affectionate. Too late he realized the deadly possibilities of the hard metallic object which he suddenly felt pressed against his ribs. In the pocket of her wrap was a pistol, its muzzle pointed in his direction.

"About turn, Mr. Aintree," she ordered. "Leave your hands exactly where they are, and keep step with me. I should never forgive myself if I allowed you to risk your valuable life by running into a shooting affray which cannot possibly concern you. Besides," she added with a return of her former manner, "you would surely not be ungallant enough to leave me unprotected after having taken me for a moonlight ramble—though, to be sure, the moon seems to be conspicuous by its absence just at the moment."

Side by side they passed through the entrance gates and up the winding drive. Not until Riggs had thrown open the door in response to her ring did she draw away from him. Then she coolly drew out a dainty cigarette-case, selected one, and offered it to him. Mechanically—his heart was too full to trust himself to words—he took one of the tubes of perfumed tobacco.

"The pipe of peace up to date," she said enigmatically.

The next moment, to his horror, she drew from the pocket nearest him a small silver-plated automatic pistol. She regarded him quizzically for a moment, then calmly pressed the trigger.

Amos gasped—the pistol clicked—a tiny flame flickered from its deadly-looking bore, from which Beryl Chalmers coolly lit her cigarette. Then she replaced in her pocket that latest novelty in the way of patent lighters, and with a smiling nod ascended the wide oak staircase which led to her room.

"You won't take me in that way the next time, my girl!" he muttered after her retreating figure.

He had not meant the words to reach her ears, but he had miscalculated the acoustic properties of the low-pitched, echoing hall.

She stopped and leant over the carved balustrade, smiling down into his upturned face.

"The next time, my dear Mr. Aintree," she said sweetly, "it will be a real one!"

By the grey light of early dawn Lee Norton and Sergeant Hattersley carefully raked through the still smouldering debris on the moor in the hope of discovering some clue to the identity of the men whose funeral pyre had been fired by their treacherous chief. Little, however, rewarded their search. A blackened watch, a long-bladed sheath-knife, and a few other unimportant metal objects— including the pair of handcuffs by which Lee had secured the two men—were all that had resisted the terrific blaze. Count Ravangar had obliterated the trail with a terrible thoroughness that had left not a single clue of any value.

Frustrated in this direction, Lee turned his attention to the task of following up the clue of the mysterious finger-prints which, according to the Record Department, were those of the convict, Lal Thaxted—the man who had been found dead on the moor nearly thirty years before.

A brief inquiry elicited the fact that the man who had been governor of the prison at the time was now dead; the chief warder had retired on a pension, and finally Lee located him as the licensee of a small public-house not far from Salisbury. The man, John Morrison by name, was perfectly willing to give Lee all the assistance he could.

"Yes, I reckon I do remember Lal Thaxted, seeing the hot water I got into over his escape," he told the detective as the two sat in the little bar-parlour after closing hours one afternoon. "Up to the time he 'hopped the twig' he was a model prisoner, quiet and well-behaved, and about the very last person that you'd expect to make a dash for liberty. He was a 'trusty'—that is, he was allowed to go about his work without having a warder over him. He had got on the soft side of the prison chaplain, and when he offered to paint some nice pretty texts on the walls of the chapel, the padre fell for it at once. Lal started all right, and being a bit of an artist—he was sent down for forgery you'll remember—he made quite a good job of it. But the last text he painted was one of his own composing. It was just 'Good-bye'. Then he just waited for the padre to come into the chapel to admire his work, jumped on him the moment he entered, knocked him senseless, mounted his bicycle, and rode out the gates as calmly as you please.

"That happened in the early dusk of a wet and misty November afternoon. By nightfall he had reached the coast, broken open a boat-house, exchanged his clerical overcoat for a suit of oilskins, and sailed across to the mainland. There we lost all trace of him until his skeleton was discovered nearly a year later.

"I was one of the men sent over to identify the remains. He had evidently crawled into one of those old, underground stone chambers where, according to the learned professor who understands such things, the Ancient Britons used to live, and there he had died of cold or starvation—leastways, that was the opinion of the surgeon who examined the remains."

"How could you identify a body that was a mere skeleton?" Lee asked.

"Well, there was his prison clothes, and the oilskins he'd stolen from the island," replied the ex-warder, somewhat surprised at Lee's question. "It's hardly likely that anyone else would dress themselves up as a convict, is it?"

"Scarcely," assented the detective with a smile. "Still, the fact remains that, so far as you are able to positively swear, the bones might have been those of another person. There was no distinguishing mark, no fracture or other peculiarity, by which they could be distinguished?" Morrison shook his head.

"All we went by were the prison clothes," he said. "Seeing that the body was wearing them, what reason had we to doubt that it was Lal Thaxted?"

"Very true," admitted Lee; "maybe any other man would have jumped to the same conclusion as you did. Still, I have a rather strong suspicion that you were mistaken." And he went on to tell Morrison of the fingerprint on the card bearing the Crimson Query. But he found the ex-warder inclined to be somewhat sceptical.

"Of course, I've heard about the Bertillon System," said Morrison, "and how every person's prints vary. But is such really the case? I know for a fact that juries will not take such evidence as conclusive. Only last week I read of a case where the prisoner, a labourer, had left his thumb-print on a glass in the house which he was accused of breaking into. Yet the man was discharged. The account of the case is in that paper over there, if you'd care to read it."

"That does not disprove the system," objected Lee. "The man might have been guilty after all." John Morrison laughed.

"Some people would say it was discredited by the fact that you've got the finger-print of a man who, although he's been dead nearly thirty years, was supposed to have made it within the last few days. Alter all, you must remember that the only people whose prints have been compared are convicted criminals—only a very small proportion of the population of the British Isles. Just because no two of them happen to be alike is no reason for assuming that there can be no two alike in the country. You might just as well argue that because nine men are honest the tenth cannot possibly be a crook!"

The other laughed good-humouredly.

"You've evidently been studying the speech for the defence in that case you were speaking of just now! But I'm very grateful to you for the information that you've supplied me with. Now I am more than ever hopeful of running Lal Thaxted to earth."

Morrison stared.

"You mean the dead convict?" he gasped.

Lee shook his head as he rose to take his departure.

"No—I mean the convict who is very much alive!"

CHAPTER XXV

mOOR LODGE, the house wherein lived Gideon Wilfer, the old archaeologist, was a large but very neglected-looking country villa standing on a by-road which ran about midway between the aerodrome and the Beaulieu River. It was not without a certain charm of its own, with its age-blackened half-timbering, lichen-spangled gables, and quaint, twisted chimneys; but so desolate and forlorn was its aspect, that a beholder, had he possessed enough curiosity to have penetrated the tangle of weeds which ran riot over what had been the drive, would have thought it uninhabited.

As the house, so its tenant. Tall and big-made, with harsh yet distinguished features, he might have made a figure both venerable and imposing had it not been for the shock of white hair which streamed from beneath his soiled grey felt hat and the long, untrimmed beard which concealed the lower portion of his face. His usual attire was a suit of tawny tweeds, very much the worse for wear, which gave him the appearance of a Rip Van Winkle of sporting tastes.

It was hardly likely that such an eccentric figure could have escaped attention on the sparsely populated moor; he was too much like the traditional mysterious miser of stage and story to avoid those vague rumours which inevitably gather round an eccentric personality in a country district where the interchange of ideas consists mainly of local gossip. He had long been looked upon as a miser-hermit, and his archaeological delvings among the prehistoric tumuli construed as a search for buried treasure. But it was not until the local handyman was admitted to Moor Lodge to attend to a leaky roof that a more sinister interpretation of his labours gained credence.

"Nothin' but skulls and old bones—'unnerds an' 'unnerds of 'em, I tells 'ee—enow to stock a village graveyard there be in them there rooms," was the burden of his tale when he returned. " 'Tis a wizard he be, for sure, else what would he want with bones that a Christian man would put under the ground? A tar-barrel be good for the likes of he—an' years agone he'd ha' got 'un, too, belike!"

And much more to the same effect; by which it will be gathered that Comparative Ethnology was a science undreamt of by the worthy villagers of West down.

But if the professor was unhonoured in his own immediate neighbourhood, it was far otherwise with those scientists who make the classification of their own species their life-study. Learned societies were proud to enrol his name on their lists of members; an address by him at the headquarters of the Prehistoric Ethnological Association was sufficient to fill that ill-ventilated Early Victorian building literally to suffocation; on more occasions than is possible to enumerate, the authorities of our great national museums had solicited his opinions on disputed points, and the mere expression of his decision was deemed final. Yet, in spite of this, Professor Gideon Wilfer was a man who considered his life-work but half accomplished. Never would he be content to cease his labours until his pet theory of the Aryan origin of the present-day inhabitants of Europe was established; and the great obstacle which lay in the way of this much-desired end was Herr Ludwig Gutzeit, late Professor of Ethnology at Heidelberg University.

In direct contradiction to Wilfer's theory that all European races are descended from a race which, ages before the dawn of history, occupied the Central Asian plateau, Gutzeit held that they were merely branches (and warped and decayed branches at that) of a wonderful nation of Teutonic warriors domiciled in his beloved Fatherland; and it is to be regretted that the expression of their conflicting views was not always marked by a spirit of scientific calm. If it be indeed true that the heat of controversy engenders the light of truth, then the solution of the problem under discussion should have shone forth like the noonday sun. For, whatever they may have lacked in other respects, the periodical wrangles in which they indulged were at least heated.

On one unforgettable occasion they had scandalized the members of a certain learned society by suddenly allowing their verbal assaults on the specimen skulls ranged before them to develop into direct assaults on the skulls of each other. The venue of the discussion had been changed abruptly from the lecture-room to the police-court, where, after delivering himself of a lecture on the unseemliness of septuagenarian fisticuffs, the magistrate had bound them over to keep the peace.

Herr Gutzeit had rented a small modern bungalow on the outskirts of Westdown, and although the rivals frequently met in the course of their digging activities among the ancient tumuli, the encounters had been of a peaceful, if frigid, nature. The labours of each were sweetened by the thought that at any moment they might bring to light evidence that would effectively demolish the preposterous vapourings of the other.

It was with a heart filled with this laudable desire that Gideon Wilfer arose at daybreak one morning, swallowed a hasty breakfast, collected his digging implements, and sallied forth on to Abbotsmoor. His objective was a fair-sized mound lying near the road which skirted the park fence of Abbot's Towers. To the casual passer-by it looked a mere natural inequality of the ground; but Wilfer's experienced eye had long since recognized its regular contour as something due to the work of men. The undisturbed state of the covering grass-grown soil showed that it was one of the few ancient burying-places which had escaped the attentions of the Heidelberg professor, and Wilfer quickened his steps as he inwardly congratulated himself on stealing a march on his Teutonic rival.

But no sooner had he come in sight of the scene of his proposed labours than his hopes in this direction were rudely shattered. Approaching the tumulus from the direction of the village was a short, stout figure which, distant though it was, he had no difficulty in recognizing as that of Herr Gutzeit. His hated rival was bound on the same errand as himself!

A less impulsive mind might have paused to marvel at the coincidence of two independent archaeologists choosing the same day on which to dig up the same tomb; but Gideon Wilfer was too enraged to indulge in abstruse speculations just then. He immediately started to run towards the tumulus with the intention of arriving there first and thus establishing prior claim to the prize. At the same instant Herr Gutzeit, perceiving his intention, also began to run.

It was an inspiring sight to see the two aged scientists charging over the broken ground. Gutzeit was short in stature, and of a portly habit that rendered his progress anything but like that of a graceful gazelle; but whereas Wilfer's long legs gave him a decided advantage, he had the greater distance to cover. It was a close finish. An impartial judge might have decided that the German was the winner, seeing that he managed to actually set foot on the mound a fraction of a second before the other; but his decision would have been complicated by the fact that Professor Wilfer, when still three yards off, cast his spade triumphantly on the top of the coveted goal.

"Mine!" gasped both men, breathlessly, triumphantly, and conclusively.

The two men glared at each other, panting. The German was the first to speak.

"So?" he said with ironical politeness. "You make der damn-fool speech when you say that. Have I not already it reached first?"

Professor Wilfer shook his head stubbornly.

"I threw my spade on it before you came up," he declared.

"Your spade?" laughed Gutzeit. "What do I of your spade know? Nuzzing! I wish to make no business with him also—I have one myself already. Your spade is to me as nuzzing. Take him and with him depart quickly. This tomb of not-as-yet-discovered bones is mine. Depart, I beg of you, or I shall fall upon you with never-to-be-forgotten frightfulness.''

Wilfer's face grew purple.

"Fall on me? You—you unspeakable Hun—"

"This sepulchre, he is mine. I have him first discovered."

The Englishman gave a grim laugh.

"Unless you quit within the next two minutes it'll be a brand-new sepulchre you'll be wanting—not a prehistoric one!"

For a moment it seemed as though the irate pair were about to revert to the traditional "trial by battle" to settle their dispute. Each man was convinced he was in the right, and—what was more to the point—was convinced of his own physical superiority over his opponent. Things had reached a stage when it seemed as though nothing could avert the coming conflict, when peace was suddenly restored in an unexpected manner.

Herr Gutzeit gave a rather rueful laugh.

"It seems, my friend, that we are quarrelling needlessly," he said, and pointed to the ground at his feet. "The entrance to this tumulus, as is usual, to the east faces. It is here—where I stand. Observe how the ground sink in just at this one spot. That means that this tomb opened has been within the past few years."

"Opened? Impossible!" Gideon Wilfer drew near and looked down at the spot indicated.

"We will soon see!" cried Herr Gutzeit, seizing his pitchfork and thrusting it into the soil; and Wilfer, everything forgotten in the ardour which the true archaeologist feels when on the brink of a discovery, ably seconded his efforts with his spade.

Half an hour's hard work was sufficient to prove that the German's words were true. There are many evidences by which the experienced archaeologist can tell whether he is digging through ancient or comparatively modern soil, but it was not until Wilfer had turned up a large stone which had the dead moss still adhering to one side that he finally gave up hope of finding the tomb unrifled.

"So, already you see that I have spoken true, mine friend!" cried Gutzeit, as he pointed to the withered growth. "Not so would it remain from the time when this tomb he was made. Twenty— thirty years would it remain so; but longer—no. Someone he open this tomb within that time."

"It seems as if you're right this time," returned the other. "Still, we may as well see all there is to be seen now we've got down so far."

It was impossible for two such enthusiasts to labour side by side in their favourite occupation and still to maintain an attitude of hostility. Long before the low entrance door of the underground chamber was unearthed Gutzeit was addressing his late enemy as *mein lieber freund;* while the conviction had gradually dawned on Wilfer that, however much his science might be at fault, the German was not such a bad fellow after all.

No doubt now remained that the tomb had been opened, for the heavy stone slab which had sealed the door lay flat on the ground. After waiting long enough for the foul air to escape, they passed through the narrow opening and examined their surroundings by the light of the electric torches with which each had provided himself.

It was a small hut-like chamber, with walls of massive blocks of unmortared stone and a roof of rough-hewn slabs, supported by a single pillar in the centre of the chamber and kept in position by the weight of the earth-mound above.

As he entered, Gutzeit's foot struck something that gave forth a metallic tinkle against the stone floor. Eagerly he turned the beam of his lamp downwards.

"Wunderschön!" he gasped in delight. "Look, mine friend, whoever has entered here has not stopped to plunder."

It was a small bronze axe-head of the socketed type which marks the Late Bronze Period. Wilfer took it in his hand and examined it critically.

"H'm! I should have expected to find weapons of a more primitive type in a tomb of this description," he mused aloud.

"Maybe it is a secondary interment of a later age than the original burial," Gutzeit suggested. "Often you may find it so."

"Maybe," said the other, and made eagerly for the remains of a human being which lay outstretched along the farther wall.

Here indeed was a find to delight the seeker after relics of by-gone days! The body was evidently that of a warrior, for it had been interred clad in the full panoply of war. A winged bronze helmet decorated the fleshless skull; the remains of a shield, studded with bosses of the same metal, lay upon the breast; a leaf-bladed sword was on the left side; a spearhead, the wooden shaft of which had long since mouldered into dust, lay upon its right; all seemingly undisturbed since that remote day when they had been reverently placed there by the vanished race whose very existence is only known by such chance discoveries as this.

"Assuredly, mine Wilfer, we have made what you call the lucky strike!" beamed Gutzeit. "Not every day do we find it so. He must have been a warrior-king at the very least—and one who fell in battle—that hole in his skull must have his death-wound been."

Professor Wilfer did not answer. He had picked up the skull and was intently examining the small hole to which the other had drawn his attention. Presently he laid the grinning relic aside and turned his attention to the remainder of the bones. When he looked up there was a strange expression in his eyes, which might have set his companion thinking had he noticed it. But in the darkness that look of speculative amazement passed unseen.

"Have you noticed the curious spiral markings on the bosses of the shield?" he asked.

"Not particularly," was the answer.

"Have a good look at them now."

Herr Gutzeit obediently turned the beam of his lamp on the object indicated and bent down to examine it. As he did so, Gideon Wilfer stooped quickly, picked up a small gold object which lay at his feet, and transferred it quickly and stealthily to his own pocket.

A second later the other turned with a shrug.

"I cannot see anything extraordinary in the marking you spoke of," he said in a tone of disappointment. "They are merely the usual type of decoration of the period of Late Bronze."

"Is that so?" returned Wilfer carelessly. "Well, I suppose we had better notify the authorities of our find. As you know, the conditions on which our permits to excavate are issued state that all objects of antiquarian interest must be handed over."

"Assuredly."

"Then would it be troubling you too much to ask you to run over to Southampton and send a wire from there?" Wilfer went on.

Gutzeit looked surprised.

"But there is a telegraph office in Westdown, which is much nearer," he protested.

The other shook his head.

"You know what gossips these local postmistresses are. If the news of our discovery leaked out we should have a mob of gaping rustics trampling all over the place. "I'll look after things here while you're gone."

More than a little mystified, the German allowed himself to be persuaded, and presently took his leave and disappeared in the direction of the railway station. No sooner was he out of sight than Wilfer rose to his feet, knocked the ashes out of his pipe, removed the helmet of the dead man, coolly placed the skull under his overcoat, and made with all speed towards his own house. Once inside, his actions were peculiar. Proceeding straight to the cabinet where he kept his numerous ethnological specimens, he selected a skull that was nearest in appearance to the one he had filched from the tumulus, and with a hammer and small chisel punched a jagged hole through the bone in exactly the same position. This accomplished to his satisfaction, he locked the stolen skull away in his safe, together with the gold sleeve-link which he had picked up from the floor of the tomb while Gutzeit's attention had been distracted towards the markings on the shield.

Hastening back to the grave upon the moor, he placed the substitute skull carefully in position and, charging his pipe, sat down patiently to await the return of the German professor.

There was a look of dreamy content in his deep-set eyes as he sat puffing clouds of smoke into the still morning air, and his lips twitched now and again in a thoughtful smile. Hitherto his researches had brought but little pecuniary advantage to himself, but this latest discovery would, he fondly hoped, render him rich for life.

For the skull of that "prehistoric warrior" had been pierced by a small-calibre revolver bullet, and three of its teeth had been filled with a dental alloy which had only been discovered during recent years. And—most significant point of all—the sleeve-link which he had picked up bore the family crest of Sir Raymond Chalmers.

CHAPTER XXVI

SO THEY HAD TO SEND FOR YOU again after all, Mr. Norton?" said Sir Raymond as he shook hands with the young detective in the study of Abbot's Towers. "You ought to feel very flattered to think that Scotland Yard cannot get on without you! I suppose you're still on this Crimson Query affair? Any clues up to date, eh? By Jove! It makes one feel quite nervous to think there is such a gang of blood-thirsty criminals at large—I, for one, do not mind admitting that I shall sleep easier when I know that they're safely under lock and key."

"Well, we are certainly doing our best to bring about that happy consummation, Sir Raymond."

Lee smiled slightly as he spoke the words. His encounter with Count Ravangar and his henchmen on the moor had rendered a continuation of his assumed character unnecessary, and it was in his own character that he had called upon the baronet that afternoon.

"I had an idea that you might be able to give us some information that would render our task easier," he went on presently.

"I?" The old man was visibly surprised. "Of course, I shall be only too delighted to be of assistance."

"Thank you, Sir Raymond." Lee assumed a careless attitude in the arm-chair, his eyes half closed and his fingers interlocked. But, indolent as his gaze appeared to be, no single shade of expression on the other's face escaped his notice. "I want you to take your mind back to the occasion of the theft of the script of the old mystery-play."

"I remember it perfectly," nodded Sir Raymond.

"In the drawer from which the book had been taken—"

"Or from which Hilda Maune *alleged* it to have been taken," corrected the other, looking up sharply. "You must take into account the possibility that the theft was a fake."

The detective nodded.

"I quite appreciate your point," he said quietly, "but I am assuming for the moment that the book was really stolen. In its place there was a card bearing the usual crimson sign. I afterwards examined the card, and on it I found a finger-print which I submitted to the Record Department at Headquarters. They, to my surprise, stated it belonged to a man who was supposed to have died many years ago. His name was Lal Thaxted."

The baronet stifled an elaborate yawn.

"Indeed?"

The tone of studied indifference in which the word was uttered told Lee more than a sudden start or change of colour would have done. Under the circumstances some little show of surprise would have been natural; but the stony, almost defiant stare with which his hearer had received the name of his old fellow-student showed that he had braced himself to remain impassive under the detective's keen scrutiny. But Lee, on his part, was equally careful to allow no hint of his suspicions to appear.

"Is the name familiar to you, Sir Raymond?" he asked.

The other man hesitated as though searching his memory. Really he was debating whether it would be a wise policy for him to utter a denial.

"It certainly seems to have a familiar ring," he temporized at length. "Why do you ask?"

"Because he was a student in the same house as you, Balliol, when he was arrested for a series of huge frauds, and I thought that such an unusual event would have impressed the man's name upon your mind."

"Oh yes, I remember whom you mean now," said Sir Raymond hastily. "He received a long sentence, and he subsequently made his escape and was found dead on the moor near here."

"So the story runs," corrected Lee. "But I have seen the man who identified the skeleton—for it was nothing more at the time of the discovery—and I am convinced that it was the clothes that were identified rather than the body itself. It is my belief that Lal Thaxted is alive at the present moment and is a member of the Crimson Query gang."

The baronet drew his watch from his pocket and glanced at it meaningly.

"Even granted that your fantastic theory be true, I fail to see your object in coming to me with it," he said coldly.

"I came for information, sir. My idea is that Thaxted made for this part of the country because he had friends hereabouts on whom he could rely to give him shelter or aid. As you were at college with him, I thought you might be able to give me a useful hint about his friends and associates."

The look of relief that leapt to Sir Raymond's eyes was not lost on Lee.

"I fear I cannot assist you in that manner," was his answer. "Really, Thaxted and I were in two very different sets, and I knew nothing whatever about his private affairs."

Lee rose to his feet.

"In that case I can only express my regret at having troubled you." On the way to the door he suddenly paused. "Oh, by the way, how is the patient this afternoon?"

"Miss Maune is still in a very grave condition. Dr. Rollinson seems to be somewhat puzzled over her case. He was saying something about calling another opinion if her condition does not improve."

Lee mentally pigeon-holed that piece of information for future consideration; aloud he said:

"Then I suppose she is not in a fit state to answer a few questions?"

Sir Raymond brought his clenched fist down on the table with a thud.

"Absolutely no, sir!" he snapped, his fingers already on the bell-push. "Must you go now, Inspector? Well, good morning, and I hope you'll be more successful in your quest than you have been up to now. Riggs, please show Inspector Norton out."

Lee went home to tea more mystified than ever. It was clear to him that Sir Raymond knew more about the forger than he cared to admit. Why had he striven to deny all knowledge of the man? What was Lal Thaxted to him? Was it a mere coincidence, or had it some deeper meaning, that the one finger-print—the solitary piece of tangible evidence they had against the mysterious Crimson Query—should have been found in his house?

Later that evening he sat down with Sergeant Hattersley to review the situation in detail. He found his subordinate rather inclined to belittle the importance of the finger-print.

"Somehow or other it doesn't seem to ring true, sir," he said. "Think of the number of cards that we've got possession of without a single trace of a print on 'em. It doesn't seem likely to me that a gang as clever as this one should fall into such a silly blunder. Why, even the cheapest burglar nowadays knows enough to wear gloves when he pays his evening call after the family is abed! If you were to ask me, I should say that the finger-print was that of somebody who handled the card *after* it had been planted there."

Lee listened to his theory in the same manner as a drowning man clutches at a straw.

"There may possibly be something in what you say," he admitted. "Let us go carefully over the events which happened immediately after the discovery of the theft." He stood for a moment in thought. "I will try to reconstruct the scene. This"—he indicated the table—"will represent the desk. You, Sergeant, are Sir Raymond. I, naturally, am myself; and we must leave the third person present, Miss Maune, to our fertile imaginations.

"Miss Maune came into the room first, switching on the lights as she entered; Sir Raymond came next, and I last. The girl crossed directly to the desk, pulled open the drawer—so—and immediately fell backwards with a scream. We came forward, saw that there was no book there; Sir Raymond picked up the card—"

"And there you've got it!" cried Hattersley triumphantly. "He picked up the card and left his own fingerprint on it as he did so!"

Lee suddenly put his hand to his head.

"I see," he said in his usual tone of voice.

In reality his heart was thumping and his brain spinning under the shock of the astounding explanation that had at the instant rushed upon him. That two sets of finger-prints could be identical in every respect he would not for a moment credit. Yet the only other alternative was even more fantastic.

If Sir Raymond had been the only person to handle that card, it meant that the father of the girl he loved was none other than Lal Thaxted—forger and escaped convict!

Moved by a sudden impulse, Lee rose to his feet, donned his hat and coat, and made his way to Dr. Rollinson's surgery. The doctor was luckily at home and disengaged, and Lee was shown straight in to him.

Lee thought it best not to beat about the bush.

"I understand that you have a certain Miss Hilda Maune under your care?" he asked.

The young doctor raised his eyebrows slightly and bowed without speaking.

"Might I inquire the nature of her illness?" was Lee's next question. "Oh, I'm quite aware that it is against medical etiquette for a medical man to discuss the affairs of his patients, but I'm not asking out of mere curiosity. I have heard—no matter from what source—that her condition is grave. What I want to know is, are you satisfied that it is due to natural illness?"

The attitude of the doctor grew perceptibly stiffer.

"I fail to see what right you have to question me," he returned.

"I am a police officer, and I have reason to know that a band of criminals have good reason for wishing that young lady safely out of the way."

Dr. Rollinson seemed unimpressed by the announcement.

"I have already made my diagnosis of the case, and am treating her in the manner which seems best for her particular complaint."

"But is she responding to your treatment?" demanded Lee.

The doctor shrugged.

"That is a question which I am unable to discuss with a layman," was the frigid reply.

Lee's lips tightened into a thin straight line.

"If your treatment is too sacred to discuss with a police officer, maybe the nursing is not. Are you satisfied with the lady who has your patient in charge?"

"Quite satisfied," was the ready answer. "Miss la Zorita is, if anything, only too tender and indulgent towards her charge." The ring of unfeigned sincerity with which he uttered the commendation showed only too plainly that the impressionable young medico had fallen beneath the sway of the angel-faced Spanish girl.

Lee Norton shrugged and crossed to the door.

"Very well, Doctor," he said calmly. "If you're so satisfied, there's nothing more to say. But a little bird whispered to me that you were thinking of calling in a second opinion. If you'll take the tip of someone who's just an ordinary crook-catcher, you'll do so without delay. And if you value your future career, let it be some body who's well up in poisons—!"

"Poisons!" The self-satisfied smile vanished from the young man's face as though wiped from it by an invisible sponge. He grasped Lee's arm. "Poison—my God! What do you mean?"

Lee came a step closer and looked him full in the face.

"I mean that the Crimson Query is after asking another of their little questions—and unless you pull up your socks and see to things in time, it'll be one that will take you all the rest of your life to answer. Got that? Then good night."

CHAPTER XXVII

THE DAYS WHICH FOLLOWED Gideon Wilfer's sensational find in the ancient grave were busy ones for him. On the following day he journeyed to London and took a room in an unpretentious hotel in Bloomsbury. In the reading-room of the British Museum near by he spent long hours poring over the old files of newspapers, patiently unearthing long-forgotten incidents, seemingly unimportant but all bearing on his self-imposed quest; jotting down dates; comparing, analysing, and thinking—always thinking.

After a fortnight's hard work, during which he had filled a note-book with a jumbled mass of data of which only he knew the value, he shifted the scene of his inquiry to the university city of Oxford. Here he was forced to adopt a different method of procedure.

There is a small public-house in a side-street near the Martyrs' Memorial, a house much frequented by the janitors and menser-vants from the surrounding colleges, where the current happenings within those temples of learning are discussed with a freedom which would greatly surprise the learned professors, and also the undergraduates, did they but know of it. In the low-ceiled "snug-gery", Gideon Wilfer took up his nightly stand, sipping his modest half-pint and listening to the conversation around him. For a long time he drew blank. Gossip he heard in plenty, and had he been interested in present-day affairs he might have obtained his infor-mation on the first night. But what he was looking for was a servi-tor who had been employed at Balliol thirty years ago; and at length, by discreet questioning and many repetitions of a story about a mythical long-lost brother, he was put in touch with such a man. From him, by the outlay of sundry silver coins, he became possessed of information that was priceless beyond rubies.

Curiously enough, at the same time that Professor Wilfer had been so industriously searching the files at the British Museum, Detective-Inspector Lee Norton had, not very far away, been con-ducting inquiries which, although approached from a different an-gle, had precisely the same end in view. But there was a source of information open to the official investigator that was denied to the other. Superintendent Woodford had been but a detective-sergeant at the time of Lal Thaxted's arrest, and in that capacity had had charge of the case; it was to him that Lee Norton went in the hope of gleaning some additional details.

"Lal Thaxted?" said Woodford, reminiscently stroking his grey moustache. "Oh yes, I remember the case well—I ought to, seeing that I got a step-up through my handling it. It was a difficult case to prove, for Lalwas a perfect genius with the pen. He could imitate any signature so perfectly that the victims themselves could not positively swear to its being a forgery. It was a series of cheque frauds that brought him into my hands."

"Was the sum total of the cheques a large one?" asked Lee.

"Yes. I could not give you the exact figures from memory after all this time, but you may take it from me that the total was somewhere in the region of £150,000."

"And how much of the loot was recovered?"

Superintendent Woodford pushed back his chair and rubbed his hands together with the air of a connoisseur who recalls the memory of a half-forgotten masterpiece.

"Ah, now you touch upon a point that brings out the real cleverness of the man!" he cried. "Lal was not only an accomplished forger; he also possessed a perfect genius for covering up the ultimate destination of the money he obtained."

Lee looked sceptical.

"I should have thought that a cheque could have easily been traced," he said.

The other shook his head with a laugh.

"The original forged cheque did not need to be traced—it came back to its supposed drawer in the usual course of banking routine, and had Thaxted left the money in the same account into which it had been paid, we should have had no difficulty in tracing the money and recovering it. But he had prepared the ground too thoroughly for that to happen. He had any amount of accounts in different names—he must have done, to have disguised the trail so completely—I mean disguised it so far as actual legal proof was concerned—but I had my own opinion where the proceeds ultimately went to. However, by the time we had laid Thaxted by the heels he had done his juggling so cunningly that Chalmers' name was never brought into the case."

"Chalmers!" Lee gasped, almost starting from his chair in his excitement. "Was Sir Raymond Chalmers in this?"

"Sir Raymond? No, it was his father's younger brother—Sir Raymond's uncle—into whose account the money ultimately found its way. But we knew all along that this Hector Chalmers was a mere tool of Lal Thaxted's—a mere blind alley in the tortuous maze of crooked finance by which the master-mind covered up all provable traces of his plunder. He was an elderly man at that time, living in Australia. He had no children of his own, and when he died a few months later he left a will bequeathing the whole of the money to his niece, Beryl Chalmers. This, of course, was part of the plan."

"How so?" demanded Lee, and he was surprised at the sudden sharpness of his tone. "I fail to see why the fact that her uncle left his fortune to her makes her a party to Thaxted's frauds."

The superintendent permitted himself to smile.

"Oh, you may rest assured that the girl was innocent enough in the matter; she was a mere schoolgirl at the time. She was another blind alley in the maze, so to speak."

Lee shook his head with a puzzled air.

"Then I don't see—"

"Ah, but you will see everything when I tell you that the two trustees who would have the handling—unrestricted handling, mind you—of the entire fortune, were Lal Thaxted himself and Sir Raymond Chalmers."

There was a hard glint in Lee's eyes as he rose to his feet and leant over the desk.

"That brings us to the main purpose of my visit." He said the words calmly enough, but the knuckles were showing white as he gripped the edge of the desk before him. "What was Sir Raymond to Lal Thaxted?"

Without hesitation the answer came.

"They were pals. Raymond Chalmers—he hadn't succeeded to the title then—was hand in glove with Thaxted, and it was only want of evidence that prevented him standing in the dock. And it's my belief," the superintendent went on impressively, "that Sir Raymond murdered Lal Thaxted in that underground vault on Abbotsmoor in order that they shouldn't have to split their loot!"

The detective quitted the great building on the Thames Embankment with his mind filled with a tangle of ideas which he strove in vain to straighten out. One fact alone stood out clearly and unmistakably amid the chaos. Superintendent Woodford had been wrong in his surmise that Lal Thaxted had been murdered by Sir Raymond; for the sole piece of firm fact in the quagmire of contradictions and uncertainties was the finger-print which proved that the ex-convict was still alive.

He had passed under the frowning stone archway which guards the entrance to the courtyard of the building he had just quitted, intending to walk across Westminster Bridge on his way to Waterloo Station. As he was about to cross the road he felt a light touch on his arm.

"Inspector Norton, I guess," said a decidedly nasal voice.

Turning, Lee recognized the sallow features of the American film producer.

"Guess I've surprised you some, eh?" laughed Amos Aintree. "No doubt you thought I was still down on the proposed location for my next film."

The detective did not immediately reply. This chance encounter seemed to be something more than a mere coincidence. Had the man been trailing him?

"That new film-drama doesn't seem to be progressing very rapidly, Mr. Aintree," he remarked rather dryly.

"Nope," admitted the other, "and that's partly why I'm talking to you at this present moment. There's a saloon over in the corner. Let's find a quiet corner where we can talk business."

Lee glanced at the man keenly. There was an air of restrained eagerness about him that roused the detective's curiosity.

"All right," he said suddenly, and suffered himself to be conducted into the small hostelry which lies in the shadow of Big Ben. The hour was still early, and the narrow, mirror-lined apartment was almost deserted.

The American waved Lee to one of the leather-covered chairs.

"Guess it's my shout," he remarked, smiling. "Name your poison."

Lee nodded, and indicated his choice.

"If you're so anxious, you can stand this time," he said.

"This time and all the time," returned the other genially. "I don't mind admitting that I'm out asking favours, Mr. Norton; I reckon I'm out to be a sure-enough, whole-piece, blown-in-the-glass benefactor to you, sir—and I'm a guy that doesn't believe in doing things by halves."

"Go ahead," said Lee, and waited.

When the refreshments had been placed before them, Aintree lost no time in plunging into business.

"See here, Mr. Norton—you remarked a few moments back that I wasn't getting on any with my new film, and your observation was pretty near the truth. The fact of the matter is that I'm stuck—held up—sidetracked and stone-walled for the want of a suitable leading man in the medieval miracle-play that is to be my next stunt."

"You surprise me," said Lee, rather taken aback by the unexpected opening, for he had thought to hear a very different subject broached. "I should have thought that you could have obtained the services of any amount of actors in London."

"I've no use for stage-actors—I'm fed to the back teeth with 'em." Amos made a grimace which reflected but little credit to the English stage. "I know 'em! I've had some—and then some more! They're too stilted—too stiff—too unadaptable for such a film as mine is to be. And as soon as you try to tell how you want things done—what do you get? 'When I was acting with Sir Henry Irving we never did it that way'; or, 'When I was playing with Wilson Barrett I always did it this way'. Gee, it makes me see red sometimes the way they carry on! They can't forget that they haven't got a row of footlights in front of 'em! No, sir; what I want is a young feller that's tolerably good-looking"—he fixed his pale-blue eyes on Lee as he went on—"tall, athletic, and with brains in his head, and who's not above carrying out the ideas of the man who's paying his salary. In short, Mr. Norton, I'm prepared to offer you the post of leading man in my new film at a salary . . ." And he named a sum which left his hearer gasping.

Now, they do not suffer fools gladly in the Metropolitan Police, and the mere fact that Lee Norton had reached his present position was in itself an indication that he possessed a more than average intellectual keenness. Before the American had finished speaking, Lee was instinctively searching for the hidden motive which had prompted this most dazzling offer. Nor had he to wait long before he was able to discern it.

"Of course," Amos went on in a casual tone, "it's a whole-time job that I'm offering. But, considering my liberal terms, you ought not to mind sending in your resignation from the detective force straight away."

Lee nodded slowly as the real meaning of the subtly offered bribe dawned upon him.

"Oh, so that's the idea!" he remarked, and a dangerous gleam came for an instant into his steady grey eyes.

"Yep, that's the little proposition; and I guess it doesn't need much brain-thrashing to enable you to make up your mind."

"You're right there," said Lee, and rose to his feet. "I've made up my mind already."

"Good!" The tone in which the other uttered the word left no doubt that he expected an immediate acceptance.

"I'm quite willing to play the dashing hero in your film at the terms you mention," Lee said deliberately, *"after* I have placed the handcuffs on the chief of the Crimson Query gang!"

The smile faded from Aintree's thin lips.

"That's no use to me," he retorted sharply. "My offer was conditional on your immediate resignation."

Lee shrugged.

"In that case I must advise you to look elsewhere for your leading man. I thank you for your flattering offer—for it is flattering to me whichever way I look at it, though I rather suspect it to be a tribute to my detective abilities than my good looks. But until I have completed the case I am now investigating, I'm afraid I cannot accept it."

The other gave a grating laugh.

"That won't be till hell pops!" he jeered. "So it's no use spilling talk. But take it from me, sir—by the time you've found the answer to the Crimson Query you'll be more fit to play the grey-headed sob-stuff grandfather than a juvenile lead!"

"Think so?" Lee queried grimly. "Well—we'll see who's right."

"If we live long enough!" said Amos with another laugh. "Well, I've made my little offer, and I'm just too sorry for words that you've seen fit to turn it down, for I'd rather taken a fancy to you." His pale, metallic eyes rested on Lee's for a second with a somewhat sinister expression. "But I guess it was just a business offer, and as you've refused it—why, there's nothing more to be said. Are you going back to Westdown straight away?" he asked, with a change of manner which seemed to indicate that he had dismissed the matter from his mind.

"I was on my way to Waterloo when you accosted me," Lee answered.

The other appeared to consider for a moment, then he laid his hand on the detective's arm.

"See here. I'm just about to run down there by road. Seeing as how I've made you miss your train, I should feel happier if you'd let me give you a lift down to your destination. It would save you at least a couple of hours—counting the connection you'd have to wait for—and I'd be glad of company on the run."

If Lee was puzzled and suspicious at this sudden demonstration of friendship, he allowed no hint of it to appear in his manner as he answered:

"If you're sure it will not inconvenience you—"

"No trouble at all, sir," was the ready reply. "My machine is garaged near by. I'll be back in ten minutes and we can start right away."

Aintree's statement that his car was garaged "near by" had not been a mere figure of speech. Lee had not been waiting more than ten minutes before a small grey-painted touring-car drew up at the kerb with the American at the driving-seat. Lee entered without hesitation, but he was careful to take his seat beside Aintree, having previously shifted his automatic to the right-hand pocket of his overcoat, where it would be available for rapid use should circumstances arise during the journey necessitating its being brought into play. For Lee fully realized that his refusal of the thinly veiled bribe—for Aintree's tempting offer had been nothing more or less—might result in other and more direct measures being taken to attain the desired end.

As the car bore westwards and turned into the Brompton Road, he felt a glow of elation to think that the mysterious chief of the Crimson Queries had valued his neutrality so highly. If anything had been wanting to convince him that his inquiries were proceeding along the right lines, this one fact would have been sufficient to set that doubt at rest; and at the back of his mind an idea was taking shape that every beat of the engine was bringing him nearer to an event that would have a direct bearing on his quest. Not without deep reason had this film director so obligingly offered to take him to the scene of his investigations. Still, he could not quite bring himself to credit that he would be made the victim of a sudden murderous attack. It would still be daylight when they arrived at their destination; most of their route lay along the well-frequented Portsmouth road, and he thought he knew the tactics of the gang well enough to be certain that the blow, when it came, would not be struck openly. But for all his reasoning, the feel of the smooth metal butt in his overcoat pocket was very comforting.

Passing through Fulham and crossing the Thames by Putney Bridge, they were soon bowling at a good speed over the breezy heights of the Heath just beyond the town. Aintree drew up at a garage in Kingston to replenish his petrol-tank, and Lee took advantage of his momentary absence to take a good look at the fittings of the car. But he could see nothing in any way suspicious.

The speaking-tube led to the driver's seat, and not to a hidden gas-tank—as had the tube of the car in which he had once taken a journey which had nearly proved to be his last earthly ride. The cushioned seats looked innocent enough, and the roof presented an unbroken surface. Convinced that he would only have to reckon with purely human agents of destruction, he resumed his seat and the journey was continued.

The hands of the clock which projects from the facade of Guildford Town Hall were pointing to half past one as they descended the steep slope of that narrow High Street. As they emerged into the open country at the other side of the town, the nervous preoccupation of Aintree seemed to increase. He seemed to be having trouble with his engine too, for one moment he would accelerate to a fair speed, then drop without apparent reason to a mere crawl. Lee, glancing at him out of the corner of his eye, saw that the American's eyes kept straying to the dial or the small watch on his left wrist.

"So that's the game, is it?" was Lee's mental comment. "He's arranged a meeting with his pals, and he wants to pass them at a particular time or place."

About seventeen miles from Winchester, just before the little village of Neatham, the high-road runs for several miles parallel to the railway. They had passed through Alton and were nearing Ropley Dean, when a loud honking, coming from a following car, caused Aintree to pull into the side of the road to let it pass. All Lee's previous suspicions returned with redoubled force as a large Rolls-Royce drew abreast. But his fingers loosened their grip on the hilt of his pistol when he saw that, save for the goggled driver, the car was empty.

Presently it forged ahead, raising a cloud of dust in its wake.

"Whew! Some dust, eh?" laughed Aintree, and at the same moment he pulled a pair of goggles from his pocket and quickly adjusted them over his face.

Although the other car had so persistently demanded a clear road, it showed no hurry to increase the distance between the car it had passed. On the contrary, the driver seemed to slow down so that the cars kept pace, the Rolls-Royce about ten yards in front— and from its passage there rose clouds of dust which enveloped the detective and his companion.

"Better slow down or I shall be half choked," Lee gasped presently. "That confounded dust—"

He broke off with the sentence unfinished. In his mind a sudden suspicion had flamed like a warning beacon. Rain had fallen earlier in the day—yet the clouds of dust that were being raised could scarcely have been surpassed on the driest day. What did it mean? Could it be possible that the clouds that billowed round them so persistently from the rear of the other car were *not* dust, but some form of stupefying gas?

"Stop!" Lee shouted, suddenly alive to his peril.

But even as he cried the words his senses reeled. The landscape, the masked figure of Aintree, the car in front—all seemed to be jumbled together in one confused whirl as he sank backwards on the cushioned seat inert and unconscious.

Aintree gave one glance at him, then sounded his klaxon thrice. Immediately the Rolls-Royce accelerated, the clouds of dust ceased to rise from its wake, and in a few minutes it had passed out of sight, for Amos Aintree had slowed to enter a narrow lane on the left of the road.

A hundred yards down it he stopped the car before a level-crossing. It was guarded by small gates, just wide enough to enable the farm-wagons, for whose use it was intended, to pass through; and, as is usual in these country level-crossings, there was no railway official in charge.

Quickly alighting, Aintree opened one gate, drove the car with its unconscious occupant on to the double row of metals of the up-line, and brought it to a standstill with the seat on which Lee Norton was sitting full in the centre of the permanent way.

Glancing at his wrist-watch, he saw with satisfaction that in two minutes the boat-express from Southampton, travelling at sixty miles an hour, was due to pass that spot. Removing his now unnecessary gas-mask, he walked some distance down the lane and crouched low among the hedge-growth, to be well out of the way of the flying debris of the impending collision.

Already his explanation of the tragedy was forming in his mind. Lee Norton—so he would sadly inform the coroner—had insisted on taking a short cut; he had opened the gate and was driving across the rails when the express had dashed upon them. He—Aintree—had managed to jump clear in time, but his friend had failed to do so. Suspicion might possibly be directed towards him—though this was unlikely—but of actual proof there was not a shred. Even if by some miracle Lee lived long enough to tell his story he could prove nothing definite against him. It would be an unfortunate accident—nothing more.

Suddenly he started. Fool that he was—he had left the engine of the car still running! He half rose to his feet to go back and correct his oversight, and as he did so a quick-panting sound in. the distance caused him to sink back again.

It was the express approaching at full speed!

At first it was a mere pulsing throb that might have passed unnoticed by ears less keenly expectant than his own; but it rapidly grew clearer—nearer. He listened intently, scarcely daring to draw breath. Now he could hear the faint, far-distant rumble coming nearer and nearer every second. In that still, silent air he could even distinguish the variations of its sound as it rumbled over a bridge or echoed through a cutting. But every gasp of its mighty iron lungs sounded louder—nearer!

In his mind's eye he could picture the rushing monster, with its heart of fire and its breath of scalding steam. Though he shut his eyes and buried his face in the grass, he could still see in his guilty imagination the long, sleekly gleaming body of the engine—the faces of the fireman and driver peering through the window of the cab—the passengers, dozing, talking, or gazing from the windows at their first glimpse of the English countryside after their voyage—but all alike unconscious of the holocaust to which they were hastening at whirlwind speed.

On and on came the tons of hurtling metal, bearing their human freight. Now Aintree could hear the quick rattle of the wheels mingling with the thunderous rumble and roar—now the hiss of the eager steam as the mighty cylinders hurled the driving-wheels onward.

A sudden ear-splitting scream of the whistle showed that the train had rounded the bend and come into sight of the car in its path. Like a living monster shrieking, appalled at the fate it was unable to avert, the sound came nearer. Aintree cowered downwards like a man waiting to receive a physical blow. He pressed his sweat-bedewed face into the grass and thrust his fingers into his ears to shut out the crash of rending metal, the roar of scalding steam, the sudden outburst of cries and groans . . .

An age of breathless waiting—then . . .

"Get up," said a voice close to him.

Fearful and wondering, Amos Aintree raised his head—to meet the coldly glittering eyes of Lee Norton and the not less ominous muzzle of the automatic he held in his hand. In the distance the clatter of the train was rapidly dying away.

"You . . . you're safe?" he gasped, striving in vain to infuse a tone of pleasure into his trembling voice. "You managed to back the car off the line in time? Thank heaven you did! I saw the train and jumped—I tried to drag you clear. Gee, what a narrow squeak!"

Lee, white and shaken though he was, recovered himself with an effort.

"It's *you* that have had the narrow squeak," he said grimly, as he engaged the safety-catch of his pistol and thrust it back in his pocket. "Get up—you unspeakable cur—and consider yourself under arrest!"

CHAPTER XXVIII

T HE LIBRARY OF ABBOT'S TOWERS was a room of sombre magnificence; its oak-panelled walls above the rows of bookshelves were hung with full-length portraits of long-dead members of the house of Chalmers; figures clad in ancestral plate-mail stood in the alcoves and on either side of the immense open fire-place. The large oriel window by which it was lighted still retained its ancient mullions, but the original blown glass had been replaced with a modern variety which permitted a clearer view of the famous stone terrace and the park beyond.

On the same afternoon that Lee Norton had so narrowly escaped death beneath the wheels of the boat-train, Sir Raymond Chalmers sat before the fire-place of that room, his eyes fixed in a thought-ful, unseeing stare on the glowing logs on the hearth. It was easy to see that he was not in the best of humours. A harassed frown creased his forehead and his lips were drawn in a thin straight line above his neatly trimmed, pointed beard. On his knee was a memo-randum book, its open pages covered with hastily scrawled figures and calculations. He had been engaged in totalling up his available funds, and the result was such as to daunt even his adventurous heart.

A light, cautious tap on the window behind him caused him to start suddenly and look round. Outlined against the grey of the early October dusk were the head and shoulders of a man. From beneath the wide brim of his battered felt hat a shock of unkempt white hair streamed; an old-fashioned goatee beard hid the lower portion of his face.

"A tramp!" was Sir Raymond's first thought, and he stretched out his hand to ring for Riggs to warn the intruder off.

The stranger saw the action, and made a gesture of such urgent, though stealthy, warning that the baronet's hand remained poised in mid-air. Presently he rose to his feet, crossed to the window, and unlatched the lower portion.

"Who are you? What do you want here?" Almost unconsciously the speaker had lowered his voice to a mere whisper.

"I want a few words with you on a matter that is both urgent and important," was the answer, delivered in the same low tone.

Sir Raymond glanced dubiously at the man, noting the griminess of his well-worn tweed suit. Yet, in spite of his shabby exterior, a sense of underlying confidence in the man's bearing seemed to hint that he was not the homeless wanderer that he had first thought him to be.

"Why did you not write to me?" he asked in a more aggressive tone.

The stranger uttered a low, almost noiseless laugh.

"Because such matters as I have to discuss are best not put into writing!"

Without another word, Sir Raymond closed the window, unlocked the small postern door which gave on to the terrace, and with a jerk of his head invited the other man to enter. Once he was inside, the baronet locked the door, drew the heavy curtains across the window, and switched on the lights.

"Well?" The word was almost a challenge, but the stranger merely smiled as he coolly seated himself in a chair on the opposite side of the fire-place.

"Pray excuse my taking a seat uninvited, Sir Raymond," he said, "but I have had a longish tramp across the moor, and our talk is likely to be somewhat protracted."

An angry flush began to creep into the other's cheeks.

"It will not be protracted unless you immediately state your name and business!" he growled.

The stranger gave a slow, mocking smile.

"It seems that you are very particular about names, my dear sir," he returned in slow, sardonic accents. "After all, as the immortal poet says, 'What's in a name?' What indeed? Many a man has for years gone under a name—yes, and sometimes *more* than a name!—that does not belong to him. Still," he added with a shrug, "there is no reason why you should not know mine. It is one that is fairly well known in certain circles, and at least it is the one under which I have always passed. Maybe you have heard of Professor Gideon Wilfer, F.S.A.?"

A look of sudden relief passed over the hearer's countenance.

"Oh—the archaeological authority?" Sir Raymond's tone was almost genial now. "Yes, of course I've heard about you, Professor. I've got your book on the prehistoric remains of Abbotsmoor somewhere in this library. Is it about your researches that you have come to see me?"

"In a sense, yes," answered Gideon Wilfer, slowly stroking his beard and regarding the other with an enigmatical smile. "It is certainly about something that I found in an ancient stone chamber on the moor. It was the one which lies under the mound not far from your own park gates. It was"—he paused and fixed his eyes on Sir Raymond's face—"a most interesting discovery."

The atmosphere of the room seemed suddenly to have changed. Sir Raymond did not move a muscle, but the stare in his hard, unblinking eyes and the sudden rigidity of his hands as they gripped the arm-rests of his chair told of the intensity of his pent-up emotions.

Presently Wilfer transferred his gaze to the ceiling, and for a space seemed to be lost in thought.

"Yes, it was a very interesting discovery," he went on in a dreamy, speculative tone. "I was thinking of writing a little monograph about it. It would be quite a trifling publication—a mere matter of two dozen pages or so—but I flatter myself that it would attract considerable attention—*very* considerable attention. It would raise many interesting questions among ethnologists—and others. Whether, for instance, the ancient Britons had reached a state of culture that included a knowledge of firearms—for the skull I found in that tomb had a very neat bullet-hole through it. It might also create some astonishment when I stated that this ancient skull had several of its teeth stopped with a dental alloy which very nearly resembles the alloy used by the present-day dentists. Yes, I certainly do flatter myself that my little work will command considerable attention from a certain class of—ah—investigators."

Sir Raymond passed his tongue over his dry lips before he spoke.

"Why do you tell me all this?" he demanded harshly.

"I thought it might interest you," Wilfer answered mildly— "especially as I happened to find a sleeve-link bearing your own crest at the same time and place. That fact, too, might raise questions that might take a good deal of answering. Who knows but what some foolish and misguided—police officer, let us say, might even go so far as to imagine that the ancient Warrior once wore a modern set of cuff-links? A very absurd supposition, as you will agree; but who can foresee the workings of the official mind?"

A dangerous gleam came into Chalmers' eyes beneath their lowered lids. For an instant it seemed as though he were about to leap upon the other man and savagely tear the life out of him. But with an effort he choked back his fury and forced his voice into an even, almost indifferent, tone.

"Do you anticipate a very extensive sale for this—ah—this monograph of yours, Professor?" he asked.

"I expect," said the other very deliberately, "to dispose of at least ten thousand at a guinea apiece. Or," he added meaningly, "I am prepared to sell the copyright for the same sum."

"£10,500!" Sir Raymond laughed aloud. "Why, my dear man, I would find it difficult to lay my hands on as many pence at the present moment!"

Gideon Wilfer smiled as he shook his head.

"I think you're mistaken in that respect. I have been up in London looking through the files of the old newspapers. I was especially interested in the trial of a certain forger named Lal Thaxted. Possibly the name is familiar to you?"

"I've heard of him," said Sir Raymond calmly. "Go on."

"I found that his forgeries brought him in a matter of £150,000, and this money—although the fact could not be legally proved— was suspected to have been paid into the account of your uncle, Hector Chalmers, who at that time was living in Sydney. He died shortly after wards, leaving the whole of the money to Miss Beryl Chalmers, naming as co-trustees Lal Thaxted and your self. Lal Thaxted, as you must be aware, escaped from prison, and a skeleton clothed in his convict uniform was subsequently found on the moor near here. His death—or presumed death—left you in sole charge of the money—"

"In trust for Miss Beryl Chalmers," put in Sir Raymond.

"In trust—exactly. But what is to prevent you from investing £10,500 of the money in purchasing the copyright of my forthcoming book? I assure you it will be a bargain at the price."

Sir Raymond started to his feet, his face convulsed with rage.

"Rob that girl to line your dirty pockets?" he cried. "Why, you blackmailing swine—"

His hand made a sudden dive towards his hip; and at the same moment Wilfer brought his hand forward, holding an old-fashioned revolver with its trigger at full cock.

"Up with your hands, Lal Thaxted!" the old professor ordered crisply. "Up with 'em—and let's have the gun you were so eager to pull on me. Ah, that's better—" He reached behind the other, possessed himself of his pistol, and transferred it to his own pocket. "You surely did not think that I was such a simp as to attempt to bargain with Lal Thaxted, forger, escaped convict, and murderer, without means to protect myself, did you? Sit over there, with your hands in front of you, and listen to what I've got to say."

Without a word, the man whom the world had known for nearly thirty years as Sir Raymond Chalmers did as he was ordered.

"I'll drop all pretence and speak plainly now," Wilfer went on, speaking across the barrel of his levelled revolver. "I don't profess to know all the details of the events which led up to your murdering the real Sir Raymond Chalmers, nor is it necessary for me to do so. It makes no difference to me whether you had that motive in your mind when, after escaping from Parkhurst, you made your way to this house. I'm quite ready to believe that it was during a sudden quarrel that you shot your one-time friend and accomplice. All I know is that you sent a bullet through his brain—"

"It was an accident, I tell you!" burst from the other man's lips. "I would have given anything to redeem that rash shot."

Wilfer laughed sardonically.

"I can well believe that, seeing that the bullet-hole in the dead man's skull precluded the possibility of passing off his body, dressed in your own convict clothes, as that of yourself. Any ordinary man might have taken panic there and then, and tried to make his escape. But I will pay you the compliment of saying that Lal Thaxted was far from being an ordinary man. But I am bound to say that, for a man who had just killed another in the heat of the moment, your plans must have been very well thought out. It was imperative that a body should be found wearing the convict-clothes, and the unfortunate fact that you had shot Sir Raymond at the *back* of the head—a place where the wound could not possibly be self-inflicted—prevented your using his body for the purpose. Your way out of the difficulty was so ingenious that it well deserved the success which it achieved.

"I am inclined to think that the murder actually took place on the moor, but on that point you are better informed than I. At any rate, you carried the body of your unfortunate friend to the ancient stone burial-chamber near the park gates, removed the clothing and everything that would lead to his identification, and placed him in the same position as the skeleton which already lay there, with the helmet, shield, and bronze weapons complete. Then you took the ancient bones, placed them in position, covered with the convict uniform bearing the number of Lal Thaxted, in another grave not far away. But, unluckily for you, you left one small article behind—the gold sleeve-link bearing the crest of the murdered man.

"Nor did your cleverness end there. Well aware that your appearance did not tally with the real Sir Raymond, you went that same night to Southampton, and from there crossed to France. Your well-known skill at imitating other people's handwriting enabled the letters that you sent from there to pass as Sir Raymond's. When you returned some years later, having grown a beard in the meantime, not a soul suspected your real identity. And not a soul ever will, if you agree to my terms. Think it over, Sir Raymond—as I will still continue to call you—and remember that the moment the money is transferred to my account you will have possession of the incriminating skull, which, at the present moment is locked up in my safe at Moor Lodge. Well, what do you say?"

The other made a helpless gesture.

"What can I say, except that I agree? You've got the whip-hand of me, and I have no other choice."

Wilfer rose to his feet and backed towards the door.

"Then it only remains for me to say good night."

Sir Raymond held out his hand.

"How about my pistol?" he asked, but Wilfer shook his head and laughed.

"I'll keep that as a guarantee of your good behaviour. Good-bye, Sir Raymond Chalmers!" He emphasized the title with a grim laugh. "It will not be necessary for us to meet again. I bank at the Southern Counties Bank, Moorgate Street. First thing in the morning I will forward a certain small, sealed parcel to the resident manager with instructions that it is to be handed to you the moment that the agreed sum is placed to my credit. I think that is all. Good-bye!"

The door opened and closed, and the man known as Sir Raymond Chalmers was alone. And yet not quite alone, for Count Ravangar, lurking unseen in the secret passage behind the panelling, had heard and carefully noted every word that had passed between them.

CHAPTER XXIX

A MOS AINTREE came before the magistrates in due course, and, having pleaded guilty to negligent driving, got off—to Lee's intense disgust—with the extremely lenient sentence of two months' imprisonment in the second division.

"Well, that disposes of him for the time being, at any rate," Lee Norton remarked, when the prisoner had been removed to the cells and the next case was called.

Sir John Lambert shrugged his shoulders as he made his way to the door.

"Yes, it was rather a fizzle," he said to the detective when they had emerged and were walking back to the station. "Still, you could scarcely expect a heavier sentence, seeing that the man had no previous convictions and that there was absolutely nothing to prove his connection with the Crimson Query crimes. I fear that you are as far as ever from solving the real mystery."

Lee nodded gloomily.

"That's true, sir. But the fact only makes me all the more eager to get a statement from Miss Hilda Maune. I'm positive that she knows enough to put us on the right track. But every time I ask to see her, the Spanish girl who is nursing her says that she is too ill—and that fool of a doctor backs her up."

The Chief Commissioner favoured him with a keen glance.

"What exactly do you suspect?" he asked.

Lee gave a hopeless shrug.

"My suspicions may be groundless, but I suspect that she will not be allowed to leave Abbot's Towers alive. I've seen the doctor who is attending her, but he seems to have made no move to call in a second opinion. From what I can judge from a second-hand description of her symptoms, I should say that she is being slowly poisoned."

"That is a grave statement, Inspector," said Sir John, shaking his head.

"But it is not lightly made, believe me, sir," Lee said earnestly. "I should feel more confident of getting her evidence if she were removed to a private hospital without delay."

It was plain that the Commissioner was impressed by Lee's words and manner.

"Very well," he said at parting. "I will instruct the Home Office expert to see Dr. Rollinson, and also to make a few independent inquiries. If what you suspect be indeed true, we must get to know what she can tell us without delay."

With this assurance Lee Norton was forced to remain content. But, though he had faith in Sir John's willingness and power to help him, he had likewise an unbounded faith in his own initiative and resource. The attitude of Sir Raymond Chalmers in the matter of the stolen play-book had both puzzled and irritated him; the manner in which the baronet had apparently resigned himself to the loss of the valuable manuscript had been anything but flattering to Lee, inasmuch as it seemed to imply a doubt as to his abilities either to detect the thief or to recover the property. But Lee had not given up the case as hopeless, and in his mind he had evolved a plan which bid fair to accomplish both these objects at one and the same time.

The plan was one that had been used before under somewhat similar circumstances, and for its successful outcome he would need the co-operation of an inmate of the Towers. He was on the point of seeking an interview with Beryl, whom he knew would be only too pleased to assist in the recovery of the family heirloom, when his thoughts and activities were switched into another direction in an abrupt and dramatic manner.

He had just emerged from the cottage in which he lodged, when he saw a short, stout man rush violently up the village street and dash into the police-station on the opposite side of the road. The expression of frozen horror on the man's flabby features, no less than his urgent haste, made Lee turn aside and enter the station.

"Ach Himmel, it was terrible—horrible!" The words, spoken with a strong foreign accent, fell on his ear as he crossed the threshold. "Mine poor, poor friend—the poor Professor Wilfer! Quarrels I had with him—yes! I strike him—yes, and was bounded over to of good behaviours be. But never would I him kill—never—never!"

And Herr Gutzeit sank on to the wooden form and openly gave way to emotion.

"Come, come!" said the sergeant, laying his hand on his shoulder. "Pull yourself together and tell us what has happened."

By degrees, with many repetitions and exclamations of horror, he told them of his tragic discovery.

He had, he stated, set out for Moor Lodge immediately after breakfast that morning, intending to inform Professor Wilfer of some discoveries which he had made on the moor the previous day. When he arrived at the house, Herr Gutzeit saw with surprise that the front door was standing wide open. He knocked and rang repeatedly without getting any response; then, puzzled and vaguely uneasy, he entered the house, to find Professor Wilfer lying dead with a bullet-wound in his forehead.

Lee stepped forward as he finished.

"Did you notice any unusual mark—on the wall, on the body—anywhere—? A mark in red?"

The German shuddered.

"Red? *Mein Gott! Ja!* There was red every-wheres!"

"I mean a mark like this"—and he rapidly traced a note of interrogation with his forefinger.

Herr Gutzeit shook his head.

"I did not see—I did not notice. My friend was dead—I come away with quickness here."

Half an hour later Lee Norton, accompanied by the local inspector and Sergeant Hattersley, arrived on the scene of the tragedy. Entering the open door, they proceeded to search the house. A room on the upper storey had been fitted up as a private museum, with rows of grinning skulls—trophies of the professor's antiquarian labours—lining the shelves of the glass cases round the walls, and here, lying staring with its glassy eyes at the ceiling, they found the body of Gideon Wilfer. It did not require much searching to reveal both the manner and means of his death. There was a wound in the centre of his forehead, and a small silver-plated automatic pistol lay upon the table.

"Suicide," said the inspector with an air of finality.

Lee bent over the body, examined the wound, measured the distance of the table from the spot where it lay. Then he rose to his feet and shook his head.

"I think it looks more like murder," he said. "There is no blackening round the wound such as you would expect to find if the muzzle had been held near the head when the shot was fired. Moreover, a right-handed man would be likely to shoot himself in the right temple, and a left-handed man in the left; it is seldom indeed that you find a self-inflicted wound in the centre of the head. Then again, look at the position of that pistol. Herr Gutzeit says that he did not touch it, yet it lies on a table six feet away from the body. Such a wound would have caused instant death, in which case the weapon would either still be clutched in the dead man's hand or else lying at his feet. As for the motive—Hullo, what's this?"

He darted across to the safe which stood in the corner and pointed to the bunch of keys which dangled from the lock.

"What did I tell you!" he exclaimed triumphantly.

"That safe has been unlocked with the keys taken from the dead man's pocket—look, the door is still ajar!"

He knelt down and, carefully avoiding touching the brass handle, swung the door open. As he did so a gasp of horrified amazement burst from Hattersley's lips. Drawn on the light buff-coloured paint of the interior of the safe was a large Crimson Query.

But the safe itself was empty.

It was in a grim, tight-lipped silence that Lee and his companions set about their task of making a thorough and methodical examination of the room. This having brought to light nothing of importance, they turned their attention to the body.

The inside pockets of the coat contained only a few receipted bills, a note-book containing some pencilled notes apparently having relation to the professor's pet hobby, and a receipt for a subscription to a well-known scientific society.

There were seven Treasury notes and some loose silver in his waistcoat pocket, a gold watch, and a few other unimportant odds and ends. It was only when Lee turned the body over that he made the first significant discovery. This was a heavy, old-fashioned revolver in the hip pocket.

"H'm—loaded in every chamber," he commented, slowly clicking the cylinder round. "That seems to indicate that he feared an attack. It will be useful if we can trace his movements last night."

"I can help you there," said Hattersley suddenly. "I was on Abbotsmoor last night just at dusk, and I saw Professor Wilfer enter the grounds of Abbot's Towers. I noticed that he seemed to be walking rather cautiously, as though he did not wish to attract attention; so, having nothing particular to do, I followed him up the drive. He went straight to the stone terrace and tapped on the library window. After a bit a door opened and he went inside. He remained there for the best part of an hour, when he emerged and set off in the direction of his home."

Lee Norton was not a little interested by this piece of information. It seemed to establish a secret and hitherto unsuspected link between the eccentric professor and somebody at present living at Abbot's Towers. He looked long and thoughtfully at the still form upon the floor, then turned his eyes to the silver-plated pistol on the table.

"There lies the key of the mystery," he said, pointing to it. "When we find the owner of this weapon we will have taken a great step forward. For it's my belief that the man who fired the shot from that pistol is the man we're after—the head of the gang whose sign manual is the Crimson Query!"

For the rest of the day Lee found his time fully occupied by the inquiries that this latest crime had made necessary. Jaded, and not a little disappointed by their negative results, he returned to his lodgings about six o'clock, hastily swallowed the first food he had tasted since early morning, and then, having unlocked a drawer and transferred a small cylindrical object to his pocket, put on his hat and sallied forth in the direction of Abbot's Towers.

Avoiding the gravelled drive, he struck into the narrow, yew-bordered alley which led direct to the steps of the stone terrace. Presently he stopped and looked about him expectantly. Immediately a dark-cloaked figure detached itself from the shadows of the tall hedge and glided towards him.

"Have you the key?" Lee whispered.

"It is here," returned Beryl in the same tone, slipping it into his hand.

"How is Miss Maune?" Lee asked.

"She is very ill indeed, Lee. It is not often that Clotilde will allow anybody to enter the room, giving as her reason that she cannot allow her patient to be disturbed. But I managed to slip in a few minutes ago, when she had gone out of the room. Poor Hilda looks very weak and ill. I tried to rouse her, but she seemed to be unconscious."

Lee remained for a moment in thought.

"All the better for our plan," was his unexpected remark. "The fear of alarming her was the only drawback to the thing I am about to do. If she is not conscious I need hesitate no longer."

She laid a trembling hand on his arm.

"You—you will be in danger?" His heart gave a sudden leap as he detected the loving tenderness in her voice. He gave a low, reassuring laugh.

"There will be more danger for another person inside that house than to myself," he told her. "And now you must return, otherwise your absence will be noticed. All you have to do is to carry on as usual. At ten o'clock make some excuse to go into Hilda's room, and, whatever happens, do not leave your post until I have accomplished what I have come here to do."

She hesitated.

"Yes," she whispered. "And that is . . .?"

"To arrest another of the Crimson Query gang!"

CHAPTER XXX

ABOUT THE SAME TIME as Inspector Lee Norton and his companions had been hastening towards Moor Lodge to investigate the murder of Professor Gideon Wilfer, Sir Raymond Chalmers had been reading a letter which had been delivered by the morning mail. It was written in neatly printed characters, and bore the heading:

To Sir Raymond Chalmers, Bart., alias Lionel Thaxted, Forger,

and beneath was the following message:

Yesterday afternoon at dusk you were visited by Professor Gideon Wilfer. Having been admitted by you to the library, he informed you of a discovery which he had made in an ancient tomb on the moor—a discovery which proved you to be the slayer of the man whose name and title you bear. At the same time he offered to hand over the incriminating skull of your victim, together with a cuff-link bearing his family crest, in consideration of the payment of £10,500. That same night he was killed by a bullet fired from your own pistol. It may interest you to know that the evidence against you is now in my possession, and it will be handed over to the police authorities unless the following conditions are complied with.

Firstly, you must suggest, and if necessary insist, that your secretary, Miss Hilda Maune, is taken for a long sea voyage on the s.y. Lapwing, *which vessel is now moored off Cowes, but will be brought up Southampton Water in order to embark the invalid. Miss Maune to be accompanied by the lady who is at present nursing her.*

Secondly, that your house, Abbot's Towers, is left entirely vacant for the space of seven days, such time to commence two days after Miss Maune has embarked on the yacht.

Thirdly, that you make no attempt to discover the identity of the writer of this letter, nor to communicate its contents to a third person.

Fourthly, that you memorize the contents of this letter and immediately destroy same.

There will be no need for you to communicate your acceptance of these terms—I will know immediately whether you are carrying them out or not. Your every movement will be watched, and, needless to say, at the first sign of your communicating with the police the whole of the facts of the disappearance of Sir Raymond Chalmers will be forwarded to Scotland Yard.

Beneath, in lieu of a signature, a note of interrogation had been drawn in red ink.

Apparently it did not need many minutes' thought to enable Sir Raymond to come to a decision. His first action showed that he appreciated the fact that the writer of the letter was one who was acquainted with the minutest detail of everything which happened within that house, and one whom it would not be wise to attempt to bluff. He took the open letter, read it for the last time, then crossed the room and deliberately dropped it into the fire.

He shivered slightly as he watched it shrivel to a wisp of blackened ash. During the past few days the man seemed to have aged ten years. His face looker thin and haggard, its lines deeper, and the eyes which used to shine with self-confidence now resembled those of some hunted animal who, footsore and exhausted, hears the eager baying of the hounds upon its track. With a weary sigh he lifted the receiver of the telephone and gave the number of Dr. Rollinson's surgery.

"Yes, Sir Raymond Chalmers speaking," he said presently. "I've rung you up to make a proposal with regard to Miss Maune, my secretary. It has struck me that a long sea voyage might result in an improvement in her condition, and, as a friend of mine has very kindly offered to put his steam-yacht at my disposal, I thought I'd put the matter to you without delay. What do you think yourself, Doctor?"

There was an appreciable pause before the answer came.

"Speaking for myself, Sir Raymond," said the doctor's voice, "I should unhesitatingly agree to your suggestion. Had you brought up the subject yesterday, I should have immediately given my consent. Now, unfortunately, I am not quite a free agent in the matter."

The listener's brows rose slightly. "I must ask you to explain yourself more fully, Doctor."

"Very good. This afternoon I received a communication from the Home Office saying that their representative, Sir Edmund Stanhope, M.D., M.R.C.S., L.R.C.P., is about to pay me a visit apparently with the laudable object of teaching me my profession." His voice took on an ironical note as he went on: "In view of the honour they have done me in sending a man with such an imposing array of letters after his name, it is hardly possible for me to refuse a consultation, so I have arranged for him to see my patient at the Towers immediately after lunch tomorrow."

Surprise was not the least of the varied emotions with which Sir Raymond heard this announcement.

"What right has the Home Office to interfere?" he demanded. "What mare's nest have they discovered now?"

"That is a matter on which I should not care to venture an opinion," was the cautious reply. "But when you remember, as you doubtless will, that Sir Edmund Stanhope is the famous toxicologist, you may be able to draw your own conclusion."

Sir Raymond's face went a shade whiter.

"Good heavens, they don't suspect that the girl is being poisoned, do they?" he gasped.

"Tomorrow will bring the answer to that question, Sir Raymond," was the non-committal response.

The baronet hung up the receiver and, thrusting his hands deep in his pockets, took a few rapid turns up and down the room, a thoughtful frown on his face. This sudden set-back of his plans was as unwelcome as it was unforeseen. It would mean a delay in carrying out the instructions of the mysterious Crimson Query—and such might well be attended by disastrous results. Coming to a sudden resolution, he quitted the room, ascended the staircase, and tapped on the door of the sick-room.

"Come in," said a low, musical voice.

A single shaded lamp cast its pool of light on one corner of the room, illuminating the white-clad figure of the girl who had glanced up from her book at the sound of the knock. Against the dark background of the time-mellowed oak panelling, the superb beauty of her creamy skin and corn-gold hair stood out, forming a picture that was more like the creation of an artist's brain than a chance, unstudied pose.

Sir Raymond felt his new-found suspicions vanish as he looked into the clear blue eyes that were raised to his. If there were indeed

a murderous conspiracy afoot, at least this pure-faced girl had
nothing to do with it.

"How is your patient tonight, Señorita?" he asked in a low
voice.

The girl clasped her slender hands with a gesture of almost
prayerful thankfulness.

"She is better, Sir Raymond—oh, how thankful I am to say that
she is better. But," she added with a warning gesture as he made a
step towards the bed, "only slightly better, alas! She is still very
weak, and must not be worried with questions. At times she is
slightly delirious too. Her mind wanders—"

"It is a lie!"

The words, weakly uttered but vibrant with fierce denial, caused
both to turn towards the bed. Hilda Maune had raised herself on
her elbow, two hectic spots showing on her marble cheeks, a light
of feverish eagerness in her dark eyes.

"Thank God that you have come here tonight!" she went on
hurriedly. "I have much to tell you. Come nearer—and send that
woman out of the room. She is in league with the Crimson Query!"

With an almost imperceptible shrug, Clotilde glanced at Sir
Raymond.

"You see I was right," she whispered, her long-fringed eyes
drooping in tender pity. "Her mind is still unbalanced, poor, poor,
girl—always harping on the Crimson Query."

Low as the words were uttered, they reached the ears of Hilda
Maune.

"No, no!" she cried fiercely. "I am not delirious. See, I am cool
and collected. Come nearer, I have something to tell you—about
the treasure that you seek—"

"Hush, hush, my poor woman!" Clotilde came forward and tenderly laid her hand on the other's shoulder to force her back on the
pillow. "Lie still now and try to sleep. Never mind about the treasure now. We will hear all about it when you are better, and
stronger, and more your own dear self."

"Don't touch me!" cried Hilda, struggling vainly in the other's
soothing yet compelling grasp. "Listen, Sir Raymond. I know the
secret of the old book—the book that was stolen. It contains a hidden cipher which shows the hiding-place—"

Clotilde released her hold and glided between the sick-bed and
Sir Raymond as he made an eager step forward.

"There, you see how it is," she whispered in a voice of infinite
compassion. "She is unstrung—excited. It would be better for you

to leave her now, Sir Raymond. I will give her a sleeping-draught—"

Hilda uttered a weak scream of terror.

"No, no—no more medicine! It parches my throat—it makes me sleep and forget. And I must remember . . . remember the thing I have to tell!"

Without heeding her, Clotilde crossed to the table, poured the contents of a small phial into a medicine-glass and returned to the bedside.

"Come, swallow this, my poor dear Hilda," she said, in a voice low and sweet as a distant vesper bell. "Drink it now and you will quite forget the things that trouble your poor mind."

Hilda turned from the proffered glass with a shudder.

"Hear me, Sir Raymond—hear what I have to say before it is too late!"

Clotilde again advanced and laid her hand urgently on Chalmers' arm.

"I must ask you—nay, I must plead with you, for the sake of my patient, to go immediately."

"First hear me!" broke urgently from the other girl. "Maybe you will not get another chance!''

Sir Raymond hesitated.

"A few words would not hurt her," he said. "Surely—"

Clotilde drew herself up and faced him squarely.

"I must ask you to leave this room at once, sir," she said, in a louder voice than she had hitherto used. "I cannot allow my patient to be disturbed. Go—go!"

Her grasp tightened on his arm, and he was surprised at the strength of those delicate, tapering fingers. Almost unconsciously he obeyed that insistent pressure and allowed himself to be gently urged towards the door.

"Sir Raymond! Sir Raymond!" Hilda had struggled up in a sitting position in the eagerness of her last appeal. "Do not leave me at her mercy. Think of the treasure—the treasure that you will never find without my help! Listen—"

"Go—go!" Clotilde cried loudly. "Go—or I will not answer for the consequences."

"Come back—come back—before it is too late!"

Bewildered, not knowing which of the frenzied demands to obey, Sir Raymond hesitated. Then, as he was about to quit the room, he chanced to glance into the face of the nurse. His action was so unexpected that the Spanish girl had not time to compose her features. Too late she saw his scrutiny and strove to alter her expression. The light of cunning triumph in the usually angelic blue eyes caused a sudden flood of understanding to sweep over the beholder's mind. He swung round and re-entered the room, making his way towards the bedside.

But he did not reach it.

Suddenly, without the slightest warning, there swirled through the open door-way a puff of acrid smoke, and at the same moment a babel of sound broke out from the floor below.

"Fire! . . . Fire!"

Immediately afterwards a woman's voice, clear and distinct, screamed the words:

"The library is ablaze!"

Clotilde spun round at the words. To her quick wits they meant a disaster more important than any revelation that the sick girl might make. Through the bedroom door and down the wide staircase she flew. Dense streams of red-tinted smoke were issuing from the library door. Impelled by a motive which overrode thought of personal danger, she dashed inside and groped desperately among the books on the shelf nearest the door.

Her hand closed upon the volume she sought, and drew it from its place among the others. Clasping it tightly, she ran towards the door—only to stop with a stifled scream as a hand fell on her shoulder.

"Let go!" she gasped, struggling. "What do you want with me?"

"I want Chicago Maud, alias Goldie, alias Señorita Clotilde la Zorita—and the stolen play-book belonging to Sir Raymond," said a quiet voice. "And it seems I've got both!"

A switch clicked. The clusters of electric globes sprang into sudden radiance, revealing the triumphant features of Detective-Inspector Lee Norton. While on the table, the last spirals of ruddy smoke still rising lazily from it, was the harmless pyrotechnic device which had induced the adventuress to betray herself.

The detective blew a short blast on his whistle, and the outer door opened and Sergeant Hattersley entered.

"Here's the lady we've been looking for, and here's the book containing the secret of the Abbey treasure. It was in full view on the bookshelves all the time we were searching for it, concealed inside the outer covers of a volume of eighteenth-century sermons—which, needless to say, was not likely to be opened from one year's end to another! You have a car waiting?"

"Sergeant Davis has it within call, sir."

Clotilde almost reeled as the handcuffs snapped on her dainty wrists.

"So much for the fourth member of the Crimson Gang," said Lee Norton. "We've got the tools—now for the hidden hand that employed them!"

CHAPTER XXXI

I T WAS A VERY CRESTFALLEN Dr. Rollinson who followed Sir Edmund Stanhope out of the sick-room after that expert in poisons had concluded the examination of Hilda Maune the following afternoon. Sir Edmund was an elderly man with thin, hawk-like features, clean-shaven, with a pair of dark, penetrating eyes whose acuity of vision had been the means of bringing many a once-confident scoundrel to the scaffold. He had not spoken much during the examination, but the few trenchant words that he had let fall had not been comforting to the youthful medico who had had the case in hand.

Pausing only to divest himself of his white surgical coat and to peel off the rubber gloves from his hands, he made his way to the adjoining room, where his coming was being anxiously awaited by the Chief Commissioner, Detective-Inspector Lee Norton, and Sergeant Hattersley.

"There will be no capital charge, gentlemen," the great toxicologist announced in his dry, incisive tones. "The patient will undoubtedly recover, for there is no trace whatever of organic disease, and her temperature is now quite normal. But," he added significantly, "it is a very fortunate circumstance, both for the patient and her medical attendant, that the nurse was arrested yesterday. I have found traces which indicate that minute doses of a vegetable alkaloid have been administered for a period extending over several weeks. Dr. Rollinson's prescription-book shows no entry of such a drug; therefore it is only logical to assume that it has been administered by some inmate of this house. And, I may add, the fact that the nurse has been found to be a well-known criminal leaves but little doubt as to the person responsible. Now that she is safely under lock and key, I think I can predict a speedy recovery for the patient."

A look of relief passed over the Commissioner's face.

"I am more than pleased to hear your report, Sir Edmund. The death of Miss Maune would have been a serious set-back for us, for she alone possesses information that will, I confidently believe, lead to the arrest and conviction of the chief of the band of assassins who have terrorized this part of the country. How long do you think it will be before we are able to take a statement from her?"

The expert hesitated.

"Is the matter urgent?" he asked.

"Most urgent," returned the Commissioner. "When you have heard what this gentleman has to say, I think you will appreciate the reason of our haste."

Lee Norton stepped forward in response to the speaker's gesture.

"In spite of the fact of the nurse's arrest, Miss Maune is still in danger," he informed Sir Edmund. "There are others who have access to the sick-room besides the inmates of Abbot's Towers. Some entries in an old diary which I found in the library, together with the legend of the death of Sir Martin Chalmers, a former head of the house, go to show that there is a secret passage leading from the interior of this house to a spot not far away—possibly to the old Abbey itself."

Sir Edmund Stanhope stroked his chin thoughtfully.

"H'm, I can scarcely say that I am surprised at what you say; it is seldom that you come across a building as ancient as this without finding something of that nature. I should advise that the patient be removed to a nursing-home at the earliest possible moment—today if arrangements can be made. In the meantime there is nothing to prevent you from obtaining a statement from Miss Maune."

"When?" Lee asked eagerly.

"At once, since the matter is so pressing," he said, and led the way into the adjoining room.

The new nurse—a middle-aged, capable-looking woman who had arrived from a Southampton hospital the previous night—rose to her feet at their entry. Sir Edmund crossed to the bedside, laid his fingers on Hilda's wrist for a moment, then beckoned the others to approach.

"You have had a very narrow escape, my dear young lady," he said, looking down with a smile breaking the customary impassiveness of his features. "But all danger is past now, thanks to the ingenuity of Inspector Norton. But, although he has exposed the dastardly plot against you, he has still to lay his hands on the man whose evil brain had planned both your destruction and that of the many previous victims of former crimes. He thinks that you have information which will assist him in that purpose."

The girl on the bed nodded.

"That is correct. I have such information, and not only will it lead to the conviction of the author of the Crimson Query crimes, but it will also clear up the mystery of the lost treasure of St. Nicholas' Abbey. Therefore I should like Sir Raymond and his daughter Beryl to be present when I tell my story."

Lee glanced questioningly at the Chief Commissioner, and in response to his almost imperceptible nod, quitted the room. A few minutes later he returned with Sir Raymond and Beryl Chalmers.

Sir Edmund Stanhope again laid his finger on the patient's pulse and nodded slightly as though satisfied that she was able to stand the strain of the coming interview. But Lee noticed that he took a small phial of colourless liquid from his inside pocket, carefully measured a few drops into a glass of water, and placed it ready to hand on a small table against the wall near the head of the bed. Subsequently all present had reason to remember the significance of this seemingly unimportant action.

"And now," said the doctor, taking a seat at the bedside," we should be glad to hear what you have to tell us."

For a few seconds Hilda Maune remained silent, as though trying to collect her thoughts into an orderly sequence. Then, in a low voice, she began:

"In the first place Hilda Maune is not my correct name, though it is the one that I have passed under all my life. I am of gipsy race—am, in fact, a lineal descendant of that Sibyl Morona who was carried to this house by Sir Martin Chalmers—'Mad Sir Martin', as he was called—and who stabbed her abductor and afterwards made her escape through the secret passage. You may well understand that oral tradition is strong in a persecuted and unlettered race, such as the gipsies were until a generation ago; and the very nature of their wandering—often hunted—lives made their wits necessarily more keen than those of the stolid, home-keeping rustics. Harried though they were, and following only the despised occupations that the law permitted them, these ragged bands of jugglers, play-actors, fortunetellers, buffoons—panderers to the universal love of pleasure and the desire to know the future—accumulated a store of secret and well-guarded knowledge, especially such as would be useful to them in their pretended occult arts. For generations we have known of the secret way which leads from the old Abbey to the passages within the walls of this house, and many a seemingly marvellous revelation of a dark-skinned fortune-teller owed its origin to chance scraps of conversation overheard through the panelling. But never had the secret of that

passage been revealed to one not of true Romany blood until it was
sold to a stranger by a traitor *chal*. His name was Juan Conreo."

"Otherwise Private John O'Connor!" exclaimed Lee.

The girl nodded in agreement.

"In spite of his foreign-sounding name, he was British born,
and, like many another man in similar circumstances, he altered his
name to a similar-sounding British one on joining the Army. He
and I were engaged to be married; yet he did not tell me that he
had revealed the secret of the underground passage until I met him
one night by appointment at the gap in the fence of the park. He
then showed me a letter which he had received from a man named
Rawlins, asking him to meet him on the moor that night, when the
agreed sum would be paid to him. I suspected foul play, and urged
him not to keep the appointment. But he laughed at my fears. With
that letter in existence, he told me, Rawlins would not dare to play
him false. He left the letter in my possession and went—to his
death, as you already know."

The Chief Commissioner glanced towards Lee.

"That places a new aspect on the matter," he said. "We have
always regarded O'Connor's death as part of the attempt on Captain St. Quentin."

A faint smile played round Hilda's lips.

"You will understand all about *that* when you have heard the
whole of my story," she said, with a peculiar and puzzling emphasis. "But to continue. I took the letter home and, happening to
glance at it again, I was surprised to see that the ink was beginning
to fade. In a flash I realized that it had been written in disappearing
ink, and in a few hours not a line of writing would remain visible. I
therefore traced each letter with ordinary ink, so that Juan would
have a hold on the writer should he refuse to pay the money—for
at that time I did not suspect anything more than a ruse to swindle
him of the promised reward. Next morning I heard of Juan's—
O'Connor's, that is—murder, and of the Crimson Query that had
been found on the body, and from that hour I resolved to devote
my life to hunting down the real head of the gang."

"Why did you not place the letter in the hands of the police?"
asked Sir John Lambert.

She shook her head fiercely and a steely glitter came into her
dark eyes.

"I come of a patient and a cunning race. Juan, during his last interview with me, had hinted at the real object which lay behind the
desire to gain possession of the secret of the underground passage.

All the attempts on Captain St. Quentin's life were merely bluff—how great a bluff you will realize when you know all. It was to get the Abbey treasure, and especially the great diamond, the 'Child of Light', that was the real object, but I did not suspect the fact until Amos Aintree came seeking information about the ancient copy of the miracle-play, *St. Nicholas and the Three Poor Maidens,* for it was a tradition of our band that the secret of the treasure was concealed in that book. But so cunningly is the secret cipher hidden that it is only by *acting* the old play and carrying out the directions exactly as set forth in the original copy that it may be read. Hitherto those who have sought to solve the riddle have merely read the words—which is useless, for it tells nothing. But the players—the gipsies—*acted* it, and thus became possessed of its secret; which, had they but had the courage to throw off their superstitious fears and brave the dead Abbot's curse, might have made them wealthy. But such scruples had no place in the mind of Count Ravangar—"

"Count Ravangar?" almost shouted the Chief Commissioner. "Is he the head of the gang?"

Hilda Maune nodded her head slowly. Throughout her long explanation her voice had been growing gradually weaker; now it seemed that she was on the verge of collapse.

Her condition did not escape the keen eyes of the Home Office toxicologist. He darted to the table against the wall, snatched up the glass which he had previously placed in readiness, and held it to the lips of the half-fainting girl.

A few sips seemed to revive her. A faint flush came into her cheeks and she struggled into a sitting position.

"Count Ravangar is the name he goes by," she said in quick, almost breathless accents. "But that is merely a cloak for his real identity—just the same as the mask that he wears hides his real features from the world. I say there is no such person as Count Ravangar . . . he is but a name . . . a symbol . . . an empty sham! The man who really evolved the Crimson Queries is a man well-known—respected—honoured . . ."

"His name . . .? His name . . .?" burst from the Commissioner.

Gasping painfully, Hilda Maune tried to speak. But an invisible hand seemed to be clutching her throat, strangling the words she strove to utter. Suddenly, with a low moan, she sank back on the pillow.

"Quick—she has fainted!" cried Lee.

Stanhope grasped her limp wrist, gasped, then bent nearer, his features startled out of their usual impassive calm.

"My God, she's dead!"

For a space during which one might count a hundred no one in the room moved or spoke. Then Sergeant Hattersley stepped forward and placed his automatic against the chest of the expert from the Home Office.

"Up with 'em—you!" he ordered. "That girl was poisoned by the medicine you took from that table! You're the only one that's been near it—and look—"

Every eye was turned in the direction in which the sergeant jerked his head. On the little table near the wall, occupying the same position as had the glass containing Hilda Maune's last draught, was a scrap of paper bearing the well-known blood-red symbol—the Crimson Query.

But Lee Norton's sharp eyes saw something else—a small hole bored through the panelling just above.

"Put up your gun, Sergeant," he ordered. "The poison was dropped into the glass by somebody on the other side—in the very secret passage that she was telling us about at the time. And it leads to the Abbey ruins. Come on—and we'll trap the scoundrel like the sewer-rat he is."

Headed by Lee Norton, the men hastened down the stairs and through the woodland path that led to the Abbey, and as they ran there came the sound of a pistol-shot from somewhere ahead.

With their weapons ready drawn for instant use, they dashed out of the woods and raced across the open space before the chapel and through the crumbling archway.

A man lay upon the steps before the altar. It was James Riggs, the butler, and there was an ominous patch of red on his white shirt-front.

Lee knelt down, raised the man's head, and bent low to catch the words which came from the bluing lips.

"He came . . . from the gallery . . . above. . . . I tried to . . . stop him . . . he shot me . . ."

The words ended in a rattling sound. Lee gently lowered the lifeless body, and as he did so the head of silvery hair came away, revealing the dark, close-cropped hair beneath. Lee Norton gasped as recognition flashed upon him.

"Lal Thaxted—the escaped convict!"

"And my half-brother!" said the voice of Sir Raymond Chalmers.

CHAPTER XXXII

T HE HOURS THAT FOLLOWED were busy ones for Lee Norton and his colleagues. Every foot of the Abbey grounds was searched, the secret passage revealed by removing a section of the interior panelling, and its many windings thoroughly explored. But the man they sought seemed to have vanished completely. Nor were the Portsmouth water-guard more successful when they boarded the *Lapwing* as she lay at anchor in the Solent. Though they searched the yacht from stem to stern, they found neither Count Ravangar nor any clue to his real identity. It seemed as though the latest and greatest problem set by the Crimson Query was destined to remain unanswered for all time.

The search of the yacht was made in consequence of information supplied by Sir Raymond Chalmers, and later he cleared up the mystery of the finger-print which had been the indirect cause of Gideon Wilfer's death.

"He came here to blackmail me," he explained to Lee. "He had found a skull with a bullet-hole in it, and had jumped to the conclusion that it belonged to Sir Raymond. In fact, he practically accused me of having murdered myself! I would have laughed at his threat of exposure, but I knew that in order to clear myself I would have to reveal the fact that Lal Thaxted was being sheltered in my house."

"Then whose skull was it that he found?" Lee asked.

"That of James Riggs, my butler, who committed suicide on the same night that Lalmade his escape from Parkhurst." Sir Raymond darted a keen glance into the detective's face, then smiled as he shook his head.

"I can see that you're rather sceptical, Mr. Norton, but I have kept the letter which Riggs wrote confessing that he had embezzled various sums of money entrusted to him, and announcing his intention of taking his own life, and saying that his body would be found in the Abbey ruins.

"I found that letter on my desk in the study, and, thinking I might be in time to prevent his rash act, I immediately hastened to the Abbey. But I arrived too late. The poor fellow had placed the muzzle of a sporting-rifle in his mouth, pressed the trigger with his toe, and the bullet had crashed through the back of his head, killing him instantly. It was the fact of the bullet-hole being in this position which made the over-clever Professor Wilfer so certain that it had not been self-inflicted, which only goes to prove the old saying that a little knowledge is a dangerous thing. Well, I was still bending over his body when Lai, wearing a suit of oilskins over his convict clothes, laid his hand on my shoulder. He had just made his escape and had come to me for help."

He paused for a moment, and the young man drew a long breath of relief. The revelation of the fact that the girl he loved was not, after all, the daughter of a convict was like a load of lead being lifted from his heart.

"As I have said, Lal Thaxted was my half-brother," the baronet resumed. "No good purpose can be served by raking up the sins and follies of the dead, so I will not go further into the details of our relationship; sufficient to say that not a living soul suspected the blood-tie which bound us. My father on his death-bed had implored me to look after him, and, in spite of his wild ways, I was really fond of him. As he stood there before me, numbed with cold, half-famished, hunted like a wild beast, I felt my heart go out to him. I resolved to help him get clear away. But the suicide of poor Riggs complicated matters, for I hesitated to make it known because it would have been dangerous to have the police making inquiries about the place. Moreover, Lal swore that he would sooner follow Riggs' example than be recaptured. Between us we carried the body indoors and then it was that the inspiration flashed across my mind. Lal had been noted for his clever amateur acting—why should he not take the place of the dead man?

"The fact that the old servant was unmarried, and of a morose and solitary disposition, with few friends, helped our deception. We carried the body to the old tomb on the moor, dressed it in the ancient bronze armour, and then closed the entrance. Then we took the actual bones of the warrior, placed them in the convict's uniform, and laid them in another tomb that had been already opened. Then, confident that I had successfully covered Lal's trail, I travelled to London early the next morning, bought a white wig at a well-known theatrical costumier's, and posted it to Lal. Then I journeyed straight to France and from there wrote and discharged the staff of servants in order to lessen the risk of his discovery. So successful was his impersonation, that what we had at first intended to be a mere temporary expedient became a permanent deception. Not a soul suspected, and even when Professor Wilfer unearthed the bones and saw the bullet-hole and the stopped teeth of the skull, he was far from suspecting the real truth. He thought them to be the remains of Sir Raymond Chalmers, and myself to be Lal Thaxted. Knowing that I could at any time prove this to be false, I played up to him; swore it was an accident, and pretended to be appalled at the prospect of exposure, and so threw him completely off the scent."

Lee looked up with a smile.

"I must confess that I fell into a similar error," he said.

"Ah, the finger-print?" said Sir Raymond with a wry smile. "I knew of the disappearance of the book long before Hilda Maune took us to the room, for Lal had already noticed its absence, and had even handled the card bearing the Crimson Query. It was lucky that I happened to pick it up and so divert your suspicion to myself. Of course, I knew that I could at any moment prove my real identity by demanding to have my fingerprints taken, but I remained silent for Lal's sake."

During the pause which followed, Lee Norton made a few entries in his note-book; but it was more with the object of gaining time than to assist his memory. Really he was doing some rapid thinking. Part of the mystery had been cleared up, but the arrest of the real criminal seemed as far off as ever.

"I thank you for the information and help that you have given us, Sir Raymond," he said presently, "and I trust it will be taken into account when you have to meet the charge of aiding and harbouring an escapee convict."

Sir Raymond Chalmers smiled, but returned no reply He had no misgivings on that score, for a highly placed official had already given that assurance when he had divulged the fact that Ravangar's headquarters was the s.y. *Lapwing.* And, truth to tell, he considered that he was entitled to some leniency in view of the fact that he had placed his life in jeopardy by revealing the contents of the letter signed by the Crimson Query. As he shook hands with the young detective at parting, he expressed a hope that he would soon have the pleasure of seeing him again.

"I have a little mystery of my own to unravel, you know," he said smilingly. "I mean, of course, the secret of the hiding-place of the Abbot's treasure. You will remember that Miss Maune was emphatic in her statement that the old miracle-play would have to be *acted* in order to make it give up its secret. Now, I do not profess to understand what she was driving at, for, on the face of it, it seems absurd to think that a play will tell more by being spoken aloud than it would by simply being read. But I propose to carry out her instructions to the very letter, and to that end I am going to give a private performance at an early date, here at the Towers and I wanted to know if you will oblige me by taking one of the parts."

Lee gave a good-humoured laugh.

"I shall be getting quite a swelled head presently," he declared. "That's the second offer to allow me to show my histrionic ability that I've received since I've been on this case. Of course, I shall be only too pleased to oblige, Sir Raymond, but I warn you fairly that I've had no stage experience. The only characters that I have assumed up to now have been those undertaken in the course of my official duties."

"You may set your mind at ease on that score," returned the other, clapping him on the shoulder. "It's to be quite an informal affair—you need not even learn your part. Beryl and I, with a few friends, are merely going to read through the play with the object of solving the hidden cipher. By the way, Captain St. Quentin is to be in the cast."

Lee looked his surprise.

"Indeed? I was not aware that he had returned to England." In spite of himself, a shade of annoyance passed across his face.

"Nor did I, until I received a letter from him yesterday. I immediately wrote back and asked him down for a few days, at the same time telling him that I had taken the liberty of assigning him the important role which is described in the old play as 'Ye Devyl'."

"I hope he won't play his part too literally!" laughed the detective as he took his departure.

CHAPTER XXXIII

I T IS A WELL-NIGH IMPOSSIBLE TASK for any organization however widespread and efficient, to unravel the past history of a man who had of set purpose shrouded his every movement and action with a veil of impenetrable secrecy. Yet in the days that followed, Scotland Yard made a determined bid to accomplish the impossible.

Under the circumstances, it was only natural that they should meet with many disappointments. The most protracted and minute questioning of the crew of the *Lapwing* failed to bring any valuable clue. With stolid indifference, they said that the private affairs of their employer were no business of theirs; they had signed on to obey orders, they maintained, and as their acts had not constituted a breach of the law, they insistently demanded either to be brought before a magistrate or else given their freedom. In the end they were released.

"There goes a pack of blooming sea-lawyers," grumbled the disappointed Sergeant Hattersley, as he watched them file back to their quarters on the yacht. "I bet they could tip us a useful hint or two if they liked."

Lee Norton shook his head.

"I doubt it, Sergeant. From what I have been able to gather of the mentality of the elusive Count Ravangar, I should say that the people who were closely connected with him would be the people who were least likely to know anything about him. Luckily we've got one or two more strings to play on."

Hattersley's manner brightened. He well knew to what his superior was referring. A search through the back files of Lloyd's Shipping List had brought to light the names of the ports at which the *Lapwing* had recently touched, and even at that moment this series of potential clues was being patiently investigated. From Cadiz to Liverpool, every recent halting-place of the yacht was being sifted for information that would demonstrate the real identity of the mysterious Count. In spite of this, however, Lee had a feeling deep down in his mind that the final act of the grim drama would take place not many miles from Abbotsmoor.

But there were other reasons why he elected to remain in the neighbourhood. Captain St. Quentin's return had occasioned a renewal of activity at the aerodrome, and the new 'plane was now well on the way to completion; and there was another reason, quite unofficial and not entirely unconnected with Beryl Chalmers' laughing eyes. It is not often that the paths of love and duty coincide, and Lee was duly thankful to Providence that they did in his case.

He was scarcely surprised, however, to find that St. Quentin was not over grateful for the solicitude with which his movements were watched.

"Personally, I think you're wasting your time here," he told the detective as they walked across the moor one morning. "It's my belief that this Count Ravangar has quitted the country for good. He must realize that his game is up now, with his gang in prison and his yacht in your hands."

There was a twisted smile on Lee's lips as he shook his head.

"Unfortunately, the *Lapwing* is not in our hands," he said. "As its owner has not been convicted—or arrested, for the matter of that—we could not hold the ship. She's lying off Cowes at the present moment."

The captain's mobile features expressed surprise.

"Rather risky, isn't it? What's to prevent this Count What's-his-name getting aboard and giving you all the slip?"

The detective gave a confident laugh.

"No fear of that. Why, the yacht is about the last place he'd make for. By the way," he went on, abruptly changing the topic, "I hear you are to take part in the little theatrical performance at the Towers this evening."

"Yes," was the answer. "I hear that you're to be in it, too."

Lee nodded.

"I have been allotted the role of St. Nicholas, who, I believe, is the original of the modern Father Christmas!"

The airman eyed him with amusement.

"In that case you'd better start growing a beaver without delay. And, when I come to think of it, I'd better look up a pair of horns and a couple of cloven hoofs from somewhere or other. I am to play 'Ye Devyl'."

"Get thee behind me, Satan!" was Lee's laughing retort. "You'd better be careful, Captain, or you'll vanish in a flash of brimstone when I come on the scene!"

The other joined in the laugh as this dire threat was uttered.

"I see you're entering into the spirit of your character. I hope you'll enjoy playing it. Speaking for myself, all I can hope for is to be funny without being vulgar. Still, I don't mind making a fool of myself in a good cause. Queer idea, acting this old miracle-play. It's something to do with the hidden treasure, isn't it?"

"It's everything to do with it," answered Lee, and went on to tell him about Hilda Maune's dying words. At the conclusion the airman shook his head dubiously.

"It sounds like a pretty thin yarn to me," he said with another laugh. "We'll look like a nice parcel of fools if we shout ourselves hoarse and nothing happens. I've heard of some queer secret ciphers, but it's the first time I've come across one that needed to be acted to be understood. Whether acted or read, the words are the same—"

"Maybe the stage directions are the clue of the mystery," was the detective's somewhat puzzling reply.

It was a merry, laughing party who gathered that night in the Great Hall of Abbot's Towers. Amateur theatricals are always popular, but when there is the added spice of mystery, as in this case, with the chance of solving the secret of a hidden diamond of almost fabulous value, the appeal was irresistible. Yet, in spite of the laughing banter which accompanied the setting of the extemporized stage, a tense undercurrent of suppressed excitement seemed to pervade the room. Each member of the cast had been provided with a typewritten copy of the old play, but the original book, with its massive covers of fifteenth-century metal-work decorated with scenes from the life of the saint, lay upon the table before them. Not the least part of the interest was the fact that each actor and actress had been given a free hand in procuring or extemporizing his or her own conception of a suitable costume.

Lee Norton presented a venerable and imposing figure with silvery locks and a long beard which flowed down over a crimson robe which, let it be whispered, bore a suspicious resemblance to a bath-robe. Beryl, by some miracle of needlecraft, had evolved a bewitching Tudor head-dress from a lace curtain, though a stickler for historical accuracy would have been bound to admit that her frock of silver tissue and pale blue was somewhat short for the period. Sir Raymond made a very tolerable Abbot in a cardboard mitre and a green velvet cope which had done duty a few minutes before as his study tablecloth. But the hit of the evening was undoubtedly "Ye Devyl", in a cloak of flaming scarlet and a grinning, horned mask of appalling hideousness.

"Thank goodness there are no children present!" said Beryl as she caught sight of him. "I'm sure you would give them all night-mares."

His Satanic Majesty laughed as he struck a posture with his barbed pitchfork.

"Great fun for the little ones, what?" came in St. Quentin's drawling voice from between the fanged lips. "I say, you might oblige me by straightening out my tail, will you? The confounded thing keeps on getting in between my legs."

Lee stepped forward.

"Ha, ha!" he exclaimed dramatically. "An involuntary tribute to my power, methinks. Even the foul fiend himself puts his tail be-tween his legs at my mere approach!"

Amid the general laugh which followed this sally the company took up their positions for the opening scene.

"Remember," warned Sir Raymond, "all the stage directions must be carried out. That is essential for the success of our play. All ready? Then we'll ring up the curtain that isn't there."

Half serious, half jesting, they read through the quaint measured lines which had originated in the brain of some unknown monkish poet so many centuries before. But it was easy to see that the minds of the actors were not on the words they spoke. Each was waiting expectantly for the impending climax—the revelation of the secret which Hilda Maune had so confidently predicted would follow. But the scenes progressed in their stilted, old-world lan-guage with never a word or sign to explain the hiding-place of the treasure.

A disappointed silence followed when Lee had spoken the final line.

"And that's that!" remarked "Ye Devyl" in the tone of one who had expected failure. "I told you the whole thing would be a frost."

Sir Raymond pushed back his mitre with a puzzled air.

"We must have omitted something," he said, shaking his head.

"I'm sure that I made an exact copy," declared Beryl. "I read it through again and again to make sure."

Lee, who had crossed to the ancient book and opened the mas-sive covers, looked round suddenly.

"I'm afraid that you did leave out something, all the same," he said.

"I'm positive I did not," the girl declared.

"How about this—" and he pointed to some words scrawled in faded ink on the first page.

Drawing nearer, she glanced down and laughed.

"Oh, *that?*" There was a note of amused contempt in her voice. "Seeing that we're no longer living in the Dark Ages, I thought there was no necessity for putting that into the stage directions. Besides, what possible bearing can it have on what we seek?"

"It may have a very important bearing," was the detective's quiet answer. "You must remember that Miss Maune stipulated that nothing—however apparently unimportant—should be left out."

"What is it, anyway?" asked Sir Raymond, drawing nearer in his turn.

Lee glanced at the writing.

"Apparently it was a ceremony that used to precede the acting of the play in the olden times. Read for yourself."

The baronet adjusted his eyeglass and with some difficulty made out the faded characters:

> *Before ye actynge of ye Playe doe ye thys: Wyth holie water takyn from ye Welle of Sainte Nycholas, sprinkle ye thys Pagye, goode and fayre, invokynge ye Blessynge of ye Sainte. Thus shall all thynges be accomplished.*

Sir Raymond turned and looked wonderingly at the detective.

"Surely you do not seriously suggest that such mummery would have any effect?" he queried with raised brows.

"It's worth trying, anyway," Lee returned briskly. "Have you any idea if the Well of St. Nicholas is still in existence?"

Sir Raymond thought for a moment.

"There is an ancient well near the old Abbey," he told him. "But I could not say if that was the 'holie welle' mentioned there. But you are never going to take that seriously?"

"That's just what I am about to do," declared Lee, as he began to divest himself of his saintly trappings. A minute later he disappeared in the direction of the servants' quarters.

Captain St. Quentin shook his head sadly as the door closed.

"No wonder that they found no answer to the Crimson Query when Scotland Yard men have their mentality still lingering in the Middle Ages!" he said with a sneer. "We'd better be careful or he'll be accusing us of witchcraft and demanding our deaths at the stake."

There was a thoughtful look in Beryl's eyes as she made a slight gesture of reproof.

"That punishment is not so obsolete as you seem to think, Captain St. Quentin," she said slowly. "Think of the two men who were burnt alive on the moor not so long ago. I should rather say that the man who compassed their deaths to save himself had a mind as evil and merciless as any witch-hunter of old. He must have been a devil indeed!"

St. Quentin shrugged his red-clad shoulders.

"I trust you do not mean anything personal." His voice showed that he was smiling beneath his mask. "There is an old saying, 'Speak of the devil and—' "

The sudden return of Lee Norton caused him to swing round with the proverb uncompleted.

"Here we are," said Lee cheerfully, depositing a small jug on the table beside the ancient book. "If the water I have here is not actually that of the same well mentioned by the monk, I trust it will answer our purpose equally well. Have I your permission to wet this page of the book, Sir Raymond?"

"Certainly, certainly!" The old baronet seemed as eager as any there to see the outcome of the bizarre experiment.

A faint smile creased Lee's mouth.

"I must confess that I do not know the traditional mode of invoking the saint's aid, so I'll substitute a modern version." He dipped his handkerchief into the water and smeared it across the vellum page. " 'Santa Claus, please bring us a nice present,' " he said gravely.

For an instant nothing happened. Then, as though they were being traced by an unseen, ghostly hand, letters began to appear upon the wetted sheet of parchment.

"Gad!" gasped Sir Raymond. "Then it is true after all! Why, man, it's a miracle—"

"Yes—a miracle of science," interrupted Lee. "Have you never heard of sympathetic ink?"

"But the water—from St. Nicholas's Well—"

"I may as well tell you that this water came from your kitchen tap!" laughed Lee. "As soon as I saw that water was mentioned I suspected sympathetic ink. Of course, I cannot tell the exact composition of this particular ink, but you may get exactly similar results by well mixing one part of linseed oil with twenty parts of water of ammonia and one hundred parts of ordinary water. Writing executed with this mixture will completely vanish when dry and will only become visible when the paper is wetted. On the moisture drying, it will again vanish, but it may be brought back as many times as you wish by again wetting it." He looked down at the page before him. "And now, as the writing seems to be perfectly legible, you had better read what it says—not necessarily aloud, you know," he added in a low tone.

"I hope that I can trust everybody here," said the baronet.

He screwed his eyeglass into position and read aloud:

"Ye Chylde of Lyghte be hydden in ye Byndynge of thys Booke."

Then he uttered a cry of amazement.

"Good heavens! It was inside the covers—here—under my very hand all the time!"

"Then take your hands off it—and put 'em up lively!" said a high-pitched voice from the other side of the table. "And all the rest of you do the same. The one who moves first will never move again!"

Hitherto the book had been the focus of every eye, but at the sound of the shrilly uttered threat everybody present looked up—to meet the unwinking stare of a brace of automatic pistols held by a man with a bearded, impassive face.

Lee recognized the man in spite of its being the first time they had come face to face.

"Count Ravangar!"

The dark eyes of the man flickered with amusement. But the muzzles of his weapons never wavered.

"That is my . . . business name," he said in his queer voice. "But you are welcome to it now that I have attained my desire."

As he spoke he made a sudden forward movement and swept the precious volume under his left arm, still keeping his pistols trained on the group.

Lee uttered a curse beneath his breath as he saw the action. Ravangar laughed.

"Thought I'd look away and give you a chance to drop me, eh?" he sneered. "You ought to rate the Crimson Query higher by this time. I'll give you a few extra details to put in your report when you hand in your resignation—for this case is going to break you, Inspector Lee Norton. They've got no use for bunglers at Scotland Yard who let themselves be bluffed into guarding a marvellous aeroplane which is really much the same as other 'planes. They don't look kindly on mugs who spend their time guarding the very man that they're out to catch! Why, you purblind bat, couldn't you see that the attempt to gas Captain St. Quentin was only a fake to cover the real motives for O'Connor's death? Didn't you know that I saw through your disguise the very moment you donned it, and that I kept up the game before and during our tussle on the moor solely to throw dust in the eyes of my own men? But there, I won't embitter your last day in the detective force by recounting the whole of your blunders. I've got the great diamond that I've been out for all the time; I'll leave the newspapers to say which of us is the smartest. I think you will admit that the latest and greatest trick of the game goes to the Crimson Query!"

Ravangar had been backing towards the door as he had been hurling the cutting gibes at the helpless detective. Rigid and motionless, well knowing that his slightest movement would be met with a stream of bullets from the ugly black snouts of the weapons that were aimed at him, Lee Norton waited until Ravangar was almost at the threshold before he answered. And then it was apparently only to admit defeat.

"It seems that you hold the winning suit, Count," he said quietly.

"A suit in diamonds, eh?" chuckled the other. "I've got the ace, anyway—"

"And I a hand of trumps!" Lee shouted suddenly. "Look behind you!"

With a snarl like a trapped beast, Count Ravangar swung round. And, even in the same instant that he realized that the well-worn ruse had been once more successful, Lee Norton's automatic cracked twice in quick succession.

Before his sagging body had touched the floor, Lee was bending over him. He fumbled for a moment at the back of the fallen man, then the mask, wig, and beard came away.

Lying there, distorted with futile rage, cold fury darting from its glazing eyes, was the face that the mysterious Crimson Query had hidden so carefully from the world.

Lee Norton took one long look, and the whole tangled skein came straight.

"Now I understand why the man they were supposed to be after was the only one who escaped," he said. "Count Ravangar was— Captain Stephen St. Quentin!"

THE END

RAMBLE HOUSE's
HARRY STEPHEN KEELER WEBWORK MYSTERIES
(RH) indicates the title is available ONLY in the RAMBLE HOUSE edition

The Ace of Spades Murder
The Affair of the Bottled Deuce (RH)
The Amazing Web
The Barking Clock
Behind That Mask
The Book with the Orange Leaves
The Bottle with the Green Wax Seal
The Box from Japan
The Case of the Canny Killer
The Case of the Crazy Corpse (RH)
The Case of the Flying Hands (RH)
The Case of the Ivory Arrow
The Case of the Jeweled Ragpicker
The Case of the Lavender Gripsack
The Case of the Mysterious Moll
The Case of the 16 Beans
The Case of the Transparent Nude (RH)
The Case of the Transposed Legs
The Case of the Two-Headed Idiot (RH)
The Case of the Two Strange Ladies
The Circus Stealers (RH)
Cleopatra's Tears
A Copy of Beowulf (RH)
The Crimson Cube (RH)
The Face of the Man From Saturn
Find the Clock
The Five Silver Buddhas
The 4th King
The Gallows Waits, My Lord! (RH)
The Green Jade Hand
Finger! Finger!
Hangman's Nights (RH)
I, Chameleon (RH)
I Killed Lincoln at 10:13! (RH)
The Iron Ring
The Man Who Changed His Skin (RH)
The Man with the Crimson Box
The Man with the Magic Eardrums
The Man with the Wooden Spectacles
The Marceau Case
The Matilda Hunter Murder
The Monocled Monster

The Murder of London Lew
The Murdered Mathematician
The Mysterious Card (RH)
The Mysterious Ivory Ball of Wong Shing Li (RH)
The Mystery of the Fiddling Cracksman
The Peacock Fan
The Photo of Lady X (RH)
The Portrait of Jirjohn Cobb
Report on Vanessa Hewstone (RH)
Riddle of the Travelling Skull
Riddle of the Wooden Parrakeet (RH)
The Scarlet Mummy (RH)
The Search for X-Y-Z
The Sharkskin Book
Sing Sing Nights
The Six From Nowhere (RH)
The Skull of the Waltzing Clown
The Spectacles of Mr. Cagliostro
Stand By—London Calling!
The Steeltown Strangler
The Stolen Gravestone (RH)
Strange Journey (RH)
The Strange Will
The Straw Hat Murders (RH)
The Street of 1000 Eyes (RH)
Thieves' Nights
Three Novellos (RH)
The Tiger Snake
The Trap (RH)
Vagabond Nights (Defrauded Yeggman)
Vagabond Nights 2 (10 Hours)
The Vanishing Gold Truck
The Voice of the Seven Sparrows
The Washington Square Enigma
When Thief Meets Thief
The White Circle (RH)
The Wonderful Scheme of Mr. Christopher Thorne
X. Jones—of Scotland Yard
Y. Cheung, Business Detective

Keeler Related Works

A To Izzard: A Harry Stephen Keeler Companion by Fender Tucker — Articles and stories about Harry, by Harry, and in his style. Included is a compleat bibliography.

Wild About Harry: Reviews of Keeler Novels — Edited by Richard Polt & Fender Tucker — 22 reviews of works by Harry Stephen Keeler from *Keeler News*. A perfect introduction to the author.

The Keeler Keyhole Collection: Annotated newsletter rants from Harry Stephen Keeler, edited by Francis M. Nevins. Over 400 pages of incredibly personal Keeleriana.

Fakealoo — Pastiches of the style of Harry Stephen Keeler by selected demented members of the HSK Society. Updated every year with the new winner.

RAMBLE HOUSE's OTHER LOONS

The End of It All and Other Stories — Ed Gorman's latest short story collection

Six Dancing Tuatara Press Books — *Beast or Man?* by Sean M'Guire; *The Whistling Ancestors* by Richard E. Goddard; *The Shadow on the House, Sorcerer's Chessmen* and *The Wizard of Berner's Abbey* by Mark Hansom, *The Trail of the Cloven Hoof* by Arlton Eadie and *The Border Line* by Walter S. Masterman. With introductions by John Pelan. Many more to come!

Death Leaves No Card — One of the most unusual murdered-in-the-tub mysteries you'll ever read. By Miles Burton.

The Dumpling — Political murder from 1907 by Coulson Kernahan

Victims & Villains — Intriguing Sherlockiana from Derham Groves

Ultra-Boiled — 23 gut-wrenching tales by our Man in Brooklyn, Gary Lovisi. Yow!

Shadows' Edge — Two early novels by Wade Wright: *Shadows Don't Bleed* and *The Sharp Edge.*

Evidence in Blue — 1938 mystery by E. Charles Vivian

The Case of the Little Green Men — Mack Reynolds wrote this love song to sci-fi fans back in 1951 and it's now back in print.

Hell Fire and **Savage Highway** — Two new hard-boiled novels by Jack Moskovitz, who developed his style writing sleaze back in the 70s. No one writes like Jack.

Researching American-Made Toy Soldiers — A 276-page collection of a lifetime of articles by toy soldier expert Richard O'Brien

Strands of the Web: Short Stories of Harry Stephen Keeler — Edited and Introduced by Fred Cleaver

Through the Looking Glass — Lewis Carroll wrote it; Gavin L. O'Keefe illustrated it.

The Sam McCain Novels — Ed Gorman's terrific series includes *The Day the Music Died, Wake Up Little Susie* and *Will You Still Love Me Tomorrow?*

A Shot Rang Out — Three decades of reviews from Jon Breen

Mysterious Martin, the Master of Murder — Two versions of a strange 1912 novel by Tod Robbins about a man who writes books that can kill.

Dago Red — 22 tales of dark suspense by Bill Pronzini

Two Robert Randisi Novels — *No Exit to Brooklyn* and *The Dead of Brooklyn.* The first two Nick Delvecchio novels.

The Night Remembers — A 1991 Jack Walsh mystery from Ed Gorman

Rough Cut & New, Improved Murder — Ed Gorman's first two novels

Hollywood Dreams — A novel of the Depression by Richard O'Brien

Seven Gelett Burgess Novels — *The Master of Mysteries, The White Cat, Two O'Clock Courage, Ladies in Boxes, Find the Woman, The Heart Line, The Picaroons*

The Organ Reader — A huge compilation of just about everything published in the 1971-1972 radical bay-area newspaper, *THE ORGAN.*

A Clear Path to Cross — Sharon Knowles short mystery stories by Ed Lynskey

Old Times' Sake — Short stories by James Reasoner from Mike Shayne Magazine

Freaks and Fantasies — Eerie tales by Tod Robbins, collaborator of Tod Browning on the film FREAKS.

Seven Jim Harmon Double Novels — *Vixen Hollow/Celluloid Scandal, The Man Who Made Maniacs/Silent Siren, Ape Rape/Wanton Witch, Sex Burns Like Fire/Twist Session, Sudden Lust/Passion Strip, Sin Unlimited/Harlot Master, Twilight Girls/Sex Institution.* Written in the early 60s.

Marblehead: A Novel of H.P. Lovecraft — A long-lost masterpiece from Richard A. Lupoff. Published for the first time!

The Compleat Ova Hamlet — Parodies of SF authors by Richard A. Lupoff – A brand new edition with more stories and more illustrations by Trina Robbins.

The Secret Adventures of Sherlock Holmes — Three Sherlockian pastiches by the Brooklyn author/publisher, Gary Lovisi.

The Universal Holmes — Richard A. Lupoff's 2007 collection of five Holmesian pastiches and a recipe for giant rat stew.

Four Joel Townsley Rogers Novels — By the author of *The Red Right Hand: Once In a Red Moon, Lady With the Dice, The Stopped Clock, Never Leave My Bed*

Two Joel Townsley Rogers Story Collections — Night of Horror and Killing Time

Twenty Norman Berrow Novels — *The Bishop's Sword, Ghost House, Don't Go Out After Dark, Claws of the Cougar, The Smokers of Hashish, The Secret Dancer, Don't Jump Mr. Boland!, The Footprints of Satan, Fingers for Ransom, The Three Tiers of Fantasy, The Spaniard's Thumb, The Eleventh Plague, Words Have Wings, One Thrilling Night, The Lady's in Danger, It Howls at Night, The Terror in the Fog, Oil Under the Window, Murder in the Melody, The Singing Room*

The N. R. De Mexico Novels — Robert Bragg presents *Marijuana Girl, Madman on a Drum, Private Chauffeur* in one volume.

Four Chelsea Quinn Yarbro Novels featuring Charlie Moon — *Ogilvie, Tallant and Moon, Music When the Sweet Voice Dies, Poisonous Fruit* and *Dead Mice*

Five Walter S. Masterman Mysteries — *The Green Toad, The Flying Beast, The Yellow Mistletoe, The Wrong Verdict* and *The Perjured Alibi.* Fantastic impossible plots.

Two Hake Talbot Novels — *Rim of the Pit, The Hangman's Handyman.* Classic locked room mysteries.

Two Alexander Laing Novels — *The Motives of Nicholas Holtz* and *Dr. Scarlett*, stories of medical mayhem and intrigue from the 30s.

Four David Hume Novels — *Corpses Never Argue, Cemetery First Stop, Make Way for the Mourners, Eternity Here I Come*, and more to come.

Three Wade Wright Novels — *Echo of Fear, Death At Nostalgia Street* and *It Leads to Murder*, with more to come!

Eight Rupert Penny Novels — *Policeman's Holiday, Policeman's Evidence, Lucky Policeman, Policeman in Armour, Sealed Room Murder, Sweet Poison, The Talkative Policeman, She had to Have Gas* and *Cut and Run* (by Martin Tanner.)

Five Jack Mann Novels — Strange murder in the English countryside. *Gees' First Case, Nightmare Farm, Grey Shapes, The Ninth Life, The Glass Too Many.*

Seven Max Afford Novels — *Owl of Darkness, Death's Mannikins, Blood on His Hands, The Dead Are Blind, The Sheep and the Wolves, Sinners in Paradise* and *Two Locked Room Mysteries and a Ripping Yarn* by one of Australia's finest novelists.

Five Joseph Shallit Novels — *The Case of the Billion Dollar Body, Lady Don't Die on My Doorstep, Kiss the Killer, Yell Bloody Murder, Take Your Last Look.* One of America's best 50's authors.

Two Crimson Clown Novels — By Johnston McCulley, author of the Zorro novels, *The Crimson Clown* and *The Crimson Clown Again.*

The Best of 10-Story Book — edited by Chris Mikul, over 35 stories from the literary magazine Harry Stephen Keeler edited.

A Young Man's Heart — A forgotten early classic by Cornell Woolrich

The Anthony Boucher Chronicles — edited by Francis M. Nevins
Book reviews by Anthony Boucher written for the *San Francisco Chronicle*, 1942 – 1947. Essential and fascinating reading.

Muddled Mind: Complete Works of Ed Wood, Jr. — David Hayes and Hayden Davis deconstruct the life and works of a mad genius.

Gadsby — A lipogram (a novel without the letter E). Ernest Vincent Wright's last work, published in 1939 right before his death.

My First Time: The One Experience You Never Forget — Michael Birchwood — 64 true first-person narratives of how they lost it.

A Roland Daniel Double: The Signal and The Return of Wu Fang — Classic thrillers from the 30s

Murder in Shawnee — Two novels of the Alleghenies by John Douglas: *Shawnee Alley Fire* and *Haunts.*

Deep Space and other Stories — A collection of SF gems by Richard A. Lupoff

Blood Moon — The first of the Robert Payne series by Ed Gorman

The Time Armada — Fox B. Holden's 1953 SF gem.

Black River Falls — Suspense from the master, Ed Gorman

Sideslip — 1968 SF masterpiece by Ted White and Dave Van Arnam

The Triune Man — Mindscrambling science fiction from Richard A. Lupoff

Detective Duff Unravels It — Episodic mysteries by Harvey O'Higgins

Automaton — Brilliant treatise on robotics: 1928-style! By H. Stafford Hatfield

The Incredible Adventures of Rowland Hern — Rousing 1928 impossible crimes by Nicholas Olde.

Slammer Days — Two full-length prison memoirs: *Men into Beasts* (1952) by George Sylvester Viereck and *Home Away From Home* (1962) by Jack Woodford

Murder in Black and White — 1931 classic tennis whodunit by Evelyn Elder

Killer's Caress — Cary Moran's 1936 hardboiled thriller

The Golden Dagger — 1951 Scotland Yard yarn by E. R. Punshon

A Smell of Smoke — 1951 English countryside thriller by Miles Burton

Ruled By Radio — 1925 futuristic novel by Robert L. Hadfield & Frank E. Farncombe

Murder in Silk — A 1937 Yellow Peril novel of the silk trade by Ralph Trevor

The Case of the Withered Hand — 1936 potboiler by John G. Brandon

Finger-prints Never Lie — A 1939 classic detective novel by John G. Brandon

Inclination to Murder — 1966 thriller by New Zealand's Harriet Hunter

Invaders from the Dark — Classic werewolf tale from Greye La Spina

Fatal Accident — Murder by automobile, a 1936 mystery by Cecil M. Wills

The Devil Drives — A prison and lost treasure novel by Virgil Markham

Dr. Odin — Douglas Newton's 1933 potboiler comes back to life.

The Chinese Jar Mystery — Murder in the manor by John Stephen Strange, 1934

The Julius Caesar Murder Case — A classic 1935 re-telling of the assassination by Wallace Irwin that's much more fun than the Shakespeare version

West Texas War and Other Western Stories — by Gary Lovisi

The Contested Earth and Other SF Stories — A never-before published space opera and seven short stories by Jim Harmon.

Tales of the Macabre and Ordinary — Modern twisted horror by Chris Mikul, author of the *Bizarrism* series.

The Gold Star Line — Seaboard adventure from L.T. Reade and Robert Eustace.

The Werewolf vs the Vampire Woman — Hard to believe ultraviolence by either Arthur M. Scarm or Arthur M. Scram.

Black Hogan Strikes Again — Australia's Peter Renwick pens a tale of the outback.

Don Diablo: Book of a Lost Film — Two-volume treatment of a western by Paul Landres, with diagrams. Intro by Francis M. Nevins.

The Charlie Chaplin Murder Mystery — Movie hijinks by Wes D. Gehring

The Koky Comics — A collection of all of the 1978-1981 Sunday and daily comic strips by Richard O'Brien and Mort Gerberg, in two volumes.

Suzy — Another collection of comic strips from Richard O'Brien and Bob Vojtko

Dime Novels: Ramble House's 10-Cent Books — *Knife in the Dark* by Robert Leslie Bellem, *Hot Lead* and *Song of Death* by Ed Earl Repp, *A Hashish House in New York* by H.H. Kane, and five more.

Blood in a Snap — The *Finnegan's Wake* of the 21st century, by Jim Weiler

Stakeout on Millennium Drive — Award-winning Indianapolis Noir — Ian Woollen.

Dope Tales #1 — Two dope-riddled classics; *Dope Runners* by Gerald Grantham and *Death Takes the Joystick* by Phillip Condé.

Dope Tales #2 — Two more narco-classics; *The Invisible Hand* by Rex Dark and *The Smokers of Hashish* by Norman Berrow.

Dope Tales #3 — Two enchanting novels of opium by the master, Sax Rohmer. *Dope* and *The Yellow Claw*.

Tenebrae — Ernest G. Henham's 1898 horror tale brought back.

The Singular Problem of the Stygian House-Boat — Two classic tales by John Kendrick Bangs about the denizens of Hades.

Tiresias — Psychotic modern horror novel by Jonathan M. Sweet.

The One After Snelling — Kickass modern noir from Richard O'Brien.

The Sign of the Scorpion — 1935 Edmund Snell tale of oriental evil.

The House of the Vampire — 1907 poetic thriller by George S. Viereck.

An Angel in the Street — Modern hardboiled noir by Peter Genovese.

The Devil's Mistress — Scottish gothic tale by J. W. Brodie-Innes.

The Lord of Terror — 1925 mystery with master-criminal, Fantômas.

The Lady of the Terraces — 1925 adventure by E. Charles Vivian.

My Deadly Angel — 1955 Cold War drama by John Chelton.

Prose Bowl — Futuristic satire — Bill Pronzini & Barry N. Malzberg .

Satan's Den Exposed — True crime in Truth or Consequences New Mexico — Award-winning journalism by the *Desert Journal*.

The Amorous Intrigues & Adventures of Aaron Burr — by Anonymous — Hot historical action.

I Stole $16,000,000 — A true story by cracksman Herbert E. Wilson.

The Black Dark Murders — Vintage 50s college murder yarn by Milt Ozaki, writing as Robert O. Saber.

Sex Slave — Potboiler of lust in the days of Cleopatra — Dion Leclerq.

You'll Die Laughing — Bruce Elliott's 1945 novel of murder at a practical joker's English countryside manor.

The Private Journal & Diary of John H. Surratt — The memoirs of the man who conspired to assassinate President Lincoln.

Dead Man Talks Too Much — Hollywood boozer by Weed Dickenson.

Red Light — History of legal prostitution in Shreveport Louisiana by Eric Brock. Includes wonderful photos of the houses and the ladies.

A Snark Selection — Lewis Carroll's *The Hunting of the Snark* with two Snarkian chapters by Harry Stephen Keeler — Illustrated by Gavin L. O'Keefe.

Ripped from the Headlines! — The Jack the Ripper story as told in the newspaper articles in the *New York* and *London Times*.

Geronimo — S. M. Barrett's 1905 autobiography of a noble American.

The White Peril in the Far East — Sidney Lewis Gulick's 1905 indictment of the West and assurance that Japan would never attack the U.S.

The Compleat Calhoon — All of Fender Tucker's works: Includes *Totah Six-Pack, Weed, Women and Song* and *Tales from the Tower*, plus a CD of all of his songs.

Totah Six-Pack — Just Fender Tucker's six tales about Farmington in one sleek volume.

RAMBLE HOUSE

Fender Tucker, Prop.   Gavin L. O'Keefe, Graphics
www.ramblehouse.com   fender@ramblehouse.com
228-826-1783   10329 Sheephead Drive, Vancleave MS 39565

www.ingramcontent.com/pod-product-compliance
Lightning Source LLC
Chambersburg PA
CBHW030322020726
47493CB00004B/1131